HOWEVER FAR AWAY

HOWEVER FAR AWAY

A NOVEL

RAJINDERPAL S. PAL

ANANSI

Published in Canada in 2024 and the USA in 2024 by House of Anansi Press Inc.
houseofanansi.com

House of Anansi Press is committed to protecting our natural environment. This book
is made of material from well-managed FSC®-certified forests, recycled materials, and
other controlled sources.

House of Anansi Press is a Global Certified Accessible™ (GCA by Benetech) publisher.
The ebook version of this book meets stringent accessibility standards and is
available to readers with print disabilities.

28 27 26 25 24   1 2 3 4 5

Library and Archives Canada Cataloguing in Publication

Title: However far away : a novel / Rajinderpal S. Pal
Names: Pal, Rajinderpal S., author.
Identifiers: Canadiana (print) 20240309596 | Canadiana (ebook) 2024030960X | ISBN
9781487012540 (softcover) | ISBN 9781487012557 (EPUB)
Subjects: LCGFT: Novels.
Classification: LCC PS8581.A486 H69 2024 | DDC C813/.54—dc23

Cover and book design: Greg Tabor
Cover image/artwork: Don Bishop/GettyImages
Anna Burns, excerpt from *Milkman*. Copyright © 2018 by Anna Burns. Reprinted with
the permission of The Permissions Company, LLC on behalf
of Graywolf Press, graywolfpress.org.

*House of Anansi Press is grateful for the privilege to work on and create from the Traditional
Territory of many Nations, including the Anishinabeg, the Wendat, and the Haudenosaunee, as
well as the Treaty Lands of the Mississaugas of the Credit.*

 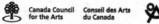

With the participation of the Government of Canada
Avec la participation du gouvernement du Canada | Canadä

*We acknowledge for their financial support of our publishing program the Canada Council for
the Arts, the Ontario Arts Council, and the Government of Canada.*

Printed and bound in Canada

For the multiple generations of my family and the push-pull of tradition we negotiate in unique and unprescribed ways.

Nobody wants to drag themselves through the endless ruins
of / All there is in this world that is not love
—Tamara Lindeman (the Weather Station), "To Talk About"

"It's not about being happy," he said, which was, and still is,
the saddest remark I've ever heard.
—Anna Burns, *Milkman*

ACT I

NAWAN DINN—NEW DAY

APNI COMMUNITY VICH *eh sabh ton vadda viah hovega. Dunian cheté rakhugi.*

Uncle Monty's command replays in Devinder's mind—that today's wedding will be the biggest Vancouver's Sikh community has ever seen and will endure in the collective memory for many years to come. An event fit for the eldest son of the eldest son of the Sandhu dynasty.

Devinder is confident that everyone will play their part, falling into their practised and predictable patterns, and that the delicate composition of his life will not go off-script.

Surely, today, of all days, everyone will be on their best behaviour. Today is not a day for surprises.

The LED display on the clock radio tells him it's four minutes to 6:00 a.m. and he flicks the alarm setting to Off before rising from bed, careful not to disturb Kuldip who lies asleep next to him. *She deserves the rest.*

By the light at the edges of the curtains he strips out of his pajamas and pulls on the T-shirt and shorts he'd selected the previous night for this morning's run. He can trace the silhouettes of clothes that drape on hangers over the top edge of the wardrobe—reminders of the day to come: his new navy Armani suit, the elaborately embroidered green-and-turquoise salwar kameez for Kuldip, and a selection of outfits for their two daughters. Everything had been meticulously ironed and organized by Kuldip the night before.

Devinder unplugs the BlackBerry that's been charging overnight, pleased to see that no new messages have come in while he slept. From a drawer of watches and jewellery he straps a weather-beaten Casio Illuminator to his wrist and places a Rolex upon the dresser for later. He steps lightly to the bathroom down the hall, wets a face cloth, spreads it wide across both hands, and rubs his face vigorously. After wiping under his armpits, he stretches the waistband of his shorts to scrub around his groin, then throws the cloth into a laundry basket filled with their daughters' clothes. He brushes his teeth and finger-combs his hair, scratches at the greying stubble on his chin.

Before heading downstairs, he peeks into the children's bedroom. They'd fallen asleep early after he and Kuldip cut short their stay at the jaggo, agreeing that their rest was a higher priority than staying up for the traditional pre-wedding night of song and dance.

Meena, eight years old, sleeps peacefully in the same position in which he'd left her, the sheets pressed tight across her body. She's a sound sleeper, yet fussy by day. Her sister, Teena, two years younger, is an agitated sleeper and yet calm during the waking hours. Meena is stubborn and never easy to please; she clings to her parents, wary of any adventure. Teena, on the other hand, accepts what is offered to her and is always keen to wander and explore her surroundings— oblivious to any worry she might cause her parents.

Teena's sheets are tangled around her legs, and one henna-painted arm—swirling vines and paisley leaves—hangs off the bed. Her pillow has fallen onto the floor. Devinder steps into the room and gently lifts her head to place the pillow underneath. As he reaches for her arm to tuck it back under the sheet, Teena mumbles, "Daddy, where are you going?" Her arm extends and her fingers tighten around his biceps.

"For a run, sweetie. Go back to sleep. Remember, today is Ranjit Bhaji's *actual* wedding day."

At the end of each of this week's pre-wedding events— the ladies' sangeet, the mehndi, and the maiya—the girls have asked if their oldest cousin-brother, Ranjit, is now *really* married. Each night Devinder and Kuldip have counted down the number of sleeps left until the *actual* ceremony.

"I don't like it when you go run, Daddy," Teena murmurs with eyes closed.

Devinder kneels beside the bed and strokes her hair to soothe her back to sleep. He looks around the newly decorated room, the subtle hint of fresh paint masked by the comforting smells of linens and lotions, lavender shampoo in Teena's hair. In the faint light he can just make out the ceiling mural, Kuldip's handiwork, a bright yellow sun with wavy beams encircling the light fixture and a crescent moon contentedly perched amongst fluffy white clouds. As his mind begins to drift, he hums the Punjabi lullaby that his mother would sing to him.

Saunja kaka saunja

Laal plungh te saunja.

DEVINDER HAD BEEN woken, as he was every school morning, with a kiss upon the cheek from his father.

"Wakey, wakey, sunshine!" Narinder Gill sang as he tousled his son's hair. Devinder opened his eyes to see him staring back—eyes that made him feel held. Loved.

He watched Pappa button his overcoat over his brown pinstriped suit and embrace Mommy tenderly before picking up his briefcase and disappearing around the corner to ascend the stairs. A short time later, after he had bathed and eaten a bowl of Weetabix in warm milk, Mommy hugged Devinder tightly and kissed his forehead at the street corner where the school bus picked him up. The smell of sesame oil from her long loose hair lingered as he waved at her from his usual seat, her bright mustard-coloured coat and red scarf made brighter against the large snowflakes that fell around her; they landed on her hair and eyelashes as she blew a kiss in his direction. Her smile as brilliant as always.

When the bus pulled up to his stop after school, Devinder looked for the familiar bright hues that made her easy to pick out of the pride of mothers that assembled every weekday afternoon. The light snow of the morning had become a blistering storm—the flakes now pellets—and the women huddled a little closer than usual to screen themselves from the sleet and piercing wind. Devinder shielded his eyes with both hands and turned his head side to side.

No mustard coat. No red scarf.

Maybe the snowstorm has made her late.

As he stepped onto the sidewalk, he noticed Auntie Deepa, the owner of the house in which he and his parents lived. They sometimes referred to her as the landlady.

Deepa moved toward him, squatted down, and embraced him hard against her chest. She took his hands and clenched them tight in her own.

"Where's Mommy?"

The wind howled around them, making her reply difficult to understand. She called him beta and then said something about how she'd be walking him home today. *Why?*

Deepa wrapped a long scarf around his neck and pulled an unfamiliar, oversized toque low over his head; the wool made his forehead itch, but he wore it without complaint, not wanting to be rude.

Devinder searched her weary almond eyes for a clue as to why she was there in place of his mother. She turned her gaze downward and tightened his boot laces.

They took short careful steps on the icy sidewalks as they walked the three blocks to the residence they shared, Deepa keeping a firm grip on his gloved hand. The sleet stung like needles against his face. He was relieved when they reached the two-storey home and entered through its black metal gate with gold-tipped posts. With the bright pink of its stucco siding and large stone lions on the stoop, the house stood out from the drab grey and olive dwellings that lined the rest of the street. At the top of the wooden door was a sign in large capital letters, black on gold: M. S. SANDHU & FAMILY.

Devinder tapped his boots to remove the ice and snow and placed them on the rubber mat in the landing. He removed the scarf and hat and held them out for Deepa. As she reached up to drop them in a cardboard box on a closet shelf, he took a couple of steps in the direction of the stairwell that led down to his family's suite, but she quickly moved to block his path.

"No. Stay up here with me, beta."

She kneeled to unzip his coat, gently pulling his arms out of the cuffed sleeves, and placed it on a hook in the hallway. Her eyes still offered no clues for why she'd been the one to pick him up today. He was apprehensive to ask her directly.

Devinder climbed onto a chair at the kitchen table and watched Deepa place two slices of thick bread in the toaster and warm a pot of milk on the stove. The air filled with the smell of ghee and garlic, as heavy and warm as a winter blanket. From another pan, the sizzle of oil and onions resounded in Devinder's ears, and a pressure cooker sent up a burst of steam. These were the same smells and sounds made when his own mother cooked, only here the garlic was more pungent and the hiss of the tadka, the tempering spice mix, louder.

Her hands moved effortlessly from pan to pan, a quick stir, an adjustment of the dials, a sudden yet smooth step aside to grab a plate from the cabinet. There was a rhythm to how she worked, a confidence and speed that he'd not seen in his own mother. A single plait of black hair rolled down

Deepa's back, as thick as the ropes in the school gymnasium, which only he and one other classmate were able to climb.

Deepa placed a mug and a plate in front of Devinder. He drank the milk—a thick skin of cream on top—and took a few bites of toast.

Karanpreet, the youngest son in the Sandhu family, came into the kitchen and sat next to him.

"Hello Dev, would you like to play a game of carrom?"

Karanpreet was several years older than Devinder and they had rarely spoken to each other except for hellos and goodbyes when they met in the front landing. On summer days, when Devinder would walk to the local park with his parents, they'd often see Karanpreet and his brothers kicking a soccer ball or playing a mysterious game called cricket that involved a lot of running between two sets of sticks. The boys would invite Devinder to play with them, but his parents always replied, "Thank you," and continued with their walk.

He was perplexed that Karanpreet addressed him as Dev. No one had called him by that name before. His teacher Mrs. Doyle had called him Dave several times at the beginning of the school year, and though Devinder was reluctant to correct her, she corrected herself soon enough. A tall kid named Graham often asked if his Christian name was Dave, to which he never had an answer.

Devinder was not sure what a game of carrom was and looked at Karanpreet with a quizzical stare.

"Hey, no problem, man. I'll teach you."

Karanpreet led him to the enormous living room—a flowered couch and two matching chairs covered in clear plastic, a wooden coffee table, a console television in the corner. His feet sank into a plush rust-orange carpet. A textured paper of thick blue stripes overlaid with enormous vines covered the walls. Mounted above the couch, as though they were watching over the room, were drawings of two elegant bearded men. The younger man wore a saffron turban with a halo of light behind his head, a quiver of arrows slung over his shoulder. He held a sword in one hand while a big beautiful blue bird sat on the opposite forearm. The older man, in a saffron turban and robe, a blue shawl over his shoulders, sat with one leg crossed over the other. His right hand was held up as though offering a blessing, with a long string of red beads entangled between his fingers and draped across his lap.

From behind the couch, Karanpreet pulled out a square plywood board—patterned with lines and circles, a hole cut in each corner, framed in thick rosewood—and placed it on the coffee table. Devinder detected the smell of mustard oil on his clothes. His face was pimpled, with faint wisps of hair above his lip and on his chin, and he wore a white handkerchief around a knot of hair on top of his head. Karanpreet then retrieved a cardboard box and emptied a stack of dark and light wooden checkers onto the table, before organizing them into a pattern on the centre of the varnished board. He sat across from Devinder. The plastic covers on the couch squeaked with every shift and move.

Devinder's attention was pulled to the door as he heard stamping boots and the jangle of keys. But it wasn't his parents, as he'd hoped; it was Uncle Monty—the landlord. The floor creaked as Monty bent down and struggled to remove his wet boots. His long dark beard was flecked with snowflakes as was his black toque—Devinder thought it strange to see him without his turban.

Karanpreet immediately stood and joined his hands together, palm to palm, holding them in a prayer pose. He bowed his head in the direction of his father and proclaimed, "Sat Sri Akaal, Pappaji!" Monty returned the greeting. Karanpreet sat back down and launched into an explanation of the rules of carrom.

"The whole point is to strike the wooden pieces into the corner holes," he said as he flicked a red plastic disc into the checkers, sending them gliding in all directions across the smooth surface.

Devinder tried the flicking motion, but the movement felt unnatural and for the first few attempts he missed the disc altogether.

"Don't worry," encouraged Karanpreet. "You'll get the hang of it."

But Devinder was distracted. He could hear Monty and Deepa talking in the kitchen. Amidst the hushed whispers, he heard his name and the names of his parents. They were speaking in Punjabi, the language Mommy and Pappa spoke on occasions when they didn't want him to understand what they were saying—or when they sang him a lullaby.

He heard the swoosh and click of the kitchen phone being dialed and then a series of yes and no answers from Monty.

The low, concerned voices were drowned out by Karanpreet's excitement as he flicked the disc across the board and a couple of the checkers ricocheted their way into the corner holes.

Uncle Monty entered and crouched down to place his hand on Devinder's head while his eyes fixed on the portraits above the couch. "Make yourself at home, son. You are our guest. If you need anything, ask. No need to be shy here."

Monty turned to Karanpreet. "Stay with our special guest, Kaka!" His voice was shaky yet thunderous, and even this gentle request reverberated like a command.

Devinder had a growing suspicion that something was amiss and more questions began to crowd his head. *Why didn't Mommy and Pappa tell me they were going to be late? What does it mean to be a "special guest"? Is it different from a regular guest?*

Over the next hour, Amarpreet and Navpreet, Karanpreet's older brothers, arrived home, weighed down by heavy school bags. With each arrival, Devinder looked toward the front door, hopeful that his parents would appear and his life would revert to its normal pattern. He heard the salutation Sat Sri Akaal exchanged, questions about school, and more hushed whispers.

Before long, Amarpreet and Navpreet had joined them in the living room where the game of carrom was in full swing—albeit tentatively on Devinder's part. Devinder observed the warmth with which the boys greeted one another: hugs and delicate touches. They took particular care to include him. Amarpreet, the eldest, with full beard and turban, and the same astonishing height as his father, kissed Devinder on the forehead and gave him a long embrace. Navpreet unwrapped a hard striped candy and handed it to him with a wink. Their familiarity surprised him.

Soon they were all taking turns to flick the disc, the sounds of the game—the hard knock of disc against checker

and the whirr of both sliding across the slippery surface—
now accompanied by the clang of karas, the thick steel bracelets that all three brothers wore around their right wrists.
They applauded as Devinder managed to sink two checkers
in successive shots.

TEENA'S BREATHING NOW returned to the steady rhythms of sleep, Devinder lifts his hand from her hair and stands. He bends to kiss her on the forehead, careful not to nudge her awake, and closes the bedroom door softly as he exits.

Downstairs, the morning sun throws light and shadows on the walls and hardwood floor, illuminating the drawings of Guru Nanak Dev Ji and Guru Gobind Singh Ji in the front hallway—the string of prayer beads and quiver of arrows sparkle. A few toys and open books lie on the area rug. On the landing, Devinder removes the gold kara from his wrist—a gift from Auntie Deepa and Uncle Monty on the day he married Kuldip—and places it on the hallway table, making a mental note to remember to put it on again before they depart for the wedding. He straps an iPod to his biceps, and with his running shoes laced and headphones looped around his neck, he leaves the house.

Across the street in Hadden Park he leans into the trunk of a Norway maple, angling his feet along the uneven mound of turf at its base—*as though the roots want to break free*. He presses his hands into the rough bark and stretches his quads and calves. In the branches above he can hear the high-pitched birdsong of robins and in the distance the intermittent caw of crows and mew of seagulls. He twists his neck to iron out the early morning kinks and pushes his middle fingers hard into the back of his right shoulder, a hopeless attempt to massage out the constant ache in his trapezius. There is a gentle throbbing in his left knee that's been there for a few days. *Perhaps the run will help.*

He glances at the Casio and notes how much time he has before he must return home, fixes the headphones firmly over his ears, presses play on his iPod, and begins a rhythmic stride. Crossing Hadden Park he spots his neighbours Allan and Lori emerging from the series of steps leading from the off-leash beach below. He shouts greetings and a "Hey Buddy!" at their black Labrador. It's only once he's on the concrete path parallel to the water's edge that he picks up his pace.

The sun warms his back, and he inhales the reassuring salt air. At the horizon, above the bay of tanker ships, red-and-black metal leviathans waiting their turn to navigate into the Burrard Inlet, the sky shows the slightest streak of coral.

Fourteen years, he thinks. That's how long he's been running the neighbourhoods of Kitsilano and Point Grey. After completing his Master of Arts in English, he'd accepted a sessional position at the University of British Columbia teaching post-colonial literature to mostly first- and second-year arts and humanities students. That spring, with Uncle Monty and Auntie Deepa's generous support, he'd put a substantial down payment on the house on Ogden Avenue. He only mentioned that he'd seen the property to them on a whim, but they quickly set things in motion. Given the current state of the market, he feels lucky to have made the purchase when he did. His home lies next to a park, next to the ocean, and is the envy of his work colleagues, especially those who have to travel great distances to get to the sprawling campus perched on the western edge of the city.

On these quiet summer mornings, Devinder witnesses the landscape stir itself to life like a waking animal. The ocean brightens into the greens, greys, and blues of a new day, and the mountains of the North Shore sharpen and announce themselves to the city. Across the bay, the trees of Stanley Park reflect and double in the water. And behind him, downtown neighbourhoods that were once filled with warehouses now present shiny high-rise structures—office towers, condominiums, and luxury hotels that soar into the ether.

Above him, a flurry of kites is sketched against the blue sky. He marvels at the skill of the kite flyers, how their hands move in quick beats as they manoeuvre the strings, always in control, making quick adjustments whenever an unexpected gust of wind comes along. This morning the long red-scaled figure of a Chinese dragon, its serpentine shape fluttering behind a fierce head spouting yellow fire, and an orca, a monochrome body with blue waves streaming in its wake, sway above the trees. He smiles at the memory of Meena and Teena as toddlers asking "Daddy, can you sing us the P'jabi song 'bout the kite?"

A group of runners is gathered in the parking lot at the end of Arbutus Street, dressed in the latest synthetic fabrics, sleek designer fitted leggings and tops, sipping from paper coffee cups. Farther along the path, as the main beach

becomes visible, he notes the kayakers and swimmers brav-
ing the cool ocean, and a woman on a stand-up paddle board
losing her balance and landing with a splash. In the distance
he recognizes the long limbs and orange cap of his former
dentist Jakob effortlessly gliding along the surface. Jakob is
seventy years old, and since his retirement it is a rare day that
he doesn't complete an ocean swim.

Devinder runs past Mr. and Mrs. Nguyen. Mr. Nguyen
strides with his arms folded behind his back, leaning forward,
and Mrs. Nguyen makes slow, rhythmic movements with her
hands and arms as she coasts along the footpath—always a
few steps between them. The Nguyens came to Vancouver
as refugees and only recently handed over their much-loved
dry-cleaning business to their eldest son. Devinder slows a
little and turns to wave at them. In return they offer nods
and gracious smiles.

If his parents were alive, they would be in their mid-sixties
now, about the same age as the Nguyens, slightly younger
than Jakob. Devinder imagines them walking along Kitsilano
Beach hand in hand—their love for each other unshackled
and free.

AUNTIE DEEPA CALLED from the kitchen and the game of carrom abruptly ended. Navpreet patted Devinder on his back. "Well done, Dev! You did really, really good!"

The brothers worked as a team to put away the game and reset the coffee table. Amarpreet took Devinder's hand and led him back into the kitchen. Uncle Monty sat at the head of the dining table while Auntie Deepa remained at the stove making fresh rotis, clapping flattened rounds of dough from one hand to the other and placing them precisely on the tawa. Each flatbread inflated like a balloon on the curved pan, and Deepa pressed a pat of ghee over the puffed-up surface, leaving behind a sheen of clarified butter. Amarpreet sat beside Devinder. Karanpreet and Navpreet sat across from them, enthusiastically scooping up yellow dhal and a sabzi of potatoes and peas with pieces of torn roti. Deepa could only just keep up. Each roti was received with gratitude, like a gift, their fingers dancing across the thin bread to tolerate the heat. Uncle Monty seemed to devour an entire roti in only two bites.

Other than the occasional request for more dhal or sabzi, there was no conversation. Devinder wondered if the quiet was due to his presence and all the unanswered questions that hung in the air. He picked at a roti that had been placed in front of him alongside a shallow steel dish of dhal and a glass of apple juice. Amarpreet gently encouraged him. "Just a few bites, Dev, and you'll get big like me."

But it was getting hard to breathe, a strange thumping filled his head. When the first tears appeared, no one noticed. It was only when the tears turned to gentle sobs that Auntie Deepa left the stove and lifted Devinder in her arms. She murmured, "Oh, poor beta," as she carried him into the living room. Uncle Monty followed.

On the couch, his head rested in Deepa's lap as she stroked his hair. Devinder's hand reached up and grabbed tight the thick braid that now draped between her breasts.

Monty declared, "We want you to know you are safe. You will stay with us for as long as you need, son."

Devinder's sobs grew more intense. He tried to speak through the tears, but the pent-up questions couldn't find a way out.

"Beta, shhhhh." Deepa rocked him tenderly with her legs.

She whispered to Monty, "We must tell him. In this weather, who knows when the social worker will get here."

And then her words tumbled out: "Beta, your pappa and your … your mommy … they were driving … driving to a meeting … and … and …"

Monty continued the sentence. "There was ice on the road …" Another long pause. "They are in a better place now, son."

As Monty spoke, he joined his hands and bowed his head toward the images of the turbaned gentlemen on the wall.

"Narinder and Mira are with Babaji now!" he said definitively.

Devinder couldn't make sense of their words. His parents didn't own a car. He'd only seen them drive a couple of times when they'd borrowed Uncle Monty's wood-panelled station wagon. *Was that what they were driving? Where were they driving to? What better place could they have gone to without me? Who was Babaji and when would he send them back?*

His chest felt heavy and his breathing became more difficult. Auntie Deepa continued to stroke his hair and rock him gently.

Devinder heard the boys cleaning up in the kitchen—the clatter of cutlery and plates being placed back in drawers and cupboards. When they'd finished, they made their way to their bedrooms after wishing him a good night, each of them bending down to hug him. Amarpreet kissed his forehead again.

Uncle Monty left through the front door a while later, wearing a black turban and his beard tied neatly beneath his chin. The house fell silent.

WHEN HE AWOKE hours later, Devinder was on the couch in his school clothes and all the lights were turned out. Auntie Deepa slept next to him, her arm curled around his body. The plastic cover squeaked as he gently lifted her arm and climbed down. He made his way to the stairwell and carefully descended in the darkness. He opened the door to the basement suite and switched on the light next to the empty coat rack. His mother's cream-coloured cardigan had fallen to the ground. Devinder picked up the sweater and held it tight against himself. He could smell sesame oil and thought of her long flowing hair—the sweet aroma that he fell asleep to every night. He stood by the entrance and surveyed the space, the narrow rectangular living room, the low ceilings and high windows. This was where he and his parents had lived their quiet lives. It was where they had fed and dressed him, bathed him, nursed him when he was sick, and—most cherished of all—listened to the stories of his day at school: what he had seen, who he had talked to, something new he had learned and was eager to share. Pappa asked him the same question every day before bedtime: "Son, what was the top thing that you saw today?" He had learned to observe, to remember, to immerse himself in his surround-ings. Devinder's response was always met with a resounding "Well done!" or "Shaabaash!"

This suite was where his parents had leaned into each other over a crumpled map as they made plans for his sixth birthday. On the bus into the city, he'd sat between them, Pappa's arm around Mommy's shoulder. They walked around Stanley Park and paid extra to see the killer whale and sea lion show at the Aquarium. Pappa lifted him on his shoulders as the enormous sea lion clapped its flippers and waddled toward its trainer to receive more fish. Then they'd taken another bus to Woodward's where they bought new school clothes: a wool sweater and a blue winter coat with cuffed sleeves. "To keep the cold away from my beautiful boy!" his mother had said.

The metallic scrape of a shovel on a nearby sidewalk clicked Devinder's mind back into the present. The curtains were open, and the few items of furniture were bathed in a soft yellow glow from the streetlight: a faded, checkered couch that folded down to become Devinder's bed, two tray tables, and a small desk. On a single shelf above the couch sat a few books and two framed photographs. One showed the three of them at Queen Elizabeth Park the previous summer and the other held photographic proofs of Devinder's recent school portrait. The kitchen was no more than a couple of short cabinets with a stove, a small refrigerator, and a sink.

Devinder knew that this would no longer be his home, but he had no idea what lay ahead. The only two people he had loved, who had loved him back unconditionally and taught him all he knew of the world, had disappeared without a goodbye.

DEVINDER'S STRIDE IS broken by the sight of a bald eagle gliding toward the park, its huge wingspan, white head, and tail feathers clearly defined against the sky. The previous summer Devinder had watched a pair of eagles attempt to make a nest in the tall cottonwood by the totem pole in Vanier Park. He observed them drift with short twigs in their beaks to the intersection of branches they'd chosen as their new home. The first few attempts ended in a pile of scraps at the base of the tree. This year the nest is cradled firmly in the upper branches. *Will this be the year for eaglets?*

Continuing on, he notices that a few seagulls are, for the moment, enjoying the calm, clear water of Kitsilano Pool. In a few hours the pool will be filled with families seeking an escape from the summer heat. *If it wasn't for the wedding this would have been a perfect day to bring the girls out to resume their swimming lessons.*

In recent years Kitsilano Park has become a refuge for some of the city's homeless population who spend their nights on the beach or under the large trees that line the road. Devinder's old friend Iqbal is among their ranks. Iqbal has been living rough for the best part of twenty years. He's easy to spot by the bright blue nylon K-Way windbreaker that he wears year-round, regardless of the weather—one of several items Devinder had given to him two years earlier.

Each time Devinder runs into him, Iqbal asks about the health of his sister, Rupi, and the nephews that he's never met. Iqbal's mother died thirteen years earlier from breast cancer and his father still declares that her son's estrangement was what made her ill, that the cancer was a result of the weight of worry his addictions placed on her heart.

Months earlier, Iqbal had grown emotional at hearing the news of Ranjit's wedding, recalling the times he held him as a newborn. He asked many questions about who would attend and where the celebrations would be held.

Devinder slows down his run and removes his headphones to peer amongst the brambles that divide the path and the ocean, determined to keep the promise he'd made to his friend that he would connect with him prior to the wedding to relay any messages he might have for Rupi. He scans along the seawall, past the Yacht Club, turns around to look back at the route he's just run. No blue jacket in sight.

At the end of the path Devinder is about to negotiate the steep concrete stairs that lead back to the street when he senses the thunder of feet approaching behind him. He removes his headphones and steps aside to let the running group pass. One by one they nod in his direction. Once, he would have challenged himself to race against them, but those days are long behind him.

He replaces the headphones over his ears and his feet hit the steps in time with the fuzzy guitar and hammering percussion of the song "Held" by Smog. He's reminded of the first time he heard their album *Knock Knock*, being taken by its desolate beauty, stories of men shedding old skin in search of escape and redress, and was gutted at the time that he had no one with whom he could share its songs.

Iqbal had first inspired Devinder's interest in music. In the latter years of high school and the first two years of university, they were forever standing in line to buy concert tickets, making trips to the A&B Sound on Seymour to grab the latest LP by the Clash or a new twelve-inch single by New Order. Back then, a new song could haunt Devinder's thoughts for days or weeks, the words, the melody, the consequent flutter in the belly. During the long commute to UBC from Ocean Park he was never without his Sony Walkman, sometimes rewinding a particular track so often that he feared the tape would unspool. Even now he occasionally likes to run with the old Walkman, listening to mixtapes that he'd made and duplicated, or others had made for him. He is reminded that he hasn't seen the Walkman in months and berates himself for having misplaced it.

Midway up the next block on Trafalgar Street he turns into an entrance between two high hedges. At the left of the housing complex, he dashes up two flights of wooden steps. On the front balcony of the apartment directly at the top of the stairs, Devinder lifts an aloe vera shrub in a red clay pot and swipes the key beneath. He unlocks the deadbolt and places the key back in its place, twists the brass doorknob, and enters. He bolts the door behind him, removes his headphones, and tears at the Velcro strap around his arm. He kicks off his shoes and continues to undress as he makes his way down the corridor; his T-shirt, soaked with sweat, sticks as he pulls it over his head; his underwear and shorts are removed in one quick motion. By the end of the hallway, he is completely naked.

He enters a sparsely furnished room with several canvases painted deep black leaning against the walls. Pinned to a large canvas are photographs of flowers—peonies, orchids, and lilies—in various stages of bloom, their petals washed in subtle light. The sweet scent of newly opened peonies fills the space.

At the kitchen sink he opens a cabinet, fills a glass, and gulps the water down in one breath. The window above the sink frames the North Shore like a painting. He rinses the glass and places it on the counter before making his way toward Emily's bedroom door.

ACT II
SAVÉRA—MORNING

THE PREVIOUS EVENING, Emily had played with her friend Sarah's sons, David and Tony, as they kicked a soccer ball into an imaginary goal, and Douglas, Sarah's husband, tended to the barbecue on the wooden patio of their Kerrisdale home, smoke rising over the maple tree that straddled their neighbour's yard. When dinner was ready, Emily picked up the ball and walked the boys to the low picnic bench where Douglas had set their plates, lifting Tony, the younger of the two, into his seat. As the boys tucked into their burgers, she sat next to Sarah on the patio steps where Douglas served them steaks, heaps of Caesar salad, and overflowing glasses of red wine.

Consumed by a conversation about Sarah's recent experiences as an emergency room nurse at St. Paul's—the downtown hospital where Sarah witnessed "the best and worst of humanity on a daily basis"—they were still picking at their plates when David and Tony, now bathed and readied for bed by Douglas, excitedly trotted out wearing superhero PJs. They insisted on a good night cuddle from Emily and sat in her lap, their hair damp and their skin soft as sable.

Tony asked, "Auntie Em, will you read us a story?" to which Sarah replied, "Boys, Em and I need to talk about some things, so not tonight. If you're good, it's possible Em can visit again tomorrow."

Emily nodded in agreement.

David asked, "Grown-up things?"

"Yes. Grown-up things," Emily and Sarah answered at the same time.

The boys hugged their auntie and planted wet kisses on her cheek before being led back into the house by Douglas.

"You're so good with them, Em."

Now alone, their glasses refilled, the women reviewed their plans for the next day.

"You still feeling okay about going?" Sarah inquired.

"Yes. I think so. Honestly, I do feel a bit nervous."

"I'll be by your side if you want to bail at any time."

Emily took a big sip of wine before she said, "Ta, Sarah. I want to be there for Ranjit and Rina, of course. They practically begged me." Even to herself she sounded unconvinced.

She took a long pause and another couple of sips before she continued. "There's a part of me that wants to see Dev and his extended family together. It's perverse, but maybe it's my one chance to catch a glimpse of the life I could have had."

Sarah stared back at her with a look of incredulity.

Emily resumed, "Remember when I came back from Northern Ireland? You asked if I'd come back for Dev."

"You told me no, that you 'didn't think so.' And then within weeks you were sleeping together."

"I know. I know. I was in such a state. I'd never felt more empty or alone. My mind was all jumbled. I thought having you nearby, painting again, and the teaching job would be enough. I thought I could see Dev now and again, as friends. I know now how naive that was."

Emily leaned her head on Sarah's shoulder.

Her voice cracked as she spoke again. "I think … I think it's time to move on."

Sarah turned her head so she could look her friend straight in the eyes. "You mean you want to leave him? You've been together, on and off, for half your lives, Em. As soon as you moved into your old apartment, I knew you two would be back together. Old apartment. Old job. Old boyfriend. It was like you came back to reclaim a life interrupted."

Emily shook her head and mumbled, "I know, I know," apologetically.

She refilled her wineglass. "I think I want … want to leave's the wrong phrase. I used to be so angry that Dev never proposed to me when the time was right, but maybe our love is strong because it's never needed to be sanctioned."

Sarah rubbed her friend's back.

"And I keep wondering if by being with him I'm not only cheating his family but cheating us—me and him. I'm sick of spending my days half worried that I'll always be trapped in this middle ground, and half worried of disappearing altogether."

Emily choked back tears and leaned her chin down. She could smell garlic on her own breath. And then, as though to draw a line to end their conversation, she said, "Once the wedding week's over, I'll speak to Dev and that'll be it. A clean break."

Sarah was not going to let her friend off so easily. "And that's why tomorrow's your one chance to see this other life, Em?"

Emily fell momentarily silent again before she replied. "I suppose so. It's hard to imagine a life without him, but yeah … I guess tomorrow's a chance to peek behind the curtain." She nervously tapped her finger against her glass. "Tell me if you think I'm an idiot."

Sarah put her arm around her shoulder. "No. You're no idiot. But you are a fine effin' mess!" They tried to contain their laughter so they wouldn't disturb David and Tony.

Douglas rejoined them on the patio with an amused expression as he tried to decipher the inside joke. Emily covered her glass with her hand as he tilted the bottle toward her. Sarah accepted before saying, "While we're still talking about 'grown-up things,' I want to say, about tomorrow, it's your call. I'll leave my place by eleven forty-five and be outside yours by noon. I'll be going to the ceremony with or without you. And I promise, as long as I'm around you'll never disappear. I need you. And my boys need their auntie Em."

In the fading evening light Emily shuddered as she straightened her back. They had joked earlier about how the invitation cards were addressed to *Mrs. Emily Rice and Family* and *Mrs. Sarah VanderVliet and Family* and must have had the same thought at the same time. They did a little dance with their shoulders and sang the chorus from "We Are Family."

"You're not an idiot, but you *are* a goof!" huffed Sarah, as once more they tried to contain their laughter.

Douglas cleared up the dishes and Sarah excused herself and went inside. A cold wind rustled through the leaves above and Emily reached into her handbag for her beige cardigan. She stood to get her arms through the sleeves.

A few minutes later Sarah returned wearing a Punjabi suit, a metallic-orange kameez with a pattern of embroidered leaves over a shiny orange salwar that hugged tight around her calves. Douglas whistled a catcall as he scraped the barbecue grill.

"It's a little tighter than the last time I wore it," she remarked as she pinched the material with her fingers.

"And when exactly was that, Sarah?" Douglas asked knowingly.

"Mmm … I think it was for Dev's wedding."

The three of them shared a muted and nervous laugh.

"You in orange and me in green. We'll be representing our motherlands well then."

Emily held up her glass and said, "Sláinte," as she swigged back the final drops of red wine.

"Proost," replied Sarah.

THE TOWN PUMP smelled of cigarettes and beer. All day Emily had been anticipating seeing one of her new favourite bands in concert—butterflies in her stomach and a sense that the show could not begin soon enough.

Sarah had dropped her off close to the bar so she'd find them a place to sit while she searched for parking. Emily looked around the dark brick-walled room and spotted Dev, busy in conversation with a tall, striking man with back-combed hair like the Cure's Robert Smith. Though she had never plucked up the courage to speak to him, she'd noticed Dev on campus before, recognized the barrel chest, his hair black as stage curtains, and an ever-present six-o'clock shadow. He was wearing his well-worn denim jacket—Emily wasn't sure that she'd ever seen him without it—over what looked like a 4AD T-shirt.

The high tables that lined either side of the hall were all taken and Emily really wanted to sit after the long week she'd had. She'd written four exams in six days and still had one more to go. Her gaze soon returned to Dev, and this time their eyes connected. He signalled with a sideways nod that there was room for her at his table. Dev and his tall friend scooted to either side and placed an empty stool between them. Noticing Sarah walking toward them, the friend vacated his seat and curtsied.

The stage crew were making the final tweaks to the sound, so introductions were quickly completed and hands were shaken—they laughed at the ironic formality of the action.

"Now that we're all inaugurated, who wants a drink?" Iqbal joked in a low voice and left to join the lineup at the bar.

Emily shifted in her seat to make it easier to look at Dev as they spoke.

"I've seen you at school. You know, I think we've had a class together?" she said, more a question than a statement—an attempt to make it seem she'd not fully placed him, though she could clearly picture the enormous lecture room and the front rows of bright orange chairs where Dev usually sat.

"Rocks for Jocks," he responded.

She laughed at his use of the popular moniker for the Earth Sciences elective and replied, "Yeah, yeah. At that time, I was confused about what I wanted to be when I grow up. I thought some lectures on plate tectonics might be just the tonic."

She was glad to see him amused by her corny wordplay and at the same time made a mental note to curb her sense of humour in case it might frighten him off.

Dev told her that he was finishing his second year.

"Why English lit?" she asked.

"I suppose I have Iqbal to blame. When we were younger, he'd recite Eliot and Joyce all the time. Then he introduced me to *Midnight's Children* and I was hooked."

After a pause, Dev asked, "And you? Have you figured out your major yet?"

"Well, I've been taking the general humanities path, so …" Emily shrugged and let out a loud and uninhibited laugh that turned a few heads. "No, not really. But I'm hoping to switch to Emily Carr come September." People often did a double take when she mentioned the art school named after her revered namesake. Dev was not fazed.

The venue was filling in and getting loud, and Emily found herself having to lean into Dev to hear him.

"You're an artist?" he asked.

"I suppose so, yeah. It's good to hear someone say that out loud. I've been drawing my whole life but recently I've taken up painting."

Iqbal came back to the table with a tray of beer bottles and wineglasses. He left the drinks on the table and shouted, "Right on!" before shimmying his way through the crowd to a spot near the stage. It was only when she reached toward the table that Emily noticed he'd brought two of each drink they'd ordered. "Oh, wow! That's generous."

She was over the moon to learn that Dev knew both 10,000 Maniacs albums inside out, could recite the lyrics. She asked what song he most wanted to hear, and he was quick to reply, "'Grey Victory.' You?"

"'My Mother the War,'" she replied.

"I love that song! What about you, Sarah? Anything you're dying to hear?" His hand touched Emily's knee as he leaned across to thoughtfully include her friend in the conversation.

"Nah! I can't say I know their music. Sorry. I'm only here 'cause Emily asked me. We haven't seen each other in a while."

"Yes," Emily added. "Sarah's a grand friend. She lets me drag her to shows even if she doesn't know the band." Dev gave them a curious look as they clinked their wineglasses and in turn exclaimed, "Sláinte," and "Proost."

A short while later the music from the PA quieted down and the lights dimmed. A rush of fans made their way toward the stage, subtly (and some not so subtly) vying for the best spot to see the show. Emily looked at Dev to see if he would take this chance to join Iqbal, whose tuft of hair was now clearly in the front row. Dev did not budge.

The audience roared as the Maniacs took the stage, and with the first few chords of "Grey Victory," Emily and Dev gazed at each other with their mouths agape. They inclined their heads and mouthed the words as the lead singer danced from foot to foot at the microphone.

With each new song Dev bent a little closer to Emily and by the end of the set they had pushed away their stools and were dancing, too.

Emily felt an electric current run through her as the band played a raucous version of "My Mother the War" during the encore. The audience started to leave but then the Maniacs surprised everyone by reappearing for another song.

Feeling euphoric and wanting to capture the evening Emily pulled a pad of paper and a STAEDTLER 2B pencil from her handbag and walked to the side of the stage. She started with a few simple lines and then began to add detail. Before the song was over she had a sketch of Natalie Merchant, her wild swing of hair, billowing skirt, and swinging arms caught in motion.

THE ROOM CLEARED quickly once the crew began dismantling the stage and the lights were back on. After the exhilaration and intimacy of the concert, there was a slight awkwardness between Emily and Dev as they tried to figure out a next step. Sarah read the signals and took her leave; Iqbal had already disappeared. Emily suggested they sit by the Gastown steam clock to unwind.

"It was good to watch the show with you, Dev."

"Thanks, Emily. Likewise."

Now that they were alone, he seemed a little unsure.

"So, d'you go to many concerts?"

"Iqbal gets me tickets through Radio Radio. He's got a weekly show."

When he failed to ask her the question in return, Emily broke the silence. "Aah," she said with a nod, "I'd go to more if I'd someone to go with. Sarah'd rather be in a noisy club with dance music pounding off the walls. Not that I mind, but nothing beats the energy of a great live band, you know?"

From the steam clock, they walked to Granville Street and found a corner table at Sugar Refinery. Dev held Emily's chair as she sat down before taking his own. They both ordered tea. English Breakfast. Sitting across from him, Emily got to more closely observe his dimpled chin, strong cheekbones, and the sparkle of his teeth. And those dark eyes.

They reminisced over their love of music, other concerts they'd seen, and what records they'd recently acquired. Emily was pleased to discover Dev's knowledge and admiration for music from Northern Ireland: not only Van Morrison, but the Undertones and Stiff Little Fingers. He claimed his favourite live album was Thin Lizzy's *Live and Dangerous*.

The subject of Irish bands got her thinking of her da; his love for music was something Emily had unquestionably inherited. She mentioned that amongst the things she'd brought from Belfast to Vancouver was her da's collection of albums from the 1960s. At the mention of Belfast, Dev looked both fascinated and concerned. *It's funny*, she thought, *that people think they understand Northern Ireland because they catch a few snippets of a story on the evening news.*

"It sounds like such a complicated place. What was it like growing up there?" he asked.

She liked the way he set up his question.

"There was a lot of unrest around the time we left."

"That must have been terrifying. I mean, you were only a child."

"Back then, it was just life. I didn't know anything else. I thought all kids had words like 'paramilitary' and 'sectarian' in their vocabulary."

Dev waved at the waiter and their teapots were refilled with hot water.

"Da disappeared when I was nine," she confessed hesitantly, fearing all this revelation might make her seem needy. "One day he left for work at Queen's University and never returned home. Ma kept reassuring me he'd be back soon, but soon never came." She curled her fingers around the mug resting in the middle of the table. "We still don't know what happened to him. He was the gentlest man I've ever known, and I can't imagine he got in with the wrong people."

Emily hadn't talked to anyone about her father's disappearance in a very long time. It was cathartic, as much of a release from the hard week as the concert had been. It was years after his disappearance before she fully understood that Da's place in the Belfast district where they'd lived was always untenable—his presence there was a remnant from days when coexistence was still possible.

"And my parents," she continued. "They were the most *in love* couple. Always embracing, touching, holding hands. I think their displays of affection were an 'eff off' to all the violence. Ma's family was Catholic and his was Presbyterian, and we lived in a Catholic area of Belfast. What they had to endure to be together was painful enough. Ma hasn't been the same since he disappeared."

There was a thin quiver in her voice that she never showed in public, let alone to a near stranger.

"Is that why you left?"

"We didn't leave right away. Da had applied to teach in Canada as a lecturer in Anglo-Irish lit. Even made a trip out this way for an interview. After his disappearance, Ma put our visas in a drawer. I'm sure she still thinks he'll come back one day. She's never given up hope, never removed his clothes, his shoes, his toothbrush from the old house and always had one ear toward the front door wishing it to open. When we did eventually move, she refused to sell the home in Belfast. Maybe it's impossible to leave someone who's vanished ..." *Rather than accept that they're dead?* She couldn't bring herself to complete the sentence out loud.

Dev gently touched her hands, which were still firmly closed around her mug, though its warmth had long dissipated. They gazed at each other across the table. She could feel a tremble in his fingertips and lifted her own fingers so that they covered his instead.

Her mother had moved back to Northern Ireland at the beginning of the school year; perhaps Emily was missing her more than she let herself think.

"So, to answer your question: three years after Da disappeared, Ma and I were walking home from the markets when we saw some kids playing war games with toy guns. We'd only just stepped onto the road to cross when we heard gunshots. Turns out not all the guns were toys. A bullet hit one of the boys in his leg and he went down hard. I can still hear his scream. And then I was on the pavement beside him."

Emily lifted her long golden-brown hair to show Dev the scar where the bullet had grazed her—a jagged ridge on her left temple.

"That's how it'd happen. People going about their day and then sudden chaos. They were just kids playing out their own version of what they saw every day. At the end of the school year, we were on a plane to Vancouver. We snuck in only a week before our visas would've expired."

Emily suddenly realized how long they'd been sitting there. The other tables were empty and the waiter was tidying up around them.

"Oh crap, it's late. I should really get home—I've got my last exam in a few days and I could use some sleep."

In reality, she wanted to stay exactly where she was, to hear *his* stories, but that would have to wait for another time.

"I've given your ears quite a bashing," she said apologetically. "Once I get started—"

"No, no, Emily, not at all."

Dev was the model of politeness.

"Which way are you going?" he asked. "I can give you a lift. Like you said, it's late."

The long day had caught up with her and she was happy to accept his offer.

"I live in Kits."

They left a few coins on the table and walked back toward Gastown. The night had cooled and Dev offered up his denim jacket. It smelled of cardamom and ginger. The sleeves hung down past her hands.

On West Cordova Street, Dev walked to the passenger side of a gold-coloured sports car, unlocked the door, and held it open for her.

"Oh, wow! What a treat. I wasn't expecting a ride in a flash car tonight!"

She noticed Dev wince at the joke.

The almost-full moon floated overhead against the ink-blue night sky as they drove over the Burrard Street Bridge into Kitsilano.

They chatted casually about their upcoming exams and favourite hangouts on campus and made plans to meet Thursday afternoon at the Nitobe Memorial Garden—Emily's choice. As he walked around to open her door, she tore a page from her sketchbook and discreetly left it on the seat before she exited.

They embraced warmly. She could sense his heart fluttering beneath his T-shirt like a bird's wings.

"Next time, Dev, I want to hear more about you. I feel like I did all the talking tonight."

"Aye, aye!" he called out as he squeezed back into the driver's seat. "By the way, I love your dress, Emily."

She looked down at the bright sundress with red flowers and was glad she'd taken the time to spruce herself up for the show. The car moved uphill and she was still smiling and waving as it disappeared around the corner and the loud purr of the engine dissolved into the night air.

A WHIFF OF coconut oil and sweat stirs Emily as Dev slips into the bed beside her. She loves the slight chill, a rush of cool air, as the covers are lifted and he shifts and curls his body to fit next to hers. She imagines if anyone saw them like this, lying side by side, they'd think they were waking from a long sleep, though, in truth, the last time they'd spent a whole night together was thirteen years ago. And that was in another country on another continent.

Their bodies have changed but there is a reassuring intimacy that Emily fears she'll never find again with anyone else. Dev is still muscular and lean, but time has had its effects: a slight softness around his middle, the hint of an arch in his upper back, fine crow's feet around his eyes. Her own body shows the marks of age, too: a heaviness in her hips and upper arms, a puffiness beneath her eyes, and her hair day by day shows more salt than pepper.

Dev's palm rests flat on the space above her breasts. With his index finger he traces the hollow beneath her throat. Still half asleep, she moves her hand to his and interlocks their fingers. After a few moments, she twists her body to face him, and their mouths open as if to kiss each other clean. It's not the intense rush of blood, the light-headedness of their early years of courtship. Not the tremor down the spine, when the slightest of caresses felt like the air was being sucked from their lungs. In those days everything around them would blur and they would become, momentarily, the only two people in the world. No. What she feels now is serenity and a tenderness that she craved during their years apart.

Emily moves her hand to Dev's face and traces the crescent scar beneath his lips—the tiny dots left by the sutures and the straight welt of skin between them. The events of the day when he sustained the injury are etched in her mind—the cry for help, the ambulance ride, the difficult waiting room encounter—along with the agonizing fear that she'd never see him again.

She looks into his eyes and he returns her gaze with the same verve she had fallen for when they'd first met; she's still taken by the deep brown, near black, of his irises. He's much more assured now, more confident, more hopeful. Although she knows him as well as anyone, she has failed to break through a thin membrane of quiet secrecy that shields him.

Twenty years ago she could never have imagined this life of acceptance and compromise. Dev will never be hers alone; they will never live together, be married, or build a life around a family. And yet their love had pulled her out of the mire after her return from Belfast. Dev's presence, no matter how ephemeral, rescued her from drowning in her own sorrow. These stolen moments have made her feel connected to the present, valued, and desired. But love is not enough.

EMILY RISES FROM bed, flicks on a light, and pulls on a paint-splattered shirt. She closes the door behind her so Dev cannot see her as she leans against the wall, hands clenched by her side. Making love to Dev has only made her decision more unbearable. She takes long, deep breaths as she walks into her studio and lifts the painting off the easel to carry it back to the bedroom.

"I made progress on Ranjit and Rina's gift," she says as calmly as she can. Dev sits up and fluffs his pillow to lean against it. He takes the canvas and holds the square image in his hands, rotating it first one way, then the other.

"I love it, Em! They'll love it, too." He pauses before adding, "That light on the petals, it's quite sensual."

Dev's ardent support of her work has never wavered. In her latest series—"Last Light"—she is attempting to capture the sun's radiance reflected on peonies in photorealistic detail.

"Do you think it's too much? It's just flowers. I don't want to shock your parents."

Dev had once told her that when they lived at home, he and his brothers would have to switch the TV channel or pretend to turn their heads whenever there was a kissing scene or any hint of nudity. In the days when Emily got to watch movies with Dev, she'd cover his eyes when the scene in a film was about to get intimate or an actor was about to disrobe. She can tell from Dev's snicker that he's thinking about the same thing.

"Not to worry. They'll find a way to pretend they don't actually see what they see."

They lie together in silence as Dev holds the painting with his stretched arms.

"It'll be ready by the time Ranjit and Rina return from their honeymoon," she eventually says—hoping that a little more time will make it clear to her whether additional brush-work is still required.

Dev carefully sets down the canvas on the floor beside the bed. They get back under the covers and hold each other tight as she breathes into his chest. Her thoughts are racing, colliding against one another. When Dev shifts to check the time she's quick to suggest, "I suppose you should be getting home. That shiny new Versace suit won't dress itself, will it?"

Dev smiles, wrapping his arms around her again and pulling her closer. "You know, I love that your accent is heaviest when you're teasing me … And it's Armani, not Versace."

Dev's tone is playful, but she knows a jolt of discomfort hits him every time she ribs him about his family's wealth—the push and pull he must navigate has been evident from the first time they met. *He can no less turn away from his adopted family than he can from his own daughters*—not that she'd ever ask him to do either.

"I should leave soon-ish."

The moment of silence that follows feels like an eternity.

Maybe it's time we stopped seeing each other. She catches herself before speaking the words out loud. *No, we need to get through today.*

"What's your week like?" she asks instead. "Any chance we can see each other?"

"I think so. After tomorrow the madness should die down. Maybe Lighthouse Park during the week?"

His suggestion, and the slight raise of his eyebrows, tells her that he doesn't suspect anything. Lighthouse Park has always been a romantic place for them. Walking beneath the red cedars and Douglas firs, sitting on the rocks at Eagle Point, gazing out at the ocean, feeling life's seemingly infinite possibilities. A lump builds in her throat.

Changing the subject, she offers, "I bet you and your brothers will look absolutely dashing in your Versace-Armani suits."

This time, she notes, Dev ignores the bait.

"Remember, everything runs on Punjabi Standard Time, so nothing will happen when it's supposed to," he says.

"Has Auntie Deepa come to terms with that?" Emily asks, remembering that Dev had told her of Deepa's initial insistence that the ceremony must end by noon or Ranjit and Rina's marriage would get off to a less than auspicious start.

"I think so. We had another meeting with the Head Granthi, the one who'll oversee the ceremony, and he assured her that the world would, indeed, not fall apart if the ceremony runs long. He said something like, 'God is timeless, only devotion matters.'"

As he sits on the edge of the bed, Dev holds his left leg and presses his fingers into the soft flesh below the kneecap, a concerned look on his face.

Emily stretches her arm toward his hair. She knows well enough that his serious tone means he's not completely sure of himself. *A breach in his armour*, she thinks.

"Sarah's picking me up at noon. We've planned it exactly as you and I discussed, Dev. We'll make our way to the gurdwara and sit in the back of the hall, well away from the family. With our heads covered no one'll be the wiser." She's intentionally chosen to wear the largest scarf she owns to best shield her face from prying eyes. "We'll congratulate Ranjit and Rina after the ceremony and apologize for not being able to make the reception." *And yes, I'll remain as inconspicuous as possible. And no, I won't go anywhere near the reception—or your family.* "Have I missed anything?"

"You forgot the bit about us synchronizing our watches."

She reaches for the spare pillow and swings it across Dev's back before bringing it to her face and letting out a long sigh. Hugging the pillow tightly against her chest, she looks over at him and asks, "Be honest. Is it best if I don't go at all?"

"No, no. Everything'll be fine. I'm glad you'll get to see Ranjit get married. Having you there will mean more to him than the hundreds of aunties and uncles he's not close to or family friends of friends of friends he doesn't even know. And I'm sure he'd rather have you there than all the business partners who'll be fawning over my brothers to get another contract. Besides," he cheekily adds, "amidst all that, no one will even notice you."

"Oh, thanks a lot!" Emily replies sarcastically as she softly pinches his arm.

"Em, you know what I mean. Stay low-key and be sure to offer Ranjit and Rina your blessing before you leave. Everything will be just hunky-dory."

She follows him into the hallway and watches him dress before they embrace. And then she leans in for what she imagines to be their last kiss.

IN MONTY'S TELLING of their journey to Canada and the subsequent lean years of adjustment and toil, Kitsilano is a sacred place that allowed them to survive and thrive.

He'd begin with the day they left their village on the back of an ox cart, then the slow journey by train to Kolkata, and an extended description of the sea voyage from Singapore, during which, he liked to say crudely, "Deepa and I were leaking from both ends, day and night."

He would continue, "By the time we got back on dry land, my Deepa was so frail I feared I might lose her. My own legs were like rubber and my stomach was as knotted as the ship's ropes. I must have lost four stone, and Deepa, well, I had to carry her off the boat in my arms. As light as dried grass, she was."

He was always full of praise for those who helped them in those early years. "We were at the mercy of strangers. The 2nd Avenue Gurdwara gave us shelter while Deepa recovered. They fed and clothed us. Arrangements were made for a doctor and we were given medicine. I don't think I fully appreciated what sewa meant until we found ourselves in need. They nursed Deepa back to health while I spent my days looking for work.

"The best way to fit in was to submit to the customs of this new country. The European workers beside us made ten cents an hour more than us but we never complained. There were neighbourhoods we weren't allowed to live in, places we couldn't go, so we stayed away. The only thing that mattered was gaining a firm foothold."

Amarpreet had been born six months after their arrival in Vancouver. By that time, they were sharing the top floor of a house with three other families. "We bought huge bags of flour and rice and split the cost. We grew our own vegetables and herbs. If one family was having a tough time with money the other families covered for them. Some of us worked two shifts to bring in extra though the work took its toll on our bodies. Once we were set here, we engaged in politics and fought for better work conditions, the right for those men who had arrived alone to bring their families over to join them. And equal pay. When new families arrived, we opened our homes and our wallets to them, tried to give them a hand up, like we'd been given ourselves."

DEVINDER HAS KNOWN and loved this neighbourhood since his first date with Emily. Even the name fascinates him: Kit-suh-laa-now—the meter of the syllables, like waves lapping against the seawall. It was Iqbal who informed him of the Squamish chief—Khatsahlano—after whom the neighbour-hood was named; that the Squamish, the Musqueam, and the Tsleil-Waututh lived here until the Indian Act displaced them in the name of what the government called "progress."

Devinder stands at the top of the concrete stairway in Point Grey Park at the end of Trafalgar Street. Across the Burrard Inlet the distinct outlines of West Vancouver and Lighthouse Park, the North Shore Mountains layered like strips of torn paper in shades of green, blue, and grey. The peaks are bare after the spring melt; their whitening and un-whitening marks the cycle of time for those who live under their gaze. Whenever Devinder needs grounding, it's this panorama that roots him in place. He takes a deep breath in through his nose and lets it out slowly through his mouth.

The pain in his knee has sharpened. It occurs to him that near the close of the sangeet three nights earlier, once the women had exhausted their repertoire of wedding songs and the dance floor was opened to the men, he'd unwisely hoisted Amarpreet into the air, catching him unawares as he bent low behind him to put his head through his legs. He'd danced for a full minute with his three-hundred-pound brother toppling around on his shoulders, both of them with their arms held aloft in celebration. *The double-decker.* He hadn't felt any pain at the time, but now he suspects that was probably when the injury occurred.

This morning, he and Kuldip are expected at Amarpreet's house by ten o'clock for the baraat—the procession that Ranjit will lead from his parental home to the gurdwara, his last journey as an unmarried man. Devinder does some quick mental calculations. *Plenty of time to shower, get dressed, and drive to Ocean Park, so long as Kuldip has managed to get Meena and Teena ready.*

His main responsibility at the baraat is to put the final touches on Ranjit's turban, to ensure it meets Uncle Monty's demanding standards, which he had adopted as a young soldier in the Indian Army. The previous afternoon Devinder had spent over an hour slowly wrapping the deep burgundy starched cotton around Ranjit's head, taking great care to get the smart lines and angles, the symmetry, as precise as those in Uncle Monty's treasured photographs.

"My pagg borrows a little from the Patiala Shahi style and a little from the Morny Dastar," Monty liked to proclaim whenever he was complimented on his turban. "Some might call it the Fortress, but it is a quite particular style I learned from one of my army comrades."

In an abundance of caution, Devinder had placed the tied turban in a hat box on top of a wardrobe in Amarpreet's bedroom. All he'll have to do this morning is set it carefully on Ranjit's head and tidy up the edges. *Easy.*

Though he's a little behind schedule, he's glad he made the time to see Emily—the first time in over two weeks. He has no doubt that their love is as strong as it was in their younger years, and some quality time together at Lighthouse Park in the upcoming week will be just the ticket.

At the bottom of the stairway, he breaks into stride and makes his way back along the path he'd tracked earlier this morning. When he's almost reached his top pace—Smog's "Left Only With Love" strumming in his ears—he notices a flash of blue down by the water. He slows his run and retraces his steps. There it is. The blue jacket. He searches for a way through the thick brambles but finds there is no easy route. He forces his way—branches snag at him and scratch his skin—until he arrives at an area covered by dark stones that have been polished by the ocean. A sycamore leans out over the water, the base of its trunk perched between giant boulders. Stacked precariously on one rock is a pile of clothes. The blue K-Way windbreaker is spread out on another. In the shallow rim a short distance ahead stands Iqbal immersed to his thighs, facing away from Devinder. Stripped down to his underwear and lathered in soap, he takes water with both hands and splashes it on his upper body like one of those sadhus in documentaries about the Ganges. Soap bubbles ripple the water's surface as he washes his hair and tips forward birdlike to immerse his head.

Devinder is amused and bewildered by the sight of his oldest friend bathing in these frigid waters. Iqbal has clearly gained weight and muscle since he last saw him, his skin is clear, and he is obviously enjoying his morning dip. Devinder tries to place the tune that Iqbal hums as he rubs soap into his armpits, around his neck, and behind his ears.

"Hey Iqqi!"

Iqbal stops mid-splash and turns around. His face has a rosy flush, and his beard is neatly trimmed. His hair has also been recently clipped and clings flat against his head. He plunges his whole body and then walks out to the stony shore, humming even louder.

"Dev, yaar. I haven't seen you in so, so long."

Devinder is unsure if the shiver in his voice is a consequence of being in the water, or the stutter that has become more pronounced in the last few years.

Iqbal dries himself with a wrinkled wool sweater— another hand-me-down that once belonged to Devinder, its original colour long faded to a murky grey. He mutters, "Aaj dinn bohut sohna charhia, Dev."

"Yes, Iqqi, it is a lovely day. But tell me, how are you doing?"

Iqbal flashes his gummy smile and reaches down to grab a plastic container from which he magically pulls out a set of dentures. He places them in his mouth and for a moment Devinder is transported back to their days together in school, when Iqbal's handsome looks and alternative style would turn heads.

"Vah-vah!" he exclaims—the Punjabi expression of approval that they'd emulated in their youth. "You're looking good, Iqqi! Love the new teeth. Isn't the water cold though? You know if you want a shower you can come to the house anytime. I can come get you during the week."

Devinder has tried over the years to convince Iqbal to visit the Ogden Avenue home. On two occasions he accepted, but his stays were short. Meena and Teena know him as "Daddy's friend from when he was little."

"I'm all clean now, Dev! And the water is lovely."

Then there are more surprises. Iqbal pulls down a new shirt from his pile of clothes, crease marks where it's been folded and packaged. He removes and stares with amusement at the strip of cardboard beneath the stiff collar, then buttons the shirt all the way to his neck. Without a hint of shame, he pulls down his wet underwear and unpacks a new pair of boxer shorts, slipping them on though he's not completely dry. Then he flicks open a pair of grey dress pants—a little wrinkled and short for his gangly legs—and tugs them over the boxers. He tucks the shirt into his trousers, which sit loosely on his waist. As he dresses, he continues to hum the familiar tune.

"What's with the smart clothes, Iqqi? Going somewhere special?"

"Like the song says, Dev, 'Oh, what a perfect day.'" Iqbal croons this last phrase, and Devinder recalls the mixed cassette Iqbal had gifted him that first introduced him to the The.

"And blessings to you and your family, Dev. Saré parivaar nu bohut bohut vadhayian."

Not only is Iqbal recalling music from their youth, but he also clearly knows that today is a special day for his family. *And why does he keep slipping back into Punjabi?*

Devinder dislikes mysteries and is flustered when Iqbal hastily packs up his belongings in a big black garbage bag, pulls the K-Way jacket over his shirt, and still barefoot, walks past him to climb the small incline. When the sound of snapping branches subsides, Devinder hears, "Later, Dev!"

He tries to retrace the path that Iqbal has climbed and his T-shirt snags on a thorny branch. Once he's back on the path, he looks in each direction. Iqbal is nowhere to be seen. Devinder paces back and forth desperate to catch another glimpse of the blue jacket. Usually, he has a lot of patience with Iqbal's skittish behaviour but today is not a day for anything unexpected.

What did he mean by 'Later, Dev'? Is Iqbal planning to show up at the wedding?

Devinder had been careful not to share any specific details of the day's events.

He makes one more attempt to spot the K-way by tracking back toward the concrete stairway. Nothing! As he scratches at his upper legs where the branches have marked him, he notices a split on one side of his T-shirt; a sliver of material hangs loose. Checking his Casio again, he is grateful for his forethought to allow a little buffer in the day's schedule, confident he can still make up the time.

He must warn Rupi or her husband, Jeevan, when he sees them later. A surprise guest and an unhappy father could easily unsettle the day.

"BEAUTIFUL. EDUCATED. PRIVATE school. Top marks in her tenth year. Speaks very good English."

In the twenty-four years since he'd been adopted by Deepa and Monty, they'd rarely spoken to Devinder about marriage. And now here was Monty openly discussing, albeit in his formal business tone, the search for a suitor for a young woman from India.

"My business associate Kash Sethi and his wife took her in when she was young. They've asked if we know of anyone in Canada to arrange a shaadi for her."

This was not the marriage talk that Devinder had witnessed between his adopted parents and his brothers. "We know better than you what's right for you. Make us proud. A man is not a man until he is a husband and a father!" In their eyes, failure to marry off your children was a shame almost as great as not having children in the first place. Devinder's brothers had never put up much resistance and were all married by their twenty-fifth birthday.

No, he wasn't being asked to marry this girl himself.

"I know you hang out in different circles than the rest of

the family, son, but why not ask," Monty continued, oblivious to Devinder's look of puzzlement.

The request did not come across as leading, and although he had plenty of single friends, *surely, they know that an arranged marriage would not be of interest to anyone in the "circles" I hang out in.*

He had to probe deeper.

"Why do you think it's been so difficult to find someone for her, Uncleji?"

Monty shook his head from side to side. "Honestly, son, you know how some people can be. The girl's background is a bit mysterious. She was found as a baby by Mrs. Sethi's older sister and her husband."

Devinder tried to decipher the hidden codes. "The girl's background is a bit mysterious" probably meant they couldn't be sure she was Sikh, let alone from the same class of landowners that the Sandhus and most of their close friends and associates belonged to. As far as Devinder knew, marrying into this class had been the number-one priority for selecting his brothers' wives.

He thought of the judgment and discrimination his birth parents had endured to be together. Not much has changed, he thought.

"Have you and Auntie met her?" he asked, surprised by his own growing curiosity.

"Oh, yes. On our last trip to India, your auntie and Mrs. Sethi took the girl with them when they went to Gurdwara Bangla Sahib. The girl even gave your auntie a tour of Hauz Khas. My legs were in pain and I was resting at the hotel, but when your auntie got back, she told me how much she liked her. Respectful, gentle, modest, and intelligent." Maybe this is a sales pitch after all?

"In fact, we chatted about her situation while we were in India," Monty continued. "Deepa felt sorry for her living in that house in Delhi. She was way ahead of me in figuring out what a bloody haramzaada Kash Sethi is!"

Monty coughed loudly and struggled to catch his breath. Devinder thought it best not to probe any deeper. Instead he left the conversation by promising that he'd think about potential candidates. But he couldn't shake the nagging feeling that maybe he had a bigger part to play.

LATER THAT WEEK, Devinder had met his brothers for lunch at Seasons, one of their regular meeting places at the top of the hill in Queen Elizabeth Park. They hadn't gathered in over a month, and it was well past time the four of them had a good "gup-shup" session.

It was a clear, slightly chilly day but they sat at their favourite table on the patio, under a heat lamp, to admire the view of the city. A light sprinkling of snow dusted the peaks of Seymour and Grouse.

As usual, a series of appetizers were ordered right away: fried squid and prawns, a charcuterie platter, mussels in white wine sauce, and meatballs.

Devinder apologized that he hadn't had a chance to attend any company meetings in the past few weeks because of the extra teaching he'd taken on. He was shocked to learn that they were considering restructuring three promising investment projects so they could finance the settlement of debts in India.

"Debts? I spoke with Uncleji a few days ago and he didn't mention anything about debts."

The brothers looked at one another as if drawing straws to see which of them would respond. Karanpreet got the signal to go ahead. "Remember a couple of years ago when Pappaji and Biji went to India, and they spent time with a businessman named Kash Sethi?"

"I know they did the trek to Hemkund Sahib," Devinder replied. "That was why we insisted that Pehalvan go with them. I didn't hear anything about any business deals though."

This time it was Navpreet who spoke. "Mr. Sethi was opening a bunch of service stations: oil changes, fluid checks, tire rotations, and such. He convinced Pappaji to invest in them, telling him the time was right and that it was a foolproof opportunity given the growing number of private cars in Delhi. We were so nervous about them hiking the trail up to Hemkund Sahib, but maybe we should have been more worried about Pappaji getting swindled. Pehalvan could help carry him up a mountain but not save him from a tricky investment."

Devinder nodded along and regretted not being more involved in the day-to-day activities of the family business; he really was out of touch. In fact, Monty and Deepa had invited him to join them for that trip to India, and as lovely as the pilgrimage to the sacred gurdwara high in the Himalayas sounded, his work schedule had been too demanding. Besides, he wasn't sure he wanted to go to India at all— his anger at what his parents had experienced stretched far beyond ill feelings for Pappa's family.

Navpreet continued, "Now Mr. Sethi is saying the service

stations are in the red and is asking us for more money to keep them afloat."

"And you know what the sneaky son-of-an-owl has done?" chimed in Karanpreet. "He's promised Pappaji that he'll buy out our share of the business if we can find a husband for this young woman he and his wife have adopted. We think that was his plan all along."

"It's entrapment!" said Navpreet, a little louder than he'd meant to. He looked around at the surrounding tables with an air of apology.

"Pappaji's being held hostage," Amarpreet added in a hushed voice.

Monty's comment about Mr. Sethi being a haramzaada, a bastard and despicable scoundrel, made more sense to Devinder now.

"We've thought of flying to Delhi to confront Mr. Sethi in person," Karanpreet confessed. "But Biji put a stop to that idea, phata-phat."

Devinder knew very well how Auntie Deepa hated even the slightest hint of a conflict. And Uncle Monty was not one to admit his own mistakes, so it wasn't a surprise to Devinder that he hadn't shared this part of the story.

Amarpreet continued, "We've all noticed that Pappaji's decision-making hasn't been at its best lately, even more so since his surgeries. Last month he wanted to break off our partnership with Patel and Sons because Sonny Patel walked out of a meeting while he was in the middle of one of his never-ending stories." They all snickered, but it was almost as though the expressed admission of their father's physical and cognitive decline was too much to disclose and they lowered their heads and said nothing for a while.

A bottle of wine arrived and the mood at the table took a turn for the better. They lapped up the appetizers and ordered their main courses: medium-cooked steaks with frites for Amarpreet, Navpreet, and Karanpreet, and a salad for Devinder.

They were briefly distracted with talk of the upcoming hockey season and how their beloved Vancouver Canucks might fare. The brothers announced that they planned to bid on a VIP suite at the newly opened GM Place. "Imagine being able to host our clients for a hockey game—right there!" Karanpreet pointed a finger at the white-domed arena in the distance, barely visible through the hilltop trees.

After they'd eaten their mains and were eyeing the dessert menu, Amarpreet turned to Devinder with a look of concern. "Hey Dev, sorry yaar, it was you who asked for this lunch. Is everything okay?"

In the excitement Devinder had forgotten the reason he'd asked for the luncheon. The conversation with Monty had haunted him. He was not given to grand gestures but thought perhaps this was his one chance to repay Deepa and Monty for the unconditional love they'd shown him since the day of his parents' passing.

He hesitated, trying to measure his words before they left his mouth.

"To be honest, guys, Uncleji spoke to me the other day about this young Sethi woman. He asked if I knew of anyone who might be a match for her." Devinder looked around the table. His brothers' heads nodded in unison, but he knew what he was about to say next would startle them. "Now that I know what you've shared with me ..." He took a moment before completing his thought. "I'm convinced that I should be the one to marry her."

It felt strange to say it out loud; his voice sounded like it belonged to another person.

Amarpreet, Navpreet, and Karanpreet looked at Devinder and then at one another. It was rare to see the three of them at a loss for words. Finally Amarpreet broke the silence. "Dev, you know we love you. Tell me you're not contemplating this because you feel you owe something to our parents?"

Devinder didn't have a chance to respond before Navpreet added, "You don't owe them or us anything, Dev. You joining this family was one of the best things that's ever happened. Ever! And …" The wine was making everyone emotional, and his words trailed off. Devinder appreciated the sentiment, though he had never doubted their love for him.

They picked at the few soggy fries remaining on their plates. Then Amarpreet asked, "Where are things at with you and Emily?"

The question caught Devinder off guard. They rarely brought up Emily in conversation, and when they did, she was always nameless.

Karanpreet, trying to add levity to the situation, said, "What the fudge, Dev? I can't believe this!" and ordered another bottle of wine.

"Emily's met someone in Ireland. One of her mother's doctors."

"Are you sure she won't come back?" Navpreet asked.

Devinder grimaced, astounded at being posed another direct question. *Why have they never shown this much interest in my relationship with Emily before?*

As if reading his thoughts, Navpreet added, his voice unable to hide a sense of guilt, "No, it's a serious question. It's too bad we never met her. I wish we had. It was always obvious to us how much she meant to you." *Obvious? Really?* Devinder hated how the cultural taboos they'd grown up with encumbered them.

"Well, that's not going to happen, guys." Devinder caught the annoyance in his voice and checked himself. In a calmer tone, he added, "Emily's future is in Belfast. And honestly, I'm happy she's moving on. I wish her the best. She'll always be special to me …" He did his best to sound assured. "But maybe it's time for me to settle down as well."

His brothers looked dumbfounded. When Devinder had first moved in with them, he quickly learned that being a Sandhu brother meant membership in an exclusive club that did much more than play carrom together. The closeness that he'd observed among them that first evening was evident in everything they did. If one of them had a problem to solve, they all got involved. But there *were* limits. If the issue didn't fit within the boundaries of what was considered proper, then silence was the preferred option. The taboo around sex made any discussion of romantic love uncomfortable. Familial love was easy, acknowledged, and celebrated. Romantic love was simultaneously convoluted and unspoken.

Sitting at the table with his brothers, staring into his empty plate and downing his second glass of Pinot Gris, Devinder thought, *It would have been good to have had these open discussions when I was younger. It would have meant so much to be asked even once, do you have someone in your life?*

They took turns to double-check with Devinder that he

was certain this was what he wanted. Trying to be helpful, Navpreet asked if he should get a photograph for him, but the question only annoyed him.

"No, Nav! What can you tell from a photograph anyway?" He turned his face aside.

There was some awkward fidgeting as Amarpreet asked the waiter for the bill and paid with the company credit card. Eventually he put his hand on Devinder's shoulder. "Take your time to think about this. It's a big commitment. Sharing a life with someone isn't exactly easy."

Navpreet and Karanpreet shook their heads vigorously in agreement.

"Of course, you know how wedding plans work; once the wheel starts to turn it'll be impossible to stop." After a pause Navpreet added somewhat sheepishly, "And it's Kuldip, by the way. Her name is Kuldip."

THAT WEEKEND, DEVINDER told Monty and Deepa what he was thinking. They appeared equally dumbfounded and looked at his brothers for guidance. Amarpreet assured them that they had talked this through with Devinder. Eventually they accepted. Wedding plans were set in motion, and three weeks later flights were booked for Kuldip to travel to Vancouver before the end of the year. At Devinder's insistence it would be a simple wedding with no fuss, but Navpreet had been right—the wheel had not simply started turning, it was speeding and there was no time for second thoughts.

KULDIP SITS ON the edge of the bed, closes her eyes, almost too tired to move. From the sounds in the en suite bathroom, the running tap and the strike of a razor against the hard porcelain of the sink, she knows that Devinder has returned from his run. He must have slipped upstairs while she was getting the girls ready in the spare bedroom.

She considers the day ahead and is proud of the role she has played in bringing the event together. Just being included in the decision-making has been a validation of her position in the family, and especially the regard that her nephew Ranjit holds for her. Yet there is always the struggle with expectations—to appear happy, to conform, and not to complain. Not only is Kuldip expected to keep an always-clean home, to be ready to prepare a meal at a moment's notice for unexpected visitors, to praise and defend Devinder and his family without question, but she must complete these tasks with an unbreakable emotional stoicism.

And the enormous effort required to care for her two young daughters is hardly considered. She loves her girls more than anything and will do whatever it takes to keep them safe and happy. But God, they can be difficult! They are sometimes spoiled, she knows, but that is through little fault of her own. She has to balance her desires with those of the family, and sometimes that means giving the girls whatever has been promised to them by Devinder's parents.

Family rules dictate that Auntie Deepa's wisdom must never be questioned; that despite her occasional pettiness, her blind refusal to see any faults in her sons, and her utter contempt for anyone who dares to do so, her word is sacrosanct. Deepa's piety is as polished as her kitchen counters. Daughters-in-law are expected to remain sober, to dress and act conservatively, to be neither too loud nor too clever.

Lately Kuldip has found herself caught between compliance and rebellion. But she is unsure how she can improve her life without upsetting the lives of her daughters. *They are the centre; the rest is only swirl*, she constantly reminds herself. *If the centre is calm, loved, and happy, nothing else matters.*

For tonight, she has gone against her mother-in-law's wishes and made her own arrangements; if her daughters should grow restless at the reception, they will be driven home by their babysitter, Alexis, who will make sure they have a comfortable sleep in their own beds. *They have endured enough this week.*

SHE WAS ALREADY awake when Devinder got out of bed, but she kept her body very still. Once she heard the front door click shut, she threw off the sheets and ran through the series of calming qigong exercises she had learned from Bawa Kaur, a family friend: clicking her teeth, back, middle, and front; circling her navel with both hands, first clockwise, then counterclockwise; shaking her limbs vigorously; and hugging her upper body with slow rhythmic hand movements down her arms.

Feeling relaxed and refreshed, she then showered and meticulously shaped her long black hair with a curling iron into the large waves she and her sisters-in-law had agreed upon. She took her time to apply her makeup, which was spare on most days, but she did not mind the extra effort to coordinate with them today.

Matching Punjabi suits with matching hair and makeup for her sons' wives—at least that should make Auntie Deepa happy.

Despite allowing Meena and Teena a little extra sleep time, they resisted her commands when she woke them— "Five more minutes, Mommy!"—until she reminded them that today was Ranjit Bhaji's *actual* wedding day. They jumped out of their beds with sleepy excitement, and she led them to the kitchen, still yawning and rubbing their eyes with closed fists. She poured them each a glass of orange juice, spooned the oatmeal that she had soaked in milk and kept in the fridge overnight into their preferred colour of cereal bowl, and sliced an apple to serve with a heap of almond butter.

"One day I'm going to have a wedding with cake and balloons and dancing and elephants," Teena announced to her sister, her voice growing louder with each addition to her list. "And so, so many balloons!"

"At my wedding there'll be a white pony, an elephant, and a tiger," Meena replied.

"A tiger? That's silly. The tiger could eat your cake." Teena had that proud look on her face she displayed whenever she thought she had outsmarted her older sister.

Meena's face scrunched into a scowl as she thought out her reply. "Oh, I know, I'll have peacocks."

"I'll have peacocks, too!" Teena agreed.

Every day they amaze Kuldip with new questions, new expressions, new ways to make her laugh.

Once they had emptied their bowls she brought them back upstairs to bathe and dress them.

She had planned simple cotton Punjabi suits for the gurdwara, but Meena insisted on wearing the three-piece lehenga Kuldip had set aside for the reception. There was no talking her out of it. Once in her outfit, Meena fussed over the stitching inside the choli, complaining it itched her sides. Kuldip had to sew extra material over the seams—a patch of velvet she kept in a pile of scraps for such emergencies. To Kuldip's relief, Teena agreed to wear a lehenga without drama or complaint.

The lehengas were off plan but the girls looked gorgeous in their long frilly skirts and sleeveless tops. Kuldip packed their cotton dupattas safely in her handbag, ready to cover their heads and shoulders as they entered the gurdwara grounds later. In a separate duffle bag, she packed a selection of extra clothes: a choice of dresses for the reception since the lehengas had moved up in the agenda; spare shoes, including comfortable white sneakers; and spare underwear—better to anticipate every possibility. Kuldip also set aside clean pajamas on their beds, in case Alexis had to bring them home early.

KULDIP HEARS THE sprinkle of the shower and as if by instinct she walks to the closet, bends over the laundry basket, and gathers up Devinder's sweaty clothes. She notices a rip in the T-shirt. Several times she has asked if she can throw out his most worn-out clothes, but he simply laughs and jokes that the wear gives them character. *Devinder hates letting go but maybe this T-shirt's time has finally come.* She lifts the material to her face. Beneath the musk of his sweat, she smells paint, turpentine, and a hint of lavender. *Her* scent.

It has been weeks since Kuldip and Devinder were intimate. These days, moments of tenderness feel more like duty than passion, more procedure than desire. Her mind wanders back to the night they first made love in the old-fashioned hotel room in Victoria that she believed was so romantic at the time, a promise of how their years together would unfold.

She takes down her outfit from the wardrobe, lays it flat on the bed and tries to shift her thoughts to the day ahead. She has attended numerous weddings over the decade since her arrival in Canada—the Sandhus are invited to all major community events, even if they do not know the host family well—but today's wedding is elevated as it is for one of their own. No cost has been spared, and no corners cut. The wedding needed to satisfy Uncle Monty and Auntie Deepa's very high expectations, which mostly meant putting together a flawless and spectacular event that would be talked about and envied, a high mark that others would strive to match. Every detail had to be reviewed, and then reviewed again.

A Tiger Team, which included Kuldip and Devinder, had been assembled to work with the wedding planners,

Pinky Brar and her assistants Bubbly and Pippi, to manage the arrangements. Their first challenge was to tell Auntie Deepa that the wedding ceremony would not be completed by noon. They had agreed that the ceremony and the reception should happen on the same day—that made Deepa nervous—and then decided that they should not leave too much time between the two functions. That made Deepa panic.

Makhan Singh, the renowned bhangra performer from Punjab, has been flown in to perform a late-night concert. Only the Tiger Team know of this special performance, and they are sure this surprise, as Amarpreet loves to say, will be "the icing on the cake."

Not like our wedding day at all, Kuldip thinks. The week she married Devinder was a series of quickly executed plans, small family gatherings, and very little celebration. There was no engagement ceremony (kudmai), no evening of traditional wedding songs (sangeet), and no jaggo oil lights were lit the night before. Of course, there was no wedding party with whom they could exchange gifts for a milni. There was not even a reception. Theirs had been a wedding arranged around a business deal, sealed with as little fuss as possible.

***

FOR THE ENTIRE week, Kuldip wondered if she had accidentally stepped into someone else's story.

Standing at the Departures gate in the Indira Gandhi International Airport, she was unsure of how exactly she should feel. She had received a generous hug and a long goodbye wave from Mrs. Sethi but there was an awkwardness in the moment that neither of them outwardly acknowledged. She was grateful, of course, to Mrs. Sethi for giving her a home for the previous twelve years, though *home* never felt like the right word for Lytton House. The gated Victorian mansion was more like an orphanage, with Kuldip its only ward. Mrs. Sethi was the younger sister of Swarno Kaur, who with her husband, Kirpa Singh, had raised Kuldip in the tiny Punjabi village of Nawabpur. The village was famous for its shrine to Sant Nirmal Singh, a holy man who it was said had been sent divine instruction to devote his life to charitable work for abandoned children. It was at this shrine that Kuldip had been found as a newborn. "Lying at the sant's feet as tiny and naked as a baby bird," Swarno liked to say. Though Kuldip called them Biji and Pappaji, they never tried to pass themselves off as her true parents; they had grandchildren close to her age.

Kuldip was dispatched to the Sethis in New Delhi when she was seven. By way of explanation, Kirpa Singh claimed that the village was no longer safe, so she was to spend a short time in the capital city. There were whispers of "dark days," which she would later come to understand was code for the conflict that had lately consumed Punjab. At the time the phrase confused her; the light in Nawabpur had not changed.

Exactly how long a "short time" was, was never made clear either.

ONE EVENING, A few months before her departure for Canada, Kuldip was tiptoeing her way back into Lytton House after a surreptitious trip to the cinema, when she overheard an argument between Mr. and Mrs. Sethi.

"If she were a boy, at least I could train her to work for me. But a girl is useless. Useless! She will never make the team!" Mr. Sethi remonstrated. "Why did your sister and that fool husband of hers take her in in the first place? They should have left her where they found her. Then she would have been someone else's problem. And they wouldn't have had to leave their village."

Kuldip struggled to contain the scream inside her. Mrs. Sethi had not mentioned her sister in years, and it was a shock to learn that Swarno and Kirpa were no longer in Nawabpur. Kuldip's knees buckled. She worried she might fall. A flurry of questions swirled through her mind. *When did they leave Nawabpur? Where are they now? Were the "dark days" the reason for their exile?*

"She is a good girl. Never causes any bother," Mrs. Sethi continued, in her practised defensive tone.

"Never a bother, huh! You think that damn school was free?"

Mr. Sethi's voice rose again and Kuldip heard his fist strike the wooden door.

She stood very still, afraid the slightest sound might give her away. Although Mr. Sethi had never been violent with her, at times she could tell the extreme restraint it took for him not to raise his hand—his face would turn several shades of red, a protruding blood vessel throbbing at his temple, and he would snort louder than usual.

"She had the best marks in her year. She was her class monitor."

"Monitor! What does it matter when no man will marry her? Maybe she's fruitless, like you. You should never have brought her here."

Kuldip could hear Mrs. Sethi sniffling through tears before she issued her final plea, "Then make the deal."

Kuldip remained frozen in place long after the Sethis had moved downstairs, both too absorbed in their argument to notice her in the dark passage leading to her bedroom. The quarrel confirmed her suspicion that the real reason for her presence at Lytton House was the hope of repairing a broken marriage—that she was a substitute for the children the Sethis could not have naturally.

She heard nothing more about a "deal" until two months later when she was told by Mrs. Sethi that she was to marry into the "prosperous and kind" Sandhu family in Canada. Kuldip recalled meeting Mrs. Deepa Sandhu, a gentle woman with a thick braid of hair that snaked down her back. Within days, Mrs. Sethi and Kuldip were traversing Old and New Delhi to obtain her passport and immigration paperwork. Brown envelopes full of money were exchanged with each mustachioed official they met.

Kuldip knew that one way or another she had to leave. If they were arranging something for her in Canada, she welcomed the chance to escape. Better that than to be surplus in Mr. Sethi's books—an expense in his business ledger. Besides, what choice did she have? She had no employment, no money, no friends she could call on. Her only confidante was Ehani, the Sethis' cook, and that friendship was unsanctioned and consequently secret.

Yet the arrangement gave her hope for what lay ahead. She remembered the generous blessing of five hundred rupees Deepa had gifted her after their tour of Hauz Khas Village and read that as a promising sign. She imagined a home and children who she would swaddle and protect. And a kind man by her side. She scrutinized the photograph of Devinder—handsome, well dressed—and dared to imagine a Bollywood-worthy romance.

The morning of her flight, Mrs. Sethi knocked on Kuldip's door carrying a heavy package wrapped in brown paper.

"Beti, I am so proud, so proud."

She pulled the twine holding the package together and the paper fell aside to reveal an assortment of fabrics for Punjabi suits. Kuldip realized she would need to make space in the scuffed plastic suitcase Mrs. Sethi had given her. The package also included two pre-sewn suits, matching chunis folded between the layers of fabric.

"This red one is for your wedding day, beti. This cream one is for you to wear today. You must make a good impression on my friend Deepa right away. Right away!" Most days Kuldip wore the kinds of Angrezi dresses that Mrs. Sethi favoured, hemmed just below the knees. It was only on their weekly trips to the Gurdwara Bangla Sahib that she was required to wear a salwar kameez, her arms and legs well covered. Was this gift an indication of how Deepa would expect her to dress?

Kuldip ran her fingers over the embroidered silks and crinkled chiffons, soft and rich to the touch—she smiled at the prospect of a brighter, more colourful life ahead.

From her purse, Mrs. Sethi pulled out a checkered handkerchief tied into a knot. She opened the bundle to show Kuldip a jewellery set: a gold necklace with matching earrings and bangles.

"These are a wedding gift to you, beti. From—from me and Swarno Bhanji."

There was a stammer in Mrs. Sethi's voice at the mention of her sister, and Kuldip hoped she might finally learn what had become of Swarno and Kirpa, but nothing more was offered. *Whatever answers she might give are useless to me now anyway*, she convinced herself.

Mrs. Sethi then reached into her dress pocket and pulled out a large wad of money wrapped in an elastic band, reddish-purple banknotes from Canada. Kuldip gaped in stunned silence until Mrs. Sethi added, "Please keep these safe, beti."

Kuldip untangled what was left unspoken—that Mr. Sethi was not aware of these gifts, and it should remain that way. To her further surprise, Mrs. Sethi placed the jewellery and money in the purse and handed it to her—a proper grown-up handbag with a metal chain strap and clasp.

Mrs. Sethi continued, "Deepa is a good woman. It was her idea to find you a husband in Canada. But I did not imagine she would marry you to her own son. What a blessing! I have heard he is a very nice boy. And he already has his own house!"

Later in the afternoon, after Kuldip had changed into the cream-coloured suit, she checked herself in the full-length mirror in her bedroom. She hung the purse over her shoulder and stared at the young woman, no longer a schoolgirl, looking back at her. The suit was very beautiful, but Kuldip worried about the prospect of spoiling or creasing during the long journey and retrieved her blue school cardigan from her pile of discarded clothes. Her stomach was in knots with anticipation. For so many years her life had revolved around Lytton House, her school, Bangla Sahib, and occasional clandestine visits to the cinema or the ancient ruins in Hauz Khas. Now she was about to travel to the other side of the world to begin a new life.

STEPPING OUT ON the tarmac, she was awestruck by the jumbo jet with its enormous, curved metal body, the height of Lytton House and the length of a cricket field. She could hardly believe that it would soon leave the ground and fly. She kept one hand tightly around her bag and the other held her chuni over her face; the air thick with smoke and the smell of jet fuel. Once on board, she found relief in knowing that she would soon be sitting comfortably for a few hours. But the relief turned to stress as she discovered that there was someone already sitting in her assigned seat. Though her schooling in New Delhi had been entirely in English, she had never had a chance to practise on a real Angrezi gentleman before.

"Excuse me, please, sir. I think you are accommodating my seat." Her voice shook with nervousness.

From his wide-brimmed hat, beaded hair, and neck and arms as red as Kashmiri chilis, she assumed the interloper was a tourist who had spent time on the beaches of Goa. He checked his boarding card.

"My mistake, love. I'm meant to be in row thirty-nine, not twenty-nine."

With a tip of his floppy hat the man made his way toward the back of the plane. A surge of pride ran through Kuldip. She had used English—in the real world!

Once her carry-on bag was stowed and she was in her seat, her purse tucked beside her, she looked around the long tubular body of the metal bird more closely, rows of cushioned seats with a big screen at the front of each section, like a long narrow cinema.

She clung to her armrests as the plane sped along the tarmac for takeoff, her right arm looped through the purse strap, her hand gripping the clasp in case it sprang loose from all the jagged movement. The luggage bins rattled and creaked and she feared the stowed bags would come crashing down on her. There was a strange popping in her ears. She was glad when the rattling subsided and a flight attendant flipped the screen at the front of her section. The opening credits to a familiar movie appeared. She tried the headphones but found the tinny sound disorienting, so she replayed the dialogue and songs in her head.

Two hours into the flight she was imagining Lata's voice singing "Didi Tera Devar Deewana" when the plane hit a patch of turbulence and she was struck with a deep sense of nausea. It remained with her for the rest of the flight. Unable to eat or drink, Kuldip turned back the trays of food placed in front of her.

The worst part was the landing at Heathrow Airport, when her stomach seemed to drop with the plane. She was glad for a reprieve to regain her land legs once safely back on the ground. As she waited to board her second plane, she recited lines from a poem she had memorized at school, a small distraction to dull her nerves.

"If you can keep your head when all about you / Are losing theirs and blaming it on you, / If you can trust yourself when all men doubt you / But make allowance for their doubting ..."

KULDIP UNPACKS THE set of peacock-blue bangles and slips them onto her wrists, shakes her arms to hear them jingle. They match the Punjabi suit, and though they cover most of her henna design, they somehow complete the ensemble. As always, Ram Dass has done a first-class job. It was Baljit who had come up with the idea that if the "boys" were wearing matching outfits, then the "girls" should too, and the four sisters-in-law met on Main Street and made a day of it. They were in the fabric store for hours and must have looked at hundreds of different materials—Ram's assistants unfurling bolt after bolt as they sat cross-legged on a cushioned platform at the centre of the showroom— before agreeing on the green-and-turquoise silk. Freshly brewed chaah arrived every thirty minutes, served piping hot in small glasses.

Once Auntie Deepa caught wind of Baljit's plan, she had her brother search the markets of Jaipur for bangle sets so all the women of the Sandhu parivaar would be coordinated. He has even brought miniature versions for Meena and Teena.

"Vah! That outfit looks great, Kuldip!" She had not heard the bathroom door open and is startled by Devinder's voice.

He stands with his head tilted to one side as he looks at himself in the full-length mirror, a bath towel around his middle.

"How were the girls this morning?" Almost all their conversations these days revolve around the well-being of their daughters.

"Fine," she says, not in the mood to elaborate.

"Have they eaten?" he asks.

"Yes, yes. They ate up everything." She could have added that she packed snacks for them in case they get hungry later but holds back.

"Good. We need to get going soon."

Of course, I know that. I'm dressed and ready to go. I'm not the one who chose to leave the house at the break of day for a morning jog. To see her.

Without removing his towel, Devinder slips a pair of boxer briefs over his legs and pulls them up to his waist. Once he is fully dressed, Kuldip adjusts the half-Windsor knot of his tie and gives a little tug to his pocket square so the right amount of fabric peeks out from his breast pocket. Despite everything, she wants him to look his best.

***

THE PLANE SHOOK violently as it began its descent. She watched the landscape change from snowy mountaintops to lush green forests to the rippled grey of the ocean's surface. Her nausea returned. Kuldip resisted closing her eyes, her mind fixated on the scene below; she had always imagined the ocean to be blue. As the plane banked right, she was stricken by an overwhelming sense of dread; the view through the window showed nothing but rough water. She lunged to grab a sick bag.

Once back on firm ground, she was interrogated in a closed room by a Canadian immigration officer, who scrutinized the photograph in her passport, holding it in one hand while glancing back at her face. She examined the birth certificate—printed on aged paper—for a long time before stamping Kuldip's passport.

At the luggage carousel her suitcase sat by itself off to the side. A kind gentleman in a blue uniform stepped in to help her lift the bag onto a wheeled trolley and left without asking for payment. In the restroom, she checked her kameez for stains from the journey, pressing her hands flat across the material to straighten out the wrinkles. She gargled hot water in the back of her throat and splashed her face. In a container for used paper towels she stuffed her crumpled school cardigan and allowed herself another smile.

More flights had arrived, so she followed the crowds exiting beneath the green NOTHING TO DECLARE sign. A series of narrowing corridors led to large frosted sliding doors where she waited patiently for the travellers ahead of her to exit. She wheeled her luggage trolley past the metal barrier that separated the passengers from their greeters, and was surprised when Deepa suddenly appeared by her side.

Kuldip bent at the waist, her hands in prayer pose as she touched Deepa's feet, mouthing the words Sat Sri Akaal as she stood up again. Deepa had changed in the two years since her visit to India, a little shrunken, frailer, and greyer than Kuldip remembered, her bright silk outfit replaced with a coarse cream-coloured cotton khaddar. Deepa held her at arm's length as she looked her up and down.

"That is a lovely suit, beti. And such a lovely purse. Zindi reh."

Kuldip beamed at the compliments. Mrs. Sethi had been right to insist she dress to impress—"You only get one chance to make a first impression."

Deepa seemed to notice Kuldip's hesitation and offered, "Call me Auntieji. That's what Devinder calls me."

At Deepa's side stood two tall, sturdy men who introduced themselves as Amarpreet Bhaji and Navpreet Bhaji. They greeted Kuldip with the same gentleness as their mother.

The brothers took turns carrying her suitcase as they walked out of the terminal into the rain and joked that a good business venture in India might be a drive-through to install wheels on old luggage. Kuldip felt a little embarrassed, but their joking was good-natured and not unkind.

Deepa held Kuldip's arm, both women bending forward against the wind and rain as they followed the brothers to the parking lot. Within minutes, they arrived at a white limousine parked in a long space. A driver in a black suit held open the back door. Kuldip immediately established that the man seated inside was Mr. Mohan Singh Sandhu, or as Mrs. Sethi sometimes called him, Mr. Monty.

He greeted her loudly as she entered—his voice disproportionately immense for the space. "Welcome, Kuldip!"

Monty was also dressed in simple khaddar. Kuldip bent forward to touch his feet and was discomfited when she realized she was reaching for metal prosthetics, a detail neither Mr. nor Mrs. Sethi had shared. She sat back in her seat and tucked her unsure hands beneath her thighs.

They travelled away from the airport along a curved road that seemed to float above the ground. In the distance Kuldip could see the rippling water that she had imagined drowning in during her descent. Auntie Deepa asked if she had eaten on the plane and Kuldip simply answered, "Yes." Deepa reached into her purse and handed her a mix of rock sugar and cardamom to ease her stomach.

Uncle Monty lifted his hand, palm facing Kuldip, and said, "I assure you, beti, that all will be okay and that you are safe with us. From now on, jo kujh saadaa hai, jo tera hai!" It was reassuring to be told that what was theirs was hers—words that Mr. Sethi would never have uttered. In fact, Mr. Sethi hadn't even bothered to say goodbye. The only guidance he had given her, a few evenings prior to her departure, was, "When you land in Vancouver you will be greeted by Mr. Sandhu, and he will answer any questions." But not only was she unsure of what questions were suitable, Kuldip felt tiny in Monty's presence.

Auntie Deepa continued to hold her hand as they travelled along a stretch of straight road. *Will this woman be the mother to finally keep me, to not abandon me or give me away?*

Kuldip stared out through the horizontal streaks of water on the window as the rain continued to fall, struck by the orderliness of the uncrowded highways—no concert of car horns, no animals sharing the road. They passed fields not dissimilar to what she recalled of the crop farms in Punjab.

Once they left the highway, they drove down wide

avenues bordered by rows of giant trees—long trunks and green canopies that reached into the clouds. The car eventually pulled into a street lined with high hedges and slowed in front of a gate that opened automatically into a long driveway. They came to a smooth stop in front of a house that reminded her of the shiny wooden lodges she had seen in movies set in the snowy mountain towns of Kashmir.

The limousine door swung open and the faces of three women stared back at her. One held a large open umbrella. She greeted them with wide eyes, trying to hide her drowsiness. Auntie Deepa insisted Kuldip wait at the doorway—stone lions standing guard on either side—as she disappeared into the house, returning a moment later with a bottle of mustard oil. Deepa poured a few drops along the trestle before she invited Kuldip inside. Kuldip trembled as she crossed the threshold into her new life.

The interior of the house was even more impressive. Dual staircases at the end of the wide hallway led to the second floor and there was an elevator to one side. Kuldip was stunned. Lytton House had expansive gardens, servants' quarters, and a security gate complete with guard, but this was far more modern with a blend of marble and polished dark wood. Compared with this home, its interior gleaming and sparkling, Lytton House seemed dismal and dated. Here, the floors reflected light up at her and seemed to whisper a soft welcome with each step.

Kuldip was led to the back of the house to a room where more family had assembled. They greeted her with enthusiasm and warmth. Even the children hugged her, some with excitement and others with shy caution as they stole looks back at their parents. Kuldip was grateful when she was finally seated on a luxurious leather chesterfield, even if it did make her feel like she was on display like a mannequin in a bazaar window.

A young woman entered carrying mugs of chaah and placed one in front of Kuldip. Then the room went quiet. Devinder entered and sat himself down beside her and the chesterfield suddenly felt small and cramped. She dared not look up. Her shoulders slumped with the weight of expectation.

A fresh cup of chaah was placed in front of Devinder and she caught a glimpse of his elegant hand and the sleeve of his checkered shirt as he reached for it. She noticed a slight tremble in his fingers and thought, *Perhaps he is as nervous as I am.* The notion calmed her. With her eyes directed toward her lap she could make out the slight flare of his blue denim trousers. *Only Bollywood stars wear jeans*, she thought.

The silence was broken by the voice of a young girl shouting, "Mmm ... ladoos!" as a plate of the round yellow sweets was passed around. The room broke into a pleasing bout of laughter. Kuldip knew the expectation was for Devinder to feed her the ladoo, and her stomach grumbled at the thought. He carefully broke off a tiny morsel, and when she turned her head to accept it, she was able to see his face more clearly—finer features than the photograph had suggested, big dark eyes, a strong chin.

Now it was her turn. She broke a tiny piece from the sweet and lifted her hand to Devinder's mouth—his breath warmed her fingers.

As the women lined up for their turn to feed them bits of

ladoo, Deepa clapped her hands and the queue was quickly broken, saving Kuldip from having to endure any more of the intense sweetness. She was introduced around the room. First to her soon-to-be brother-in-law Karanpreet and his wife, Kiran; then to Baljit and Harpal, the wives of Amarpreet and Navpreet. *How promising that my three sisters-in-law greeted me at the car.* Kuldip paid close attention as she was introduced to her nephew and nieces: Ranjit and Manjit (the latter being the "mmm ... ladoos" girl), the son and daughter of Amarpreet and Baljit; Surinder and Balwinder, the daughters of Navpreet and Harpal; and Mandeep and Paramdeep, the daughters of Karanpreet and Kiran. By the time she met the remainder of the guests, including a clutch of aunties and uncles and first and second cousins, she was losing track of the names and her head was swirling from the number of relations she would have to quickly learn. She feared she would never keep them all straight.

Kuldip's hand shook as she placed her empty cup on the large glass coffee table and the rattle of the cup on the saucer echoed across the room. Devinder nodded at Auntie Deepa and she clapped her hands once more. The gathering came to an abrupt close.

Kuldip was led upstairs to a bedroom, where a tray of food sat on a bedside table. Her suitcase stood in one corner looking tawdry against the shiny wooden floor.

"Sorry for the quick introductions, beti. We wanted to give you a bigger welcome but Devinder worried it would be too much after your long journey."

"It was fine, Auntieji." Kuldip's voice cracked.

"Eat and get some rest, beti."

Kuldip suddenly remembered her purse. She had not seen it since she was in the limousine. As she looked around the room Deepa sensed her panic.

"I will bring your other things to you right away." Deepa gave her a knowing nod, as though she was aware of the jewellery and the wad of money. Kuldip pondered the scheming it must have taken between Mrs. Sethi and Auntie Deepa to make this arrangement happen.

She ate the simple meal alone—a cucumber, tomato, and cheese sandwich with ginger soup. In the adjoining bathroom, she changed into a night suit, which had been left folded neatly on the vanity along with a set of towels.

Then she lay down on top of the sheets and was just falling asleep when Auntie Deepa returned with her purse. Kuldip immediately clicked open the clasp and breathed a sigh of relief upon seeing the knotted handkerchief and the roll of Canadian banknotes.

TWO DAYS LATER she tried on the wedding outfit and jewellery in front of Kiran and found the suit was a little loose around her waist. Kiran suggested they pay a visit to Ram Dass, the family tailor.

"He can fix anything," she explained. "Besides, don't you also want to get those lovely materials sewn into suits?" Kiran pointed at the rich fabrics still folded inside her suitcase.

Kuldip was glad for the offer of an outing after being stuck inside the enormous house. Uncle Monty had filled her ears with endless stories of his and Auntie Deepa's lives in Canada, their hardships and accomplishments. The stories were insightful, but she was relieved to get a break. And she was hoping Kiran would offer her some advice and guidance.

Kuldip's most pressing question was about the health of her soon-to-be in-laws. Kiran explained that Monty's health had declined sharply after their return from India and had led to the loss of his lower legs.

"The past two years have been rough on the entire family."

After the surgeries, Monty and Deepa had dedicated themselves to religious and charitable causes. First they had taken the Amrit Ceremony to be baptized as Sikhs and made a sacred promise to lead a life of devotion. Monty had given up alcohol and meat, and Deepa, already a vegetarian, committed herself to volunteer at soup kitchens to feed Vancouver's homeless population. They had plans to start an orphanage near Monty's birth village and often spoke of returning to find a suitable location. But given Monty's lack of mobility a long trip back to Punjab seemed to Kiran to be a dream too far.

"It's all in the name of simplifying their lives, clearing their debts, and making up for past mistakes," Kiran said.

Kuldip mulled this over. She wondered what mistakes Monty and Deepa might have made.

"And how long have you been in this family, Kiran?"

"Twelve years now. I came from India like you and didn't meet Karanpreet until a week before our wedding. You will lack for nothing, I promise. But you will find that sometimes things are a muddle. Everyone assumes you understand what's expected of you and sometimes you need to ask to be sure. I'm always happy to help."

Kuldip was thrilled by the thought of having someone to confide in—she had always dreamed of having a sister.

On the drive home—Ram Dass had quickly made the required alterations to the wedding attire and promised to have the other suits ready within the week—Kuldip plucked up the courage to ask Kiran about Devinder.

"Oh, Dev's such a good man. You got the best of the lot, Kuldip. I'm sure you already know that he was adopted when he was only a little boy. His own parents were killed in a car accident. If it was not for the Sandhus, God only knows what might have become of him. And I really do not know what they would do without him either. Everybody loves Devinder."

Kuldip turned her head away and smiled at her own reflection in the car window. *Everything is going to be fine!*

THE NIGHT BEFORE the wedding her stomach was in knots, as though a rough stone had lodged inside her. Kiran was the only one she could speak to about the doubts that had suddenly appeared.

"I felt the same way before my wedding. It is nothing. Try to focus on all that you have to gain and all that you get to leave behind."

It was not so much that Kuldip had thoughts about backing out, but she was marrying a man she had only met for a few minutes. Kiran spoke highly of Devinder, but Kuldip was the one who would have to spend her life with him. That night, she slept restlessly.

In the morning, the family and a handful of additional guests assembled at the gurdwara. Kuldip's wedding outfit felt heavy, but its warmth was a welcome buffer from the cold.

Auntie Deepa walked her into the prayer hall over the sound of kirtan and sat her next to Devinder. Kuldip gave a quick sideways glance and glimpsed his beige sherwani and red turban, the beard he had grown out over the past few days.

For the four lawaan, Devinder's brothers filled the role of what would traditionally be that of the bride's brothers and led her around the Guru Granth Sahib, the sacred book of Sikh scripture. The ceremony was over in fifteen minutes. The stone in her stomach seemed to diminish, but she was surprised by how little emotion she felt, as though the day had been a mere formality. What mattered was that Kuldip was a wife now and would need to assume her new duties with care.

She remained sitting at Devinder's side for the minutes it took for the congregation to offer them sagan. Soon after, in the parking lot, they were approached by a few guests for another round of congratulations. It was easy to see that Devinder was adored as he joked and laughed with them. Amongst the select guests was a friend named Sarah who gifted them a certificate to a store called Ten Thousand Villages.

The immediate family returned to Monty and Deepa's home and had a simple dinner prepared by the house cook. Deepa made a show of removing Devinder's stainless steel kara and replacing it with one made of "twenty-two-carat Indian gold." Her sisters-in-law accompanied Kuldip as she followed Devinder into Monty's limousine and the driver took them to a beautiful hotel in the city centre. The suite smelled of jasmine, the white flowers arranged in several vases on the low dressers. From the window she could see hundreds of large white boats along the waterfront, a forest of thin wooden masts, and snow on the mountain peaks in the distance.

That night, as they lay down on opposite sides of the king-size bed, Kuldip realized that they had still not spoken directly to each other.

BY THE TIME they arrive outside Amarpreet's home both sides of the road are filled with cars. Sandhu Properties had been early investors in this development in Ocean Park. While it's now sought out by those who want "easy access to the city and seascapes," for the Semiahmoo, the people who lived on these high bluffs before the settlers arrived, this was a place of renewal and vision, and the vistas of the Salish Sea and the Gulf Islands provided a tactical vantage point. There are wide tree-lined streets, broad driveways, but no sidewalks; houses recede into the surrounding woods, hidden behind manicured English laurel hedges. The neighbourhood is officially called Harmony Estates—with a sign made from large brass letters on a curved brick wall at its entrance—but when Uncle Monty first invested here Iqbal had nicknamed it Shantih Estates because of its popularity with retiring Punjabi Sikhs, and that sobriquet remains stuck in Devinder's mind. Whenever they'd meet here Iqbal would greet Devinder by cheekily chanting "shantih" before giving dramatic recitals of long passages from *The Waste Land*.

This entire week has served as a tribute to Uncle Monty, who repeatedly claims this will be the last family wedding before his body fails him altogether. The prospect of Monty's demise is whispered very quietly amongst the family, as though speaking it out loud could hasten it. Monty has decided to remain in his car and not be present in either the gurdwara or the reception hall, but his shadow will loom large over the day's events. Devinder knows there will be many who'll want a few minutes with Vancouver's most revered businessman and community leader; a meeting with Mr. Mohan Singh Sandhu has become a symbol of achievement, something to be strived for, something to be coveted. Devinder understands that for Monty the lesser shame is to conduct meetings in his limousine rather than show any infirmity. Monty's always been very conscious of his public image but in the past few years it's become an obsession.

Amarpreet and Baljit have been trying to persuade Monty and Deepa to move in with them—though they're only a stone's throw away, they worry about their ageing parents' ability to manage on their own, particularly now that Deepa's health is also showing signs of decline. Amarpreet sees it as his duty as the eldest son, and the argument that he and Baljit have more than enough space in their home has grown louder and more frequent, especially now that Ranjit will be married and moving out. They've even had an elevator installed. But Deepa insists, "We didn't raise ourselves out of poverty to make our children's lives more difficult. We are happy in our own home!"

Monty and Deepa continue to use the defence that they have Pehalvan Singh, as well as a team of housecleaners, cooks, and social workers, and their sons are compelled to coordinate their schedules and the schedules of their spouses and grown children to make sure there is hardly a moment in the day when someone is not with them.

Devinder pulls up beside Monty's limousine and is evaluating his parking options when he spots Ranjit's sister, Manjit, rushing toward them, zigzagging between the parked cars on the driveway. She's a little short of breath and has an impish smile on her face.

"Sat Sri Akaal, Chachaji, Chachiji!"

Manjit offers the slightest of bows and blows kisses at Meena and Teena who wave enthusiastically at their cousin-sister from the back seat. "Chachaji, your brothers are all in a panic. I'll park your car. But you should go in quick before one of them has a bird." She winks at Devinder and the girls giggle at her audacious joke.

As Manjit drives away, Kuldip and Devinder carry Meena and Teena to the window of the limousine. Although Monty's voice does not have the timbre it once had, he maintains a commanding presence. "Aah, Maninder, Tejinder. My lovely angels. How beautiful you look!"

He struggles to stretch his arm out of the window to bless his youngest granddaughters, and they bow their heads to meet his hand. With prodding from Kuldip, they hold their hands together in front of their faces and sing in unison, "Sat Sri Akaal, Dadaji."

A worrying line of sweat circles Monty's neckline and brushes the edges of his turban, so Devinder asks Kuldip to take the girls into the house by herself and climbs inside. He knocks on the glass screen separating them from Pehalvan. "Turn up the AC, yaar! Uncleji is melting back here."

Devinder reaches for Monty's swollen hands, skin the texture of rice paper.

"I'm fine." Monty takes a moment to compose himself before he continues. "Tip-top. Don't you worry about me, son."

His persistent bronchial cough has worsened over the last couple of months, and he places a handkerchief over his mouth as he tries to suppress the rattle and wheeze that emanates from his congested lungs. Despite his illness, Monty looks sharp in his white turban and cream-coloured khaddar suit—Pehalvan, no doubt, had spent an extra-long time getting him ready this morning. The beard, which he once kept tied flat against his chin, hangs down mid-chest. Pehalvan has been instructed to make sure Monty does not overexert himself today, and has the full trust of the family to decide when he needs a break.

Devinder notices Monty's old briefcase tucked in the space beside him. *Even on his grandson's wedding day, he's ready to show himself as the master businessman and empire builder.*

In truth, it is Amarpreet, Navpreet, and Karanpreet who run the company these days, and Monty is simply a figure-head. Ever since the imprudent investment with Mr. Sethi, the brothers have developed a ruse that allows their father to think he's critically involved in the decision-making while in reality he lacks the ability to impact the day-to-day finances. With his short-term memory deteriorating year by year, the ruse is becoming easier—and more necessary.

They make small talk about the day ahead, and Devinder recollects the last time he was alone with Monty. The Tiger Team had been meeting at Monty and Deepa's home to review some final details for the wedding day and seek their approval and blessing. Deepa contributed several changes:

a few minor tweaks to the layout in the reception hall and suggestions for the dinner menu. Monty stayed quiet, and as soon as the meeting was finished claimed he was tired and in need of rest. Pehalvan was busy washing the limousine in the driveway, so Devinder offered to take Monty upstairs.

In Monty's bedroom, he noticed the old family albums were open and a stack of photographs lay on the dresser. *Perhaps for the slide show at the wedding?* More curiously, the box frame in which Devinder had mounted Monty's army medals many years earlier—including the Burma Star, the Defence Medal, and the Independence Medal—had been removed from the wall and sat empty on the bedside table.

Now, as he holds Monty's hand, Devinder regrets not asking him about the empty frame and missing medals. He imagines a conversation as enlightening as those they had in the years after his brothers had all married and he was the last son living at home. In those days Devinder often had Monty all to himself and was able to be inquisitive in a way he never could with his brothers around. And Monty was only too eager to divulge.

He wishes he could stay with him but is aware that he's expected inside. He gives Monty's hand one last squeeze before commanding Pehalvan to keep a close eye on his passenger.

WITH ITS EXTERIOR of Douglas fir cladding and enormous tempered-glass windows, Amarpreet and Baljit's house merges seamlessly into the treescape—towering western hemlocks and giant cedars. The four-storey home backs onto a steep decline to the ocean. A public staircase next to the property winds down to a tiny public beach. The crowning feature is the rooftop terrace that rises above the trees to give a 360-degree view of the Pacific Ocean, the Lower Gulf Islands, the growing downtown core of Surrey, and, on clear days, the distant Pacific Ranges of the Coast Mountains.

The front door is open, and Devinder can hear chatter from inside as he works his way past the parked cars on the driveway. He nods in the direction of the dhol player who is standing in the shade lightly tapping the barrel-shaped two-sided drum strapped to his shoulder. The marble floor of the large foyer and the hardwood of the main living room are covered with crisp white sheets—the furniture has been moved to the garage. Relatives from near and far, about three dozen in total, stand conversing in the open space, and Devinder is greeted with warm smiles and fervent waves. Natural light floods the room through the skylight in the foyer's ceiling. Speckled Italian marble lines the height of the far wall where the photographers have set up a tall chair for Ranjit to sit for the pre-baraat portraits; the captain's dining chair, mahogany with red velvet covers, sits empty and ignored on the marble hearth for now, but will soon be the central focus.

Devinder catches the comforting smell of chaah as it drifts in from the kitchen and realizes in the rush of the morning he has forgotten to eat breakfast.

He can sense the mix of excitement and apprehension for the celebrations to reach their culmination. Monty's two younger sisters have driven in from Abbotsford with their families. Deepa's younger sister, Chhoti Masiji, and older brother, Vaddé Maamaji, have flown in from Jaipur. Devinder's nieces are making their rounds, checking to make sure everyone is taken care of. A few select close friends of the family are also present, including former residents of Haripur, Monty's ancestral village. Devinder finds it fascinating that the first connection between Punjabi Sikhs is often through identifying the pind, the village, they are from and uncovering common acquaintances—almost always less than three villages of separation. On those rare occasions these days when he meets somebody from the community who does not know of the Sandhus, Devinder's standard response to the obligatory question is always "Haripur"—much easier than having to disseminate the story of Narinder and Mira.

Circling through the room is the audiovisual team—a photographer, a videographer, and their assistants—doing their best to be inconspicuous as they try, without much success, to take candid shots of the gathering. Devinder notes the quick movements and exaggerated smiles, attempts for more traditional poses, when anyone notices they have a camera on them. The caterers carry and distribute platters of samosas and Indian sweets, trays balancing dozens of small cups of chaah.

Devinder shakes hands and offers greetings as he walks the room, all the while searching for Auntie Deepa. He finally sees her in the kitchen in conversation with Kuldip. Whatever they're talking about, Deepa looks serious and a little flustered. She shakes a finger at Kuldip but then her expression changes dramatically as she bends low to embrace Meena and Teena. By the time Devinder is beside her, she has her hands placed on his daughters' heads and is smiling broadly while whispering, "Zindian raho," her customary blessing—"stay alive and be well." As she straightens, Deepa grabs Devinder's hand to steady herself.

Kuldip looks at their daughters and asks, "What do you say to Dadiji, girls?" In unison again, they hold their hands in a prayer pose and bow their heads slightly. "Sat Sri Akaal, Dadiji!"

Devinder can tell that standing up too quickly has caused one of Deepa's occasional bouts of dizziness and gives her a minute to regain her balance. The doctors have prescribed medication for her blood pressure, but he worries that something else is going on that they have not yet diagnosed.

"Beta, your brothers need your help. That turban you tied last night…"

She does not need to finish her sentence.

"Auntieji, don't worry I'll take care of it."

"I know, beta. You always do."

Deepa calls out a quick "Zinda reh!" as Devinder departs. In the dining room, he finds his brothers gathered around Ranjit, dressed in his sparkling wedding outfit; gold threaded diamonds on the tailor-made burgundy sherwani, the tunic that ends below his knees, over a gold-coloured salwar that narrows around his calves and ankles, and gold fringes on the crinkled chiffon scarf around his neck. The traditional pointed leather shoes, beside him, are also embroidered with gold thread and sequins. Only the turban is needed to complete the ensemble.

Seeing his nephew crowded by his father and uncles, Devinder cannot help but grin at the absurdity of the matching outfits he and his brothers are wearing. From the navy suits to the spread-collared white shirts, silver ties, and shiny black patent-leather shoes, every item matches. Even their socks. His brothers look back and forth at one another and try to restrain their laughter. *We look like an eighties boy band. But if it makes Auntie Deepa happy, it's worth it.*

Ranjit, as if reading his uncle's thoughts, laughs out loud and says, "Guys, I know who the lead singer would be! Just saying." They all turn to look at Devinder whose suit sits perfectly on his frame.

"Nah, kid," says Devinder. "The groom has to be the lead. You look seriously dapper!"

His brothers nod in agreement while making small adjustments to their own ties and pocket squares. Devinder spots the length of burgundy fabric, formerly the completed turban, the pagg, that he had painstakingly tied the night before, draped over an empty chair.

"Dev, sorry, yaar. Thank goodness you're here," says Amarpreet with a trace of guilt. "We were all trying to call you."

"I noticed. And you know I don't answer my cell if I'm driving with my girls." He does his best to veil any frustration.

While Devinder is carefully examining the material, Ranjit asks with a knowing grin, "So, Dev Chachaji, how is it that you're the only one who can fix this?"

HOME FROM SCHOOL, his grade four homework completed, Devinder had just turned on the TV for an episode of *Swiss Family Robinson* when he heard the rattle of keys in the front door. Amarpreet walked in with his hair hanging loose around his shoulders. At first Dev thought it was a practical joke. Karanpreet loved to play the joker, but Amarpreet and Navpreet were not beyond playing up to get a laugh. Auntie Deepa, having heard the front door open, came into the living room and gasped at the sight of her eldest son in such an unkempt state. If this was a joke, then Deepa was obviously not amused.

It was only when Amarpreet came closer that they noticed the cuts and bruises on his face; one eye was swollen and there was dried blood around his nose. Amarpreet's body trembled and his legs crumpled as he began to cry on his mother's shoulder. Devinder grabbed him by the arm and guided him to the couch before turning off the TV.

"Biji, I'm so sorry! I'm so sorry!"

"Beta, what has happened? I don't understand." Deepa's eyes searched her son's face for an explanation.

For a few minutes, Amarpreet struggled to get any sound

out at all. Devinder, also shaken but desperate to help, went to the kitchen, brought back two glasses of water, and urged them both to take a sip.

Finally Amarpreet's words spilled out in short spurts. "I was walking back to the car ... after class ..." he mumbled, before needing to catch his breath again. "I was jumped ... I didn't see them coming. The first punch was to the back of my head. It knocked off my pagg. Then they knocked me to the ground ... and started to kick me."

Deepa couldn't contain herself any longer and let out a deep wail as she held her hands over her face and shook her head furiously. Devinder recalled the posters on the wall of the gurdwara classroom with images of the Five Sacred *K*s. The kesh, the unshorn hair—God's natural gift—was the most treasured.

Once Deepa's sorrow had settled, Amarpreet reached into his backpack and pulled out the dishevelled pagg, the length of black cotton Devinder had seen him wearing that morning.

"I don't know how many of them there were ... I couldn't stand up to fight back. All I could see was their leather boots coming at me again and again."

Amarpreet could lift nine-year-old Devinder with one arm. It was hard to imagine him not being able to stand his ground in a fight.

"I curled my body ... to protect myself. It was all I could do."

"Was there no one else around, beta, to help you?"

Amarpreet explained that there was a man, perhaps a teacher at the college, who ran toward his attackers, screaming for them to stop. It was only when he was close that they ran off.

His sobs started up again. With his head held in his hands, he managed to say, "The gentleman helped me sit up … stayed with me … to make sure I was okay. He used his own jacket to stop the bleeding. He sat with me … until I was strong enough to stand again. He offered to drive me home."

THAT EVENING, THE family sat together in the living room with the rumpled turban lying on the coffee table between them. For the longest time no one uttered a word until, finally, Uncle Monty pounded his fist on the table, making everyone jump.

"Nobody does this to a son of mine!" he shouted, repeating, "nobody!" several times until his breath gave out.

His fury filled the room, and though Navpreet and Karanpreet stayed silent, Devinder could read anger and fear on their faces. Auntie Deepa recited prayers to herself.

Monty reached for his car keys. "I will find those bloody bastards!"

"Pappaji, please. You're not going to find them now. It happened hours ago."

But the more Amarpreet tried to calm him down, the more agitated Monty became, and the brothers had to pull at their father's arms to keep him from leaving.

The room fell silent again but not for long. "How dare they do this to us!" Monty yelled. "I will go to the college tomorrow and ask them to expel these haramzaadai!"

"They weren't students, Pappaji. They were only there to make trouble." It was Navpreet's turn to talk down their father.

Monty swore out loud: Punjabi words that Devinder had never heard before but knew were the type his adopted father would never use in front of him ordinarily.

The family sat in uneasy silence for the next twenty minutes, each lost in their own thoughts. Eventually Uncle Monty picked up the unravelled pagg and walked out of the room with it cradled in his arms.

***

A WEEK LATER, after numerous family debates and Deepa's pre-emptive prayers asking for forgiveness, they drove to an Italian barbershop on Main Street—the place where Amarpreet took Devinder once a month to get his short back and sides. The brothers had decided that this was an "all-for-one and one-for-all" moment, that together they would make the sacrifice.

They sat in a row facing the mirrored wall. One by one they removed their turbans and unbraided their hair so it canopied over the backs of the red leather chairs, nearly touching the floor. Karanpreet, still new to wearing an adult pagg, having only recently graduated from the large handkerchief, the patka, to cover his topknot, looked to his older brothers. His hair was not nearly as long as theirs but had the same shiny, almost silken texture. Devinder collected the lengths of cotton in a plastic bag and sat back on a chair in the waiting area. One of the stylists returned from the stockroom with the largest pair of scissors he'd ever seen. The head barber, with a concerned look on his face, asked them if they were sure they really wanted to proceed. They looked back and forth at one another for reassurance before they each held their eyes tightly shut and nodded. Navpreet reached a hand over and touched Karanpreet's arm to comfort him.

Their lifetime of commitment to the sacred tenet came to an end with three quick cuts from the large scissors. The detached braids lay on the barbershop counter—end to end they made a nine-foot rope of hair.

On the walls around the salon were photographs of young men with the latest popular hairstyles and the brothers were asked to choose which one they wanted. Amarpreet pulled a folded piece of paper from his shirt pocket showing the poster for the film *Sholay*, which he'd torn from a magazine. He pointed his finger at Dharmendra, the lead actor. The team of barbers passed the page around and had a little conference amongst themselves. Finally one of them turned back to the brothers. "You all want the same cut?"

Devinder stared wide-eyed at his brothers' reflections as the barbers got to work, taking short strips of hair between their fingers and making careful, angled cuts. At one point, Navpreet asked for a pause as he reached over to Karanpreet, who was now in tears.

Two other customers stuck around even after they'd paid for their own cuts, looking sad and concerned.

Later an electric trimmer was run over his brothers' beards and a straight razor shaved their faces down to the skin. As was the fashion, all three opted to keep lengthy sideburns.

When the job was done, the barbers nodded at each other in recognition of their own skill, but they did not break the sombre mood. Devinder barely recognized his brothers; they hardly resembled the three young Sardars who had entered the shop forty-five minutes earlier.

On the drive home Devinder kept looking from one face to the other in disbelief. He clutched the plastic bags that held their turbans and their braids, labelled *A*, *N*, and *K*. Navpreet took a cassette from the glovebox and played "Yeh Dosti Hum Nahi Todenge," a song from *Sholay*, which lightened the mood considerably. All four of them sang along, with Karanpreet, in the back seat, adding hand gestures for revving a motorcycle and a harmonica solo to close.

DEVINDER CARRIED TWO towels and a bottle of coconut oil onto the deck. He unrolled one towel on the wooden slats beneath Monty's feet, and on the other set the open bottle. Despite his escalating infirmity Monty's legs were still as thick as tree trunks and the routine of applying the oil in gentle circles was a kind of meditation—accompanied by the whisper of wind through the treetops. After twenty minutes on each leg, Devinder moved on to his hands. Of his early health ailments, nothing frustrated Monty more than the arthritis in his fingers, which some mornings made it impossible for him to wash and comb his kesh or tie his turban with the meticulousness that he demanded of himself. Lace-up shoes were a problem, too, but that was easily fixed with the purchase of slip-ons—though the move away from his traditional Oxfords took some convincing. On those painful mornings, Deepa was able to wash and comb her husband's hair and then plait and knot it into a bun. But the turban was a more difficult proposition. Monty struggled with shaping the fabric into the front-peaked style, his preferred fashion. Every morning, before leaving the house, he would ask Deepa and Devinder how his turban looked, and they would reassure him that it looked fine, even on days when it was lacking its required symmetry.

"Uncleji, when did you first learn how to tie a turban?" Devinder asked as he pulled at the knotted joints on Monty's thick fingers.

"I was fifteen years old, son." Monty grimaced and closed his eyes. Devinder was unsure if the expression was from the pain in his joints or from the memory of the story he was about to recite.

For the next twenty minutes Monty regaled him with the story of Tarsem Singh, a fellow army recruit, who he had been stationed with in Peshawar, on the North-West Frontier.

"Tarsem was always very particular about how he looked. He'd be up at the crack of dawn to tie a fresh turban, even if the one he had tied the previous day still looked fine. He was quick at completing the tasks that were assigned to him, but he never hurried his pagg. Even the Angrezi soldiers would remark how much they adored his style. Soon all the Sikh soldiers wanted their turbans to look exactly like his.

"We were issued two khaki turbans each. Tarsem would be wearing one while the other was washed and dried. Soon me and the other Sardars began to do the same. Up till then, I would wear the same pagg for many days and think nothing of it.

"I'll never forget the sight of dozens of turbans hanging to dry on the ropes we had rigged up for ourselves. Imagine it, dozens of khaki paggs, each six yards long, drying in a line, swaying in the wind like giant flags. In the daytime heat they would dry in no time."

In that moment the treetops rustled a little louder as though they were listening in.

"Tarsem took a liking to me," Monty continued. "I think he'd figured out my secret. That I was younger than the rest of the squad. That I probably shouldn't have been there. Though I was big and strong, I wasn't the most coordinated or the quickest. Other soldiers would make fun of me as I struggled to hike a hill or reload a rifle. All that stopped when Tarsem took me under his wing. In the evenings, he taught me how to tie a turban in his own distinct style."

Monty went silent, sadness etched around his eyes. He explained that after their time on the North-West Frontier, he never saw his mentor again. Tarsem was assigned to the 26th Indian Infantry Division that took Rangoon away from the Japanese during the Burma Campaign. And two years later when the lines of Partition were drawn, Tarsem and Monty ended up on different sides of the border as Punjab was split between West Pakistan and India.

"Poor Tarsem! He helped the Angrezi win the war, but then they drew him out of the country he loved. We lost touch with each other as did so many who were separated by Partition."

Monty scowled as Devinder held his thumbs in a firm grip and worked the joints.

"Aah ..." Monty said, as though he'd suddenly remembered that his story was not complete. "What I learned from Tarsem I've believed in ever since. I asked him once why he didn't just wear yesterday's turban and he replied, 'Begin every day by respecting how you look, and the rest will fall into place.'"

As Devinder was rolling down Monty's trouser legs, wanting this intimate moment to continue, he asked, "Will you teach me how to tie a turban like Tarsem Singh, Uncleji?"

Monty had a surprised look on his face. "Are you planning to become a Sardar, son?"

"No, but maybe I could help you on days when your hands hurt," Devinder replied.

Monty reached out to bless Devinder and then tilted his head back to let the sun warm his face, the trace of tears in the corners of his eyes.

WITH THE STRAIN of studies over for another year, Emily was ready for a summer of rejuvenation—ocean swims, a much-needed visit with her mother, hikes with Sarah—before, hopefully, starting a program at Emily Carr College. She was certain now that the best path forward was to pursue her passion in the fine arts, rather than medicine or nursing, the professions most encouraged for young girls back in Belfast. A year in the general studies program had made it abundantly clear that while she had an aptitude for maths and science, her real strength was in the arts and humanities. Besides, her grade point average was a half point higher in those courses. *Wasn't that reason enough?*

Emily hadn't needed the full three hours allotted for the exam on Impressionism, which meant that there was now plenty of time before her date with Dev. Arriving home, she immediately switched on the stereo and unwrapped a new TDK SA90 cassette tape—a step up from the regular TDK D90. In between showering and dressing she filled the ninety minutes of blank space, hitting Pause on the cassette deck, cueing up the next record, dropping the needle, and checking the VU levels before dropping the needle for a second time and pressing Record at the exact moment when the song began. By the time side B was complete the floor was strewn with album covers, inner sleeves, vinyl records, and an assortment of clothes she had tried on and rejected, finally settling on a simple white cotton dress.

On her way out she grabbed Dev's denim jacket and stopped to look at her reflection in the mirror by her front door. She rolled up the sleeves, popped the collar, and gave her reflection a thumbs-up. On the bus back to campus she used each stop to cautiously inscribe in her best handwriting a title for the mixtape—the name of the song that had been playing in her head since her time with Dev the previous weekend: A CASE OF YOU. She read over the song list several times and was pleased with her selections; the tape had the right mix of old and new tracks without anything too sentimental or earnest.

As she sat on the sidewalk outside Nitobe Memorial Garden, her hidden sanctuary in the northwest corner of the UBC grounds, her mind strayed to what she would miss the most about the campus once she changed schools. The garden was by far top of the list; she'd been here in all weathers, whenever she needed a moment alone.

Emily rotated the cassette case between her thumb and index finger. As soon as she spotted Dev walking toward her, the muscles in her cheeks lifted. She took a deep breath and slipped the cassette safely into her bag. He was wearing an R.E.M. *Chronic Town* T-shirt and carrying a heavy backpack that bulged at the seams. Compared to the previous weekend, he looked tired and dishevelled.

She hesitated before she leaned into him for a hug but

was reassured when he also leaned toward her. They held each other until it seemed awkward to hold on any longer; she resisted the urge to place her hand over the flutter of his heart.

"Hey Emily. Been waiting long?"

"No, not at all." She laughed. "Tough exam?" She couldn't help but stare at the cowlick on his forehead.

Dev's eyes darted down and his hand reached up to tame any stray hairs. "The exam was fine. But I was up all night studying."

"Aah …" Emily smiled. She noted his nervousness was back. *Probably a good sign*, she thought. "Are you still up for a walk then?"

"For sure. But it's not fair," he replied.

Emily furrowed her brow, wondering what he would say next.

"You look so put-together and …" He looked down sheepishly at his clothes, his hands buried deep in his pockets. "I haven't shaved since Saturday."

Emily ran her index finger across the dark stubble on Dev's cheek. "Ouch," she cried as she quickly drew her hand away and flicked her fingers.

"Ha ha," was Dev's quick reply.

Emily nudged Dev's arm and took a step back. "Doesn't this look flash on me?" She struck a pose to model the denim jacket.

ONCE THEY WERE through the gated entrance with its tiled gable roof, Dev followed her lead and placed a few dollars inside the donation box.

"I can't believe I've never made it to this part of campus before," he confessed. "This is beautiful!"

It was the tail end of cherry blossom season and the blooms hung like pink clouds over the pond that ran through the garden. The leaning Garry oaks, also in full bloom, shone green and gold, making a gateway over the footpath. To their left, a line of visitors waited to enter the teahouse, the angled rooftop peeking above a miniature fence and garden. A sweet honey smell filled the air. She watched as Dev inhaled deeply and his face brightened.

Emily led Dev to a wooden pavilion next to a log bridge that spanned the pond. Here they could sit sheltered from the bright sun and take in a broad view of the campus oasis. Dev sighed as he took off his backpack and his shoulders immediately straightened.

"I forgot to ask, what exam did you have today?"

"Twentieth-century poetry," he replied. "A bunch of short answers and a long essay."

She asked with interest what Dev had written about.

He replied, "The importance of time in T. S. Eliot's *The Waste Land*," but seemed distracted as he fumbled around in his backpack.

She thought he was about to pull out a book to show her—perhaps a beaten-up copy of *Selected Poems*—but instead he presented her with a cassette tape. She laughed out loud, a little miffed that he'd beaten her to the punch but thrilled to see she was also deemed worthy of a Super Avilyn 90.

Not wanting to delay it any longer, she reached into her bag and said, "Ta-da! Great minds …" as she handed him A CASE OF YOU.

They took a few minutes to look at their track listings, both beaming with delight. Included on her tape were two songs she'd also recorded on his: "The Morning Fog" by Kate Bush and "Well I Wonder" by the Smiths. Written on the edge of the case in neat block letters was OUT ON THE WEEKEND.

Emily touched his hand, and he didn't resist; the tremble was gone.

"And here I was," she said, "thinking you'd been busy studying this whole time."

He looped his little finger around hers. "Well, I did have some time to spare, Emily." She could tell he was trying to play it cool. "First the lovely sketch of Natalie Merchant and now—now a mixtape."

They sat pressed against each other. Emily pointed out the surrounding trees: the coast redwood, the red alder, the Torrey pine, and of course the Japanese cherries and Garry oaks. She listed the shrubs across the pond: the mountain laurel, the Japanese Pieris, the Alpen rose. Dev followed her finger and scrutinized the small island in the pond until he could distinguish the shape of a turtle—the rock feet beneath its domed grass shell.

"So, tell me, Dev, the last time we spoke—or should I say the last time *I* spoke—you didn't share much about yourself. In fact, you're still a bit of a mystery to me."

"I guess I prefer listening to talking. And besides, I loved hearing your stories." He stared into her eyes and asked,

"Okay, what would you like to know?"

She thought about a safe first question. "Tell me about your parents?"

Dev contemplated for a moment, as though solving a puzzle in his mind. "Well, the family I live with aren't my birth family. I was adopted."

She immediately felt conflicted but let him speak on. He told her about the day his parents died, the last time he saw them, his father's business suit and the snow on his mother's eyelashes as she waved him goodbye, his confusion and disbelief when Deepa showed up to collect him from the bus stop after school.

"My parents were my entire world. They were all I knew. That night, I remember sitting alone in the dark of the basement wishing for them to walk through the door, almost sure it would happen. I felt so lost and empty, not knowing if I'd ever be loved again." Emily reached over and wiped a warm tear from Dev's cheek. She held her hand on his face a moment longer.

"Sorry. I haven't discussed this with anyone in a long time," he said. "I still dream about my mother's mustard coat and the kindness of my father's eyes."

"Dev, you don't have to apologize for the way you feel." She added, "Not to me. Ever." She gripped his hand, a little tighter this time.

He continued: "Auntie Deepa and Uncle Monty didn't have to take me in. They could have passed me on to a foster home like the social worker recommended. Instead, they made sure I became a part of their family and never let me lack for anything. And I gained three brothers who are now my friends, my guardians, and my teammates. I'll be in their debt forever."

There was a long silence before Dev asked, "So, what are your plans for the holidays, Emily?"

She gave herself a moment to take everything in, still a little dazed by Dev's revelations. She'd shared more than she had expected with him the previous Saturday, but it was time for her to let go of a secret, too. She replied, as casually as she could manage, "My mother's visiting for two weeks in early May."

"Visiting?" Dev asked with a puzzled look.

"Yeah," she said hesitantly. "She moved back to Belfast at the end of last summer."

Dev looked concerned.

"It's all right. I'm all right," Emily said. She was twenty-one years old and living alone in a country without any family; she could see how that would concern Dev.

"I'm looking forward to seeing her. And then hopefully I'll get work at Opus, like I've done the last two summers. And you? What do you have planned?"

She could sense he wanted to hear more about Ma and why she was back in Belfast but appreciated that he didn't pry any further. "My summers are always the same," he said. "I work in the family business. Real estate. My brothers all work there, too. It's quite dull really, compared to a few months in an art supply store on Granville Island!"

He wasn't wrong. Emily found the subject of property ownership uninteresting and the Vancouver obsession with equity rather annoying, but she wanted to know everything about him. "And tell me what is working in the 'family business' like?" She made air quotes with her fingers.

"Well, we're not the 'Corleones' or anything," he said with a grin and air quotes in return. Emily gave him a wink. "The business is … comfortable. Mostly, it's organizing and filing. But I sit in on all the planning meetings and tend bar at our events."

Emily detected reluctance in his voice, perhaps conflicted emotions. "Did your brothers have a say in working for the 'family business'?"

Dev smiled at her persistent joke but then his face turned serious again. "I can't say for sure if they did or not. I know that once each of them completed their college diplomas they went straight to work for our father. I think they always accepted that that was the way things were, just as they accepted …" He took a pause and gritted his teeth. "That they'd go along with our parents' wishes when it came time to marry. They accepted that having a choice isn't always possible, that certain decisions would be made for them. Refusing to go along with their wishes would be disrespectful, and they'd never tolerate that in themselves."

He turned his head away, but Emily wasn't about to let it go. "Do you mean your brothers have all had arranged marriages?" she asked, trying not to sound disapproving.

"Yes," was his short reply.

She wanted reassurance that Dev's future wasn't already decided. "And what about you? Do you feel obliged to follow your parents' every wish?"

"They treat me like a son, and in some ways no different to how they treat my brothers." He looked across the pond for a minute before he continued—the tremble in his fingers returned. "They've always given me more leeway, more rope, supported my hobbies and interests in a way they never did for Amarpreet, Navpreet, or Karanpreet. I think, in some ways, Monty and Deepa feel that with me they can let go of their own expectations of themselves, of what it means to be the perfect Punjabi Sikh parents."

"Do you mean they're giving themselves a break? That by going easy on you, they're going easy on themselves?"

Dev shrugged. "Or they feel they're not allowed that same control over me, that because I'm adopted they don't have the same authority."

Emily was taking it all in. She could relate to people acting the way they thought they were expected to behave. "Have you ever just asked them, Dev?"

The question seemed to surprise him. She imagined a family life of restraint, of unexpressed thoughts and questions.

He was looking tired again. Emily couldn't tell if the lack of sleep was catching up to him or if it was the topic of conversation. She decided to lighten the mood. "Your brothers' names all rhyme? What's up with that?"

Dev's eyes brightened. "Ha! I guess it's a Punjabi thing. And every Punjabi boy or girl has to have a nickname. When they were growing up Amarpreet was Shera, Navpreet was Papu, and Karanpreet was Kaka, which normally refers to a baby, but poor Karanpreet had to endure that nickname right up to the time he got married. To make things more complicated, they go by Amar, Nav, and Kaz with their friends."

"And I thought García Márquez novels were difficult to follow. You'll have to draw me a family tree if I'm ever going to remember all that."

"That's not all." Dev laughed, clearly enjoying the moment—he'd obviously not talked himself out at all. "Not only does everyone have multiple names, but there's an endless list of uncles and aunties. Some are real relatives, others are friends or acquaintances that have been given family status. A kind of forced familiarity. For years I thought we had this massive family and I'd go around thinking all these people were related just because I'd seen them at some function."

Emily put her hand over her mouth to contain her laughter.

"Do you have a nickname, Dev?" she whispered.

"Well, 'Dev' is my nickname. It's short for my full name, Devinder. Uncle Monty and Auntie Deepa call me that, though my brothers will shorten it to Dev usually."

"Tell me more about your auntie and her role in the family ..." Emily paused before elevating her voice to add, "Devinder."

"Deepa's the quiet controller. If Monty's tilting in a direction she doesn't agree with, she'll find a way to turn him around, while still letting him think he's in charge. That way she gets her way and Uncle Monty gets the credit—or will claim the credit at least. Deepa's the one who keeps everything together. The woman letting the man think he's in control, that's a Punjabi thing, too, I suppose."

"Oh, Dev, that's a universal thing! We're so good at it you don't realize you're being duped."

As they resumed their walk through the petal-covered pathways, Dev, wide-eyed once more as he looked up at the trees, asked, "What do you like most about this place?"

She held her arms apart and turned her head from side

to side, grinning from ear to ear. "Look around, Dev." She waved her arms at the meticulously manicured grounds, the canopy of native maple trees, and the imported azaleas and irises. "People walk past all sorts of beauty every day without noticing it. I used to do the same. When I moved here from Northern Ireland, I was so taken by the variety of greenery, these enormous trees, these flowers, these smells. As much as the ocean and the mountains, the birds and the sky, I fell for the plant life. Don't get me wrong, Ireland is lush and beautiful, rich and verdant. The countryside's spectacular. Da used to take me to the Botanic Gardens close to his work and we'd picnic beneath the shade of the lindens and oaks. I loved it. But I was cooped up indoors whenever there was a whiff of danger. When I arrived here, I felt for the first time like I was free to wander, like my senses were finally awake. Even the shrubs and the moss fascinate me. I mean, check out the moss!" She pointed at a nearby patch of hair moss, and they bent down together to look at the sprout-like ground cover, luxurious and inviting.

"It sounds like it was tough growing up in Belfast."

Emily was hesitant to return to the subject of her child-hood, but she was the one who'd brought it up and he seemed genuinely interested.

"Well, we were living in a war zone essentially," she replied in a matter-of-fact way. "But it wasn't all Bloody Sundays and car bombs. As a kid, you don't crave for anything as long as you feel loved. Ma and Da sheltered me the best they could. I guess they hoped their love would act as a barricade. To be fair, though, the sense of uncertainty and lingering dread was never far from my thoughts."

They sat for a moment on a bench beneath the Japanese cherry blossoms, their names a kind of silent meditation: Kanzan, Ojochin, Taki-nioi. A breeze blew through the tree-tops and blossoms rained down, settling on the pond's surface.

When they started walking again, Dev thanked her for suggesting the garden as a meeting place. He seemed genuinely happy to have spent the afternoon with her. Emily was thinking how easy it was to be around him and wondered if they might spend the remainder of the day together.

Before she could ask, Dev said, "By the way, I've promised my family that I'll be home for dinner this evening. They want to celebrate the end of the school year with me. I should probably get going soon." He must have noticed the look of disappointment on her face. "I can drop you off in Kits on my way though, and I'd like it if we could see each other again soon."

Emily was quick to reply, "Well, it's supposed to be warm tomorrow. I'm planning to go to the beach in the afternoon." She was thinking on the spot, creating plans for herself, in the hope that he'd join her. "I'll be at Spanish Banks around two-ish."

She chided herself, worried her eagerness might come across as desperate. Devinder intrigued her and she didn't want to scare him off. Fortunately, he wasn't troubled one bit.

"I have plans, but I'll shift a couple of things around. Tomorrow afternoon is perfect, Em."

Hearing him call her "Em" made her feel as if they'd known each other forever, not merely the last week. In that moment she realized her own nervousness and doubts had disappeared completely.

DEV SEARCHED FOR Emily amongst the sunbathers at Jericho Beach and Spanish Banks. She'd been right; it was a warm day for late April, much too warm for the jeans and sweatshirt he'd worn. Before stepping onto the sand, he removed his running shoes and gym socks, stuffed them into his backpack, and rolled up his jeans. A group of men in neon-yellow and -green tank tops were practising Ultimate Frisbee moves nearby, and farther along the shore a couple of dog owners were throwing sticks into the ocean.

It took a few minutes before he spotted Emily lying on a beach towel beside one of the large tree stumps that lay horizontal in the sand. She was wearing a dandelion-coloured dress and a pair of oversized sunglasses that made her look like a movie star. An open book resting on her chest. Dev unfurled his beach towel next to hers as quietly as he could. He lightly brushed her hand by mistake as he removed his sweatshirt. She sat up and pushed her glasses to her forehead.

"Dev! I'm glad you came." Emily stretched her arms over her head and let out a yawn. "I fell asleep," she said, turning the book cover toward him. *The Good Terrorist* by Doris Lessing. In the bright sun her eyes were noticeably greener—almost India jade.

"It's busier than I'd expected. Have you had a swim yet?"

"No, but I should probably get in the water soon, while it's still warm. Besides it'll wake me up." She stood up and held out her hand. "Care to join me?"

He was unsure of what to say, afraid of appearing uncool. "No, I think I'll just get comfortable for a bit, if that's okay?" He didn't want to turn down her outstretched hand, but also didn't want to embarrass himself.

Emily peeled off her dress to reveal a yellow swimsuit and long, thin limbs, freckles on her shoulders. As she walked away, she threw her sunglasses toward him and with no time to react, they bounced off his shoulder onto the ground. She laughed as he picked them up and blew the sand from them. "Ta!" she yelled.

Thirty metres into the water Emily disappeared beneath the shimmering surface and reappeared much farther out. Her arms and legs moved with ease and rhythm. Dev squinted to keep sight of her as she floated in the distance.

THE WATER SPARKLED on Emily's skin as she walked toward him, and he noticed a slight shudder as she lay down on her towel. "The water's cool. But really lovely all the same," she said, as she rubbed the goosebumps on her skin. She pulled a shawl from her beach bag to wrap around herself.

"How deep does the water get where you were swimming?"

As soon as he asked the question, Dev realized it sounded awkward.

"Not as deep as you might think. At low tide you can walk quite far out. Why? Have you never swum at this beach before?"

He thought it best to be truthful. "I've never swum in the ocean at all." He looked at her for a reaction. Nothing. "In my family the ocean's something to admire from a distance, not something to play in. It's mostly a feature to determine listing prices." He laughed, but knew it sounded a little disingenuous.

Emily looked surprised. "You've lived your whole life by the ocean and you've never been in it? You know how to swim though, right?"

"I can manage, I suppose. I learned in school but that was ages ago. And honestly, I never worked up the nerve to leave the shallow end of the pool. When we came to the beach as kids, we were only allowed to dip our feet in."

"Well, that's smart. The ocean can be a wild beast; it can surprise you with its ferocity. How do you feel about going in with me?"

"We could try that," he replied. "Sure."

Her eyes lit up and she did a little dance with her shoulders.

He added nervously, looking out at the infinite body of water, "But maybe in like twenty minutes."

Emily lay back and covered herself with the shawl, shielding her eyes from the sun. He reached over and placed the sunglasses on her face. He'd been expecting that she might tease him for his mediocre swimming skills and inexperience, that it might be taken as a mark against him, but it hardly seemed to matter to her.

A few minutes later Emily suddenly sat up on one elbow to face him. "I'm sorry, Dev. I didn't ask how you are. How was your time with your family last night?"

He was quick to respond. "Fabulous! My brothers were there. Even my little nephew."

"Oh, a nephew. How old is he?"

Dev reached into his jeans pocket for his wallet and pulled out a passport-sized photograph of Ranjit. "He only just turned one."

She examined the picture closely. "He's so cute, Dev. Look at those eyes; they're massive! I love that you carry a photo of your wee nephew with you. I'm sure the girls dig that."

Dev hoped Emily couldn't see him blush, and he continued to talk about his previous evening. Auntie Deepa had cooked lamb curry, his favourite, and they'd sat on the back deck talking well into the night. His brothers teased him by calling him "Professor" since he was on a path to becoming the first in the family to complete a university degree. He didn't mention that all evening his head felt light and he had no appetite, that he kept remembering the feeling of her hand holding his.

"What about you, Em? What did you do last night?"

She sounded somewhat forlorn as she shared that she'd gone alone to Fifth Avenue Cinemas to watch the movie *Brazil*. Iqbal had mentioned the film to him, but he knew nothing about it.

"We'll have to go together. I'd love to see it again. It's fucking brilliant!"

His face must have shown alarm.

"Sorry. I do go on with my cursing and blinding sometimes."

"No, no, it's okay. You surprised me, that's all."

"Are girls not supposed to swear? Is that another rule I need to be aware of?" Now she was teasing him.

He tried to sound unruffled. "Honestly, in my family boys aren't supposed to swear either. We're expected to be polite and stay composed at all times. Smoking is forbidden and even the mention of drugs can land us in trouble. Oh, and we should never tell a lie. Lying is a cardinal sin and getting caught out in a lie is the biggest shame you can bring upon yourself."

He surprised himself. This was the type of conversation he could only ever have with Iqbal—something they might include in one of their "Top Ten Lists," fashioned after the *Late Night with David Letterman* skits. Yes, the next time he saw Iqbal he'd suggest "The Top Ten Forbidden Things in Your Punjabi Friend's Home."

Emily remained silent, perhaps mulling over his words, and he thought it best to switch the subject. He stood up quickly and declared, "Okay, the weather's getting cooler so either we try the water now or I'm going to have to layer up again."

Emily clapped her hands with delight. "The first thing we need to do is to get you to float in the ocean."

Dev removed his jeans to reveal his long swimming shorts. She took his hand and walked him slowly into the water. It was colder than he'd expected, and he had to stop every few steps to let his body adjust. The occasional swirl of seaweed grabbed at his ankles, unsettling him.

Emily urged him on. "It's okay, Dev. The deeper you get, the easier it'll be. It's best to quickly dip your whole body in."

"What?" Dev's teeth chattered. "I don't think I can do that."

Emily splashed his torso sending him farther into the water as he tried to get away. Almost belly button deep, he froze. She took his hands again and guided him until the water was up to his chest. He was fine as long as he could feel the sand beneath his feet. Emily wrapped her arms around him and gave a friendly, reassuring squeeze.

"It's okay, I won't let you drown. Promise." She let go and stood to his side. "Tilt back into my arms, Dev."

He slowly reclined until his ears touched the water, her hands beneath him. "Now kick your legs up and keep them straight. Let the salt water do the work." He relaxed enough to trust that she would brace him. "I've got you, Dev. I've got you. Take a deep breath and fill your lungs."

The sun shone on his face and the world became very quiet. *It's no different from being in the pool*, he told himself as he breathed in slowly, deliberately, gently moving his hands and feet, no longer aware of the cold or the depth. There was only the powder-blue sky and the silhouette of Emily's face glistening silver at the edges of his vision. He could see her lips move but couldn't make out what she was saying. He floated for what seemed like an eternity, his fear forgotten.

"Fuck!" he said. "This feels so good."

As he spoke an errant wave pushed water across his face, and in a panic he flailed his arms and legs until his feet were firmly back on the sea floor. Emily howled with laughter. The swimmers around them stopped to check they were not in distress, only continuing when she waved a hand casually in their direction. "We're okay, we're okay!" She took a few deep breaths into her stomach to quell her remaining laughter.

"That was good, Dev. We'll have you out with the dolphins in no time. And swearing like a sailor, too!"

BACK ON THE beach, they dried off and curled up beneath Emily's shawl. Dev hadn't known that another body could generate so much heat. They spent the next hour at Spanish Banks and went into the ocean together one more time, keeping close enough to the shore that his feet could find the sandy bottom when needed. Emily took another short swim by herself but mostly they lay side by side. When the sun disappeared behind the clouds, the air suddenly turned cooler, and they changed out of their swimsuits in the public changing rooms.

As Emily approached, now with a windbreaker over her sundress, Dev reached into his bag and pulled out a bottle of wine, holding it across his forearm like a waiter at a swanky restaurant. "I thought maybe we could share a drink? Then maybe dinner?"

He hunched his shoulders, worried it was too bold a move, too soon, but she grinned warmly back at him. "Ooh-la-la! Châteauneuf-du-Pape."

He felt himself blushing again and tried to sound valiant. "I may have swiped it from Uncle Monty's cellar. It's one he always likes to have on hand."

She took the bottle from him and turned it on its side, holding it up against the profile of the North Shore. He'd never thought of the shape as that of a mountain range, but it worked. She pointed across the water. "That's my favourite view, you know. I can draw every ridge and peak from memory." She stood behind him and used his finger to point at two sharp mountain peaks on the North Shore skyline. "People call them 'the Lions' but the Squamish name for them translates to 'Twin Sisters.' Sarah and I climbed the western peak last spring."

"I've lived here my entire life and sometimes feel I hardly know this place," he confessed.

They walked through Jericho Beach Park and along Point Grey Road. Passing the gated houses with their tall hedges, palm trees, and fountains, Emily said, "I give my head a shake sometimes about living so close to these mansions."

Thinking of the expansive family home in Harmony Estates, Dev remained silent.

By the time they made it to Trafalgar Street, the sky had darkened. Instead of turning south to where he'd dropped her off on their previous dates, she led him down a stairway back toward the water. At the bottom of the steps by the seawall lay a giant sawn-off log, half immersed in the water.

"You see, the ocean's so formidable it can shift this enormous piece of wood around. Last week it would have been too far to jump onto."

With that, she leapt from the pathway onto the log and stared back as if she expected him to do the same. He hesitated a moment before following, but his footing was not as sure. As he straightened himself to stand upright, Emily grabbed his hands. Once he was balanced their faces almost touched.

She winked as she said, "Be careful, Dev, I'd hate for you to break that lovely bottle of wine."

They stood on the log with their arms wrapped around each other. Their first kiss almost unsteadied him. They held on to each other until the scattered drops of rain became a downpour.

By the time they reached her apartment he was soaked through to the skin. Emily grabbed a towel and dried his hair with swift movements of her hands.

"Just relax," she said, as she peeled his sweatshirt over his head.

An hour later, as they lay naked on Emily's futon, their limbs twisted in the sheets, he could still taste the ocean on his tongue and sense the soft touch of her hands holding him afloat. The smell of wet soil drifted into the room as raindrops tapped against the window. The bottle of wine stood unopened on the kitchen counter.

KULDIP PREPARED BREAKFAST while Devinder showered and dressed for work. She sprinkled a dash of ground pepper into his freshly squeezed orange juice, as she had seen him do at the seaside hotel the morning after their Anand Karaj, and placed the glass next to his mushroom-and-onion omelette with buttered toast. They were in the third month of their marriage and their lives were falling into daily routines. After the wedding there had been family gatherings over the Christmas and New Year's holidays, but in January everyone returned to their previous schedule. There was talk of a spectacular celebration for Vaisakhi, marking the spring harvest in Punjab and the anniversary of the founding of the Khalsa, the kinship of baptized Sikhs, with bhangra and music, poetry and skits, but that was months away. And so far, no one had asked for her assistance.

Devinder devoured the omelette and complimented her on the chaah. He asked that she add less sugar next time or else brew it without sugar and he would add his own. He was always kind, never moody or brusque.

Kuldip felt an emptiness once he waved goodbye and closed the door behind him; the house immediately seemed colder and she ran upstairs to grab a sweater from the pile that Kiran had brought over for her.

She had made up her mind that today she would venture out alone but as she stepped through the front door the sky turned dark and a sudden heavy rain stopped her.

Back in the house, she checked the windows every few minutes to see if the sky had lightened, while she continued the daily investigation of her new home. In the office on the main floor, she surveyed Devinder's collection of books, organized neatly by author name on wooden shelves. From the row marked CANADIAN LITERATURE she pulled out books based on the appeal of their titles, having no other gauge to guide her. She was particularly intrigued by *A Jest of God* and *Lives of Girls and Women*, and decided she would ask Devinder if she could take them out of his office to read. In addition to the hundreds of books were rows and rows of vinyl records. She flipped through them: not a single familiar title. On a bookshelf marked REFERENCE was a well-worn copy of the *Oxford Children's Encyclopedia*, which she leafed through to look up names of places she had heard mentioned lately on TV—Quebec, Ontario, the Prairies, the Maritimes.

Once the rain had finally subsided, she wrapped a shawl beneath her raincoat and set off in no particular direction. She admired the rows of colourful two- and three-storey houses and low apartment buildings, enormous old trees and lush hedges, told herself that she would not let the damp keep her from settling in.

She practised the street names and learned the names of the trees, speaking them out loud: "Arbutus—balsam—cypress—maple." Farther along she practised what she would later learn were the names of famous battles and dead politicians: "Trafalgar—Macdonald—Blenheim—Waterloo."

She had gone as far as Jericho Beach when she heard a ringing inside her purse; Devinder had insisted on getting her the cellphone in case of an emergency and she flipped it open with a sense of dread. She was delighted to hear Kiran's voice telling her that she would be dropping by. Kuldip hurried home to tidy up the living room and prepare a fresh sabzi for the visit.

OVER LUNCH SHE learned that plans for the Vaisakhi celebration were progressing and Kiran asked if she would help in choosing the vendor for the dinner.

"Your cooking is so fine, Kuldip. I think you should taste the food from the two suppliers and help me decide. And you must teach me how you get your gobi to taste so sweet."

Kuldip smiled to herself at the thought of Ehani's recipe finding an enthusiastic fan so far away from home and imagined her secret Lytton House friend squatting by her fire, cackling loudly in the secondary servants' quarters, concocting dishes for the "Master and Masterani." Kuldip missed their conversations and her blunt motherly advice; "Sometimes, beti, you have to blend the best masala you can with the spices at hand."

After tidying up the dishes, she started to brew another pot of chaah. *Now is as good a time as I'll get*, she thought, and plucked up the courage to tell Kiran that Devinder had never once touched her, though they slept in the same bed every night.

"Don't worry too much, Kuldip. These things can take time. You have moved into Devinder's life and his house. It's a big change for him, too. He is getting over his own loss."

"What do you mean?" Kuldip asked, as the mix of water, black tea, and spices boiled on the stove.

Kiran hesitated before she replied. "I think it's only fair that you know. Devinder had a girlfriend for a long time. Someone he went to university with. She broke it off with him last winter."

Kuldip was momentarily lost in the steam from the pot of chaah. All sorts of questions were flooding her head and she was unsure of what was acceptable to ask. As she added milk to the bubbling mix, she posed the one question that seemed most immediate, "What if he never gets over her, Kiran?"

Her sister-in-law was quick to reply. "He will. Trust me. She lives across the ocean now. I hear she's with someone else. A doctor, I think. Give it time. You'll see."

Kuldip carried a plate of biscuits and two steamy mugs of tea to the kitchen nook.

"You also make the best chaah! I can never seem to get the mix of cardamom and ginger right." Kiran took another sip and added with a playful grin, "How can Devinder *not* fall in love with someone who cooks sabzis and makes chaah that taste this good?"

Kuldip asked about her children's well-being and noticed how animated Kiran became when she spoke of Mandeep and Paramdeep, who were both doing "splendidly" in grades one and three. "Once you and Devinder have little ones, everything will change," Kiran said. "Your love for them will bring you together."

Before Kiran left, Kuldip handed her a glass jar of chaah masala mix—Ehani's special blend.

***

WHENEVER SHE COMPLAINED about the weather, Devinder's standard reply was, "Wait till spring." *Wait, wait, wait,* she thought. *Will the waiting ever end?*

He was right, though. By mid-March, the clouds had lifted and everything seemed to blossom all at once. The surrounding gardens and parks were suffused with fresh buds and new smells. Light filled their home, and by April she'd thrown open the windows and doors. Her daytime sadness slowly abated. She turned the sill of the kitchen window into a herb garden, clay pots of basil, thyme, parsley, coriander. In the backyard she dug up an area near the fence and created a vegetable patch for zucchini, spring onions, varieties of squash, peas, and carrots. Late afternoons she sliced and diced for the evening meal, soaked lentils and rice, kneaded dough for rotis. She was eager to perfect what Ehani had taught her: the layering of oil, cumin seeds, onions, ginger, garlic, turmeric, and tomatoes into a thick paste, the tadka, that served as the base for many dishes. From the Apple Farm Market, she brought home vegetables, both familiar and unfamiliar, to make sabzis. One day, searching for brinjals, she was surprised when the shopkeeper failed to understand her. She gestured to make an oval shape by opening her hands, so her fingers touched their opposite, and then closing them together as she pulled them away from each other. She mouthed the word *purple* and was happy to be led to a stack of Japanese eggplants. She selected unripe fruits to pickle: limes, lemons, apples, and green mangoes. On weekends, she and Devinder made trips to Fruiticana for bitter melons, ladyfingers, and ground spices. In a high kitchen closet, she found a brand-new Crock-Pot, a gift from Auntie Deepa that Devinder had never used. She cultured milk in the ceramic pot to make dahi, the thick yogurt that soon accompanied every dinner.

Spring also brought a change in Devinder. Some mornings, rather than running alone, he would ask her to accompany him, and together they would walk the pathway along the beach. She was impressed that he could name the trees and every mountain peak across the water. After dinner, they often strolled to an ice cream shop on Cornwall Avenue and then back to Hadden Park to sit on the grass; the ocean's inlet on one side and their beautiful home on the other.

Toward the end of his semester, Devinder mentioned a faculty conference in Victoria and she plucked up the courage to ask if she could go with him. He was hesitant at first but finally agreed after explaining that he would be busy in meetings during the days and that she would likely be spending most of her time alone. *How does he think I spend my days when he is at work?*

They drove to the terminal at Tsawwassen, and after a long wait in their assigned lane, during which Devinder insisted that she take two small ginger-flavoured tablets to avoid being seasick, they finally looped their way onto the enormous ferry. Once parked, they climbed the clanking metal staircase to the passenger cabin and found forward-facing seats by a large window. She felt like a child, quietly overwhelmed by a deep nervous excitement. Captivated by the strange world of blue, green, and white waters that surrounded them, she swivelled her head at a loss for which direction she should look. She wanted to see it all.

Thirty minutes after leaving the dock, with the Channel Islands in view, they heard some commotion and noticed a crowd gathering on the opposite side of the ship, fingers pointing excitedly at the water. Devinder grabbed her hand and led her toward the crush of excited passengers. They found an opening where they leaned over the cold railing, the sea breeze blowing hard and sharp into their faces. Kuldip held tight with both hands and hesitantly leaned out while pressing her legs into the metal deck to steady herself. After a few seconds Devinder pointed a finger toward the water and a flash of gleaming silver appeared. She gasped at the first sight of the sleek body swimming alongside the ferry, arcing itself out of the water and disappearing beneath the surface again. Before long, she noticed more dark shadows and realized there was a whole pod of dolphins swimming alongside the hull. They appeared, disappeared, and appeared again. As the ferry steered between a couple of islands, the pod broke away at an angle from the ship.

Long after the crowd had dispersed, she remained at the railing, hardly noticing that her fingers had gone numb. Devinder went back inside and returned a few minutes later with two cups of hot chocolate. He reached around her waist, his arm touching her side. Kuldip trembled slightly and her feet melded into the deck. He put his chin on her shoulder, his warm breath on her neck. The intimacy thrilled her after months of barely brushing past each other. She leaned back and let go of the railing. His hand reached beneath her shawl and rested flat against her stomach. She remembered Kiran's words that "these things can take time" and wondered if this day would mark a new beginning for their marriage.

That evening they checked into the Empress Hotel. At the opening reception in the Bengal Lounge he curled his arm around her and introduced her to his colleagues as his wife. They shook her hand and offered congratulations. Devinder's department head, Dr. Williams, a short man with odd mannerisms, winked as he teased Devinder, "Nice job, my boy!" Devinder flitted between conversations, and she could tell how much these people admired him. Though the talk was primarily about work and what he referred to as "department politics," she was happy to be by his side.

That night, in a room with red-and-gold wallpaper, dark velvet curtains, and a faint smell of mothballs, Devinder slowly undressed her in the darkness. Kuldip unbraided her hair and fell back into the feather duvet. *His warm breath, the rough stubble on his chin, heartbeat like butterfly wings.* She did not offer up the coy resistance of Bollywood movie heroines but let him guide and instruct her step by step.

Falling asleep she sensed an unfamiliar, faintly disorienting, but pleasing calmness. *This day is indeed a new beginning.*

HIS BROTHERS HAVE reluctantly left the room and Devinder is alone with his nephew. He will need to move quickly. Time is of the essence.

"Chachaji, I told Dad we should wait, but you know how anxious he gets. Sometimes he seems lost without you. They all do!" It's good to see that Ranjit is relaxed and good-humoured despite missing the most critical piece of his wedding attire— the rest of the outfit hardly matters if the turban is not tied right. Though the younger generation is better at taking things in stride and able to talk more freely with one another about what matters to them, there are cross-generational barriers they still struggle to overcome. Devinder had been the first to learn of Ranjit's girlfriend Rina when they started dating in their final year of high school. Two years later, once the word was out, he acted as mediator to get the family to agree that Ranjit could marry someone of his own choosing.

"The times are changing," he'd explained to Monty and Deepa. "Your grandchildren don't care about their life partner's religion, class, or social standing." Eventually they'd come around but only after Ranjit committed to working in the family business. *One victory at a time.*

Devinder puts his hand on his nephew's shoulder. "Let's get you looking like a proper Sardar, shall we?" He takes the crumpled length of material and hands one end to Ranjit. "First we need to untangle this mess and pleat it properly." They stand at opposite ends of the dining room stretching the material diagonally and folding it into a four-inch width just as they'd done the previous afternoon. As the cotton passes between his hands, Devinder gauges the texture to know how much starch has been retained and consequently how much water he'll need to apply to get the cotton to the right level of firmness. Luckily, the material has not been handled too much and the starch is still active.

Devinder coils the precisely folded fabric, places it in Ranjit's lap, and arranges the accoutrements on a chair: a white ribbon, a metal container of pins, a glass of water, and a salai, a blunt needle the length of a pencil. He takes a long sip of chaah to settle his nerves. *Here we go.* First, he ties the white ribbon around Ranjit's forehead, then steps back to make sure it sits straight and at the right height. Next, he asks Ranjit to hold one end of the fabric in his teeth as he begins wrapping it around his head, from the back to the front in overlapping circles, steadily higher on the left side, steadily lower on the right. Before each turn he wets his fingertips in the glass of water and runs them across the material. Five turns exactly and the hard frame of the turban is complete. He presses his hands against the cloth to smooth the edges.

Meena and Teena have snuck into the room and are captivated by their father's meticulous work. "Dad, where did you learn how to do this?" asks Meena.

"From your Dadaji, sweetie."

"Why do only boys wear turbans?" follows Teena.

"Some women wear turbans, too. The important thing is to make sure you have your head covered when you're at the gurdwara. That's why Mommy has the dupattas packed for you." These are familiar questions and Devinder's responses are well-rehearsed.

Teena then asks, "Dad, why do we need to cover our heads?"

He takes a moment to think so his response does not sound curt. "It's to show respect, sweetie. To God and the Guru Granth Sahib."

Teena offers a soft, "Hmm …"

Devinder is happy his answers have satisfied them for now, though he's certain that more questions will follow. He looks forward to the day when they'll be old enough to have candid debates with him; they're already more inquisitive and unafraid than he and his brothers ever were. He and Kuldip have signed them up for Punjabi language classes this winter, knowing that in addition to the basics of reading and writing they'll acquire a foundation of the history and culture of Sikhism. They've agreed that when the girls are older, they will not hold them to any doctrine; they'll be free to choose their own paths. When it comes to parenting, he and Kuldip are an excellent match.

The all-important final turn requires Devinder to tuck the loose end of the material over the front peak. Then the stretch of fabric over the top of Ranjit's head is tucked into the frame, so no hair is left showing. He takes the strand that Ranjit has held in his mouth and pulls it tightly over the place where the back folds meet. As a final touch, Devinder tucks in the loose hair at the nape with the salai and presses in a couple of pins where the folds overlap to give the front and back an extra sturdiness. He quietly reviews Tarsem's rules. The turban ticks all the boxes: the right size, shape, and symmetry, smart lines, and not a single stray hair in sight. Ranjit looks strikingly similar to young Monty in his Indian Army uniform.

"How does it look, girls?"

"Ranjit Bhaji looks like a prince!" exclaims Meena, to which Teena offers up vigorous applause and a little skip-and-dance. They both run to hug their oldest cousin.

Ranjit inspects himself in a hand-held mirror, angling it to view the side and back. "Vah! You've outdone yourself, Chachaji! It's perfect, even better than the one you tied yesterday."

Devinder's not so sure but he's proud of his accomplishment nonetheless. *Anyway, it's the illusion of perfection that matters, not perfection itself.*

LATE SUMMER, THE vegetable garden was thriving, her daily routines of preparing Devinder's meals and keeping the house orderly were old hat, and Kuldip was in search of new projects. She had been registered to begin school in September, a diploma in accounting, to prepare her for a position at Sandhu Properties one day. But her pregnancy and the fatigue of the first trimester had delayed those plans. There was so much she wanted to fix up or replace but she was aware of how busy Dev was with teaching summer classes. If she was going to influence him, she better make it count; asking about two projects at the same time might just work.

"Ji, how would you feel about buying some new furniture? Or maybe we could paint our home?" She was convinced that brightening up the place would make the coming winter more tolerable, not to mention more welcoming for the baby when it arrived in January. Nothing in the house matched: everything looked rather battered and dull. The walls were covered in scuff marks, the baseboards scratched and stripped of paint.

"What do you have in mind, Kuldip? Do you have a plan?"

"I do."

Kuldip had been scouring magazines and paying extra attention when they visited the homes of friends and family. Gradually her scheme had taken shape. The most pressing need was to replace the worn-out chesterfield and the cracked leather armchair in the living room—an Italian leather sectional and recliner would do the trick, similar to what Kiran and Karanpreet had in their home, modern and slick. And the Formica kitchen table and chairs would be swapped out for a glass Scandinavian set from a store in Richmond.

She was always careful to check with Devinder that her choices were within their means, but he would simply shrug and say, "If you like it, let's buy it."

Kuldip began taking walks to West 4th Avenue and West Broadway to roam the lighting stores, the designer galleries, and the paint shops. Devinder's thrift store dinnerware, chipped and marked, was replaced with new ceramic plates and bowls. Cups, mugs, glasses, and cutlery were put in a box and left in a nearby alley where she had noticed others leaving unwanted household items. They always disappeared, no matter their condition. Together she and Devinder drove to high-end department stores and bought bedding and towels to replace the sets that were frayed and thinning. Room by room their home was refurbished and began to look more like the homes of her sisters-in-law.

As for painting the walls she told Devinder that she was up to the task of doing the job herself, but he convinced her that given the height of the walls in the stairwells it would be best to hire a work crew. "I don't want you falling off any ladders," he said with the caring look that had displaced the indifference of their first few months together.

She adored the paint shops with their little swatches—
more colours than an Indian fabric shop! she mused—and was
happy to select the shades of white and grey for the living
room and stairway. Devinder teased her that her choices were
based on the swatch names rather than the colour palette.
"Of course you'd hate November Rain and White Ice, and
prefer Silver Moon and Floral White!" She had begun to
enjoy his good-natured teasing.

She complained about the absence of portraits of Guru
Nanak Dev Ji and Guru Gobind Singh Ji in the house and was
adamant they should add them. "Even Mr. Sethi had paintings
of the first and last Gurus in the hallway of Lytton House,"
she explained, though she had to admit that amongst the
faded paintings of the English countryside, men on horses,
fox hunts, and stuffy portraits, the images seemed somewhat
underappreciated and out of place.

Shortly after the house was painted, Auntie Deepa popped
over one Sunday afternoon. Amarpreet, who had driven her,
carried a large rectangular package wrapped in brown paper
and twine. To Kuldip's surprise, Deepa unwrapped the package and revealed two gold framed drawings of the Gurus.

"Your home will be blessed for the baby's arrival," Deepa
said, nodding in approval of the new colours on the walls.
"Zindi reh!"

The only room off limits to Kuldip's redecorating was
Devinder's office. In the window sat a beautiful blue vase that
Kuldip wanted to move out to the living room, but he insisted
it remain in the office untouched. "We can find other vases
to match the updated furniture and paint," he explained.
Even the plant with huge perforated leaves, which would

have looked perfect next to the sectional, had to remain in
its place beside his desk.

LATE IN KULDIP'S pregnancy, Kiran's visits became more
frequent—to check on Kuldip and get her out of the house
now that the days were shorter and darker. They explored
the surrounding neighbourhoods, often finding themselves
in cozy coffee shops where Kiran would catch her up on the
latest community "gup-shup." Kuldip even once tried drinking what the chalked menu board called "chai tea" but tasted
to her like the barista had been overgenerous with the milk
and not generous enough with the masala.

During one of their mornings together, Kuldip was struck
by a brightly coloured painting in the window of a gallery
on South Granville. It was a depiction of the view from
Kitsilano Beach, with orcas and dolphins swimming in the
foreground. The sky was orange with pink waves and the
ocean was a shimmering blue. The North Shore Mountains
were shades of jade and calabash.

"Do you think Devinder might like this for our home?"
she asked Kiran.

"I don't know, Kuldip. That's something you'll have to
ask him."

She admired the mix of art pieces in Devinder's office:
drawings and paintings of various sizes and shapes covered
an entire wall. Centering the display was a small drawing of
a singer whirling in front of a microphone as her long hair
and ankle-length skirt swung around her.

Kiran and Kuldip entered the gallery to take a closer look. The owner, a smartly dressed Eastern European woman, took the painting from the window and hung it on an empty wall near the back of the gallery to give them a better look.

"I'm always happy to see new faces in here," declared the owner. "When I was a teenager in Prague, I dreamed of running a gallery." She looked directly at Kuldip, as though she knew she had a potential buyer in her sights.

Kuldip had to take a deep gulp of air to disguise her shock when she was told the price.

Back on the street she turned to Kiran, "Four thousand dollars? That is more than one lakh rupees. How can it cost so much?"

Kiran shrugged as if to say *why not*.

Later that week Devinder came home from work with a package wrapped in brown paper. Kuldip acted surprised though she had guessed its contents right away.

"Ji, how did you know?"

"Kiran told me about your trip to the gallery and I phoned them right away."

"Are you sure it is not too much money? We can take it back."

They hung the painting in the space between the two windows in their front room, above the leather sectional, opposite the drawings of the Gurus. The blue of the ocean matched the blue of the baseboards and window frames perfectly.

WHEN EMILY TOLD Dev the news that Ranjit would be joining her art class, he acted like it was no big deal. "So, he'll be one of your students. That's fine. Just treat him like all the others."

But when she first saw Ranjit in her introductory print-making class, she had a tough time shaking the image of the baby in the photo that Dev had carried in his wallet when they'd first met. The young man in the front row—handsome, with shoulder-length shiny black hair, chiselled cheekbones, and deep haunting eyes—was built like a boxer. When the class stood to watch a demonstration of the various carving tools, she was startled to see that Ranjit stood over six-and-a-half feet tall.

A month into the course, as she was moving through the classroom while students practised etching portraits into pieces of basswood, she stopped at Ranjit's station. When he noticed Emily looking over his shoulder, Ranjit offered, "It's from an old photograph, Miss. My granddad was in the army back in India." Emily was transported in time to a conversation with Dev. "What do you think?" Ranjit asked, catching her lost in thought.

"Hmm ... that's a good start," was the only reply she could manage.

At the next class she decided she had to let him know that she knew Dev, so it did not come up in the future as a surprise. Leaning in to inspect and offer feedback on the etching he was still working on, she offered, "Your uncle and I were at UBC together. We were ... friends ... We're *still* friends." She tried to sound casual although she feared the overly cautious words might give her away.

Ranjit didn't seem fazed. "That's so cool that you know him!"

By the end of the semester, Ranjit had become Emily's star pupil, and they had regular discussions after class and during her office hours. Over the next year, with Emily's tutelage, Ranjit specialized in oil painting. Though he was no longer in any of her classes, she passed on what she knew about texture and tone, one-point and two-point perspectives, depth, and the potency of empty space. He was always eager to share his new work with her. He learned to restrain his sometimes heavy hand, both in composition and brush stroke. Emily arranged for him to attend life-drawing sessions in her college studio, and at the end of each sitting he would have a list of questions about her technique: how she held her brush, the exact curve of her fingers and angle of her wrist, the pressure she used to apply paint to her canvases, the ratios required to mix particular tones. He was endlessly inquisitive and engaged her in long conversations about why she felt this urge to create, how her art fed and nourished her. If she could teach her students anything, it was to be present, to be open to astonishment, to discern nature's wondrous patterns, variations in colour, and the quality of light. Ranjit quickly absorbed all that and more.

Emily became not only a mentor but a confidante. One night, after one of their longer sessions, she said, "You've got real talent, Ranjit. I hope you'll keep painting."

Ranjit looked deflated. He confessed that his family had expectations for him to run their business someday and avoiding this obligation—by studying anything unrelated to the company, especially something as "frivolous" as art—was only a temporary option. "Art will never be anything more than a sideline for me."

ONE DAY EMILY was in her office preparing for a faculty presentation when she heard a knock at the door. She was happy to see Ranjit but short on time.

"What is it, Ranjit? I'm in a bit of a hurry."

"I'll be quick, Miss. I just wanted to share some news with you."

It was a slight annoyance that he refused to address her as Emily or Em, but after more than a year of trying to get him to do so, maybe she had to accept it. "Yes?"

He seemed hesitant, sensing her tone. "Miss, it's just that I'm getting married to Rina."

Emily suddenly felt guilty for being so short with him. She tried her best to feign surprise, though Dev had revealed this news to her weeks earlier. He'd told her how hard he'd fought to get Monty and Deepa on board. "Congratulations, Ranjit! That's grand! I really like Rina, you know. I'm so happy for you both." She'd met Ranjit's girlfriend several times, and it was obvious they loved each other.

"We kept our relationship from our families for the longest time," Ranjit explained. "We knew that telling them would be like releasing the genie from the bottle, and there'd be no putting it back. We're honestly a little terrified of how quickly the wedding plans are coming together. A date's already been set."

On the one hand, she thought, *that's a lot of pressure for a young couple. But then again, if they love each other, what difference does it make?* She found herself speculating on what would have happened if she'd ever met Dev's family. *Perhaps that explains why he was so reluctant to take the next step. It still doesn't excuse him, of course.*

Emily looked at her watch. She was cutting it close, but Ranjit still stood in the doorway looking like he had more to say. She nodded at him expectantly, giving him the okay to continue.

"You see, the other news I wanted to share is that I've made a deal with my family that hopefully means I can continue painting."

"A deal?" she asked.

"I'll finish this school year and then start work full-time at the family business. But my grandfather's building me a studio."

It was obvious from the huge smile on his face that he was thrilled, but Emily felt a lump form in her throat. The conversation was hitting too close to home, and she imagined the negotiation Dev would have had to fashion if they'd ever pursued marriage.

Before Ranjit was out the door, she'd begun to collect the materials she needed for her meeting, but his words were playing on a loop in her mind. She remembered that Ranjit had told her on several occasions, "I'm the oldest grandchild and have to set an example for the others." *Too much pressure*, she thought.

She locked her office door behind her, waved at Ranjit, and made her way to the faculty washrooms to splash cold water on her face. She'd have to compose herself before being in a room with her colleagues.

TWO MONTHS LATER Ranjit and Rina appeared at her office door holding a gold envelope. "We wanted to give you this personally. We want everyone that matters to us to be there."

She saw how the invitation was addressed and grimaced.

"Don't mind that, Miss. My mom wrote the cards. Our wedding invitations are always to the extended family. Feel free to bring whoever you want. We can promise it'll be an event you'll never forget."

"I really appreciate the invite. Of course I'll do my best to be there," she replied.

Rina chimed in, "Please, Miss. You've been such a big part of Ranj's life for the past two years. It would mean a lot!"

EMILY CONSIDERS CALLING Sarah to say she's had a change of heart. Her fingers hover above the keypad but she cannot bring herself to dial. Instead, she grabs a towel and walks to Jericho Beach for a swim. As her limbs cut through the water, memories of her years with Dev flood her mind: evenings spent lying side by side on the floor of her apartment listening to music; driving to Squamish for the salmon run; watching anxiously from the shore as he completed his first solo swim in the ocean—it was brief but she was proud of her role in helping him overcome his fear.

Perhaps love is as much about letting go as it is about holding on? she contemplates as she drifts on the surface. *If Ma had let go of Da rather than holding on to that thin wire of hope, would things have been different for her? She might have been happy here. She might have stayed.*

The water nudges her back and forth, side to side, but she is lost in her ruminations.

After today she will see him one last time. She'll suggest an early morning walk close to home, *not* Lighthouse Park. In fact, she'll meet him here at Jericho Beach. She will tell him quickly, calmly, with no drama, and that'll be it. She can already picture his response. His *non*-response. He'll turn frightfully quiet. And once she leaves, she will not look back. He can continue his run or return home. That will be his choice. It will hurt for sure, but it's long overdue and it's best for them both.

Maybe it's finally time to submit to the West Coast pressure to own real estate. There's a low-rise condo building in the West End that she's always adored, close to the water and only minutes from Stanley Park and the seawall, that has a listing for a two-bedroom apartment on the top floor. Her studio would have a view of the ocean. Her paintings are selling, and the money from the sale of the Belfast home is just sitting in a savings account. She can afford an upgrade.

Walking home, she catches herself picturing scenarios in which things worked out differently for her and Dev. If her mother had not fallen ill and she had returned as planned and met Dev's brothers; or if she had accepted his wild offer to move to Belfast to be with her. An expression from her grandmother pops into her head: "If ifs and ands were pots and pans, there'd be no work for tinkers' hands." She takes a deep breath and shrugs to shake off the thoughts.

BACK IN HER apartment, minutes before she is to be picked up by Sarah, Emily takes off her bright emerald leggings and opts instead for cream-coloured slacks. She sticks with the long-sleeved white kurta that Dev had bought for her the first time they went to Main Street together. On Dev's guidance she has stuffed a thin cardigan into her handbag in case the prayer hall becomes too cool from the air-conditioning. On her way out, she picks up the large cream-coloured scarf and drapes it around her neck.

"BUT IS IT Uncle Monty-level vah-vah?" asks Devinder.

His brothers assist with positioning the palla, the gold-laced red scarf that will later connect Ranjit and Rina for the lawaan. Amarpreet pins the middle of the palla onto his son's shoulder, so he doesn't have to worry about it sliding off. Ranjit stands in front of the mirror adjusting and read-justing the sheath and sword around his waist. He holds the sword's silver hilt as he paces the dining room, striving to walk with a natural gait. More adjustments are required.

"It feels so much heavier than when I tried it on earlier," he says, as the sheath knocks awkwardly against his leg.

After a few more tries, he manages to find the correct height and angle to allow him to walk with an easy stride. A bead of sweat on his brow, Ranjit signals to his father that he is ready to be led into the living room for the final stage of the morning's preparations.

The guests shift around to create a passage to the high-backed chair positioned in front of the picture-perfect marble fireplace. Everyone wants a good view of the groom, so the photographer has to jostle the crowd as his assistant sets up two light diffusing umbrellas. Devinder savours the scattering of compliments for Ranjit's impeccably put-together ensemble. The photographer calls out to let everyone know he is ready to start shooting, unperturbed by the hubbub.

The next addition to the wedding outfit is made by Manjit who pins the kalgi, a gold-coloured brooch adorned with a single feather, into the front of her brother's turban. Since Ranjit does not have a sister-in-law, the final touch, the application of kohl, has been assigned to Kuldip. Devinder, observing from a distance, knows how much this honour means to her. He notices a slight shake in her hand as she applies a token stripe of the liner beneath each of Ranjit's eyes. The photographer is discreet and quietly captures the intimacy of the moment.

The first of the posed portraits is reserved for Auntie Deepa. She touches Ranjit's face gently, kisses his cheek, and stands beside him with her hand on his shoulder as the photographer clicks the shutter button several times. He takes a quick look at the camera's LCD screen and gives a thumbs-up. Then Amarpreet and Baljit take their places either side of their son. Click. Click. Click. Manjit joins them, standing behind Ranjit. More clicks. Then a posed shot of the two siblings, who are trying very hard to keep straight faces through all the formalities and rituals. And then a few more to be sure, and "less smiley," Deepa suggests. Then the various combinations are taken with Navpreet's family, Karanpreet's family, and finally Devinder, Kuldip, Meena, and Teena.

Next, the remainder of the guests promptly queue for their portraits with the groom. There's a lot of straightening of clothes, men fastening the top buttons on their suit jackets, women carefully evaluating the drape of their chunis. No one wants to be left out. Everyone wants to look their best. First it is the turn of the uncles and aunties from the maternal side of the family, and all the combinations and permutations are staged and photographed.

Devinder checks his Rolex when the final pair of guests have had their turn. They're already more than an hour late in leaving for the gurdwara and he gestures to the photographer to wrap it up. Immediately, the photographer's assistants start to disassemble the diffusing umbrellas.

"Wait, wait, wait!" Manjit calls out over everyone's heads with an arm in the air. "We missed the cousins' group shot!" She gives a pleading look at both Devinder and her father and they oblige. The first cousins gather and position themselves around Ranjit. After some cajoling, Meena joins them. Everyone is present except Teena.

Kuldip has already noticed that her daughter is missing and is making her way from the room calling Teena's name. Devinder follows. They search the house, Kuldip's voice growing shakier as they encounter empty room after empty room. Devinder knows not to worry—this is what Teena does—but he's conscious of the time.

When they finally find her alone in one of the spare bedrooms, she's attempting to read a copy of the wedding invitation.

"Hey sweetheart, what are you doing?" asks Devinder.

"I'm reading, Dad," she answers with a huff. Staring intently at the elaborate lettering, she stumbles over the words as she asks, "What's an An ... and Ka ... raj?"

Kuldip perches next to her. "It's pronounced An-und

Ka-ruj, sweetheart. It's the wedding ceremony. You'll see Ranjit Bhaji and Rina Bhabhiji have their Anand Karaj today at the gurdwara."

Teena looks puzzled. "Did you and Dad have an Anand Karaj?"

"Yes, of course we did," adds Devinder. "But sweetie, right now we need you for a photograph with your cousin-brother and -sisters."

"Oh, Dad! More photos?" She pouts her bottom lip and looks up at him in exasperation.

Devinder sighs. Teena makes a good point. *More photos? Really?*

"Come on, sweetie. This'll be the last one. Promise."

"OKAY, EVERYONE, THAT'S it for the indoor shots." Devinder expects a collective sigh of disappointment, but it seems the guests are excited to move on to the next part of the festivities. He checks the time; a further thirty minutes behind schedule, but there is one critical gap in the portraits that needs to be filled.

The family gathers by the large front window as Ranjit and Deepa make their way down the driveway and slide into the back of Uncle Monty's limousine followed closely by the photographer. Camera flashes light up the tinted glass.

A few minutes later groom and grandmother walk solemnly back into the house, and everyone starts readying themselves to begin the baraat. A tear runs down Devinder's cheek. Kuldip, next to him, is also choking up, her lips trembling. Today is supposed to be a happy day, but she must also be feeling the dread of inevitability about Uncle Monty's health. Devinder places his hand on the small of her back.

By the front door Amarpreet quietly hands Ranjit a tissue to wipe his eyes as the photographer and videographer stand outside waiting for the exodus onto the driveway. With a quick shake of his shoulders, Ranjit straightens his body before stepping into the sunshine. As he walks slowly over the trestle, his tunic sparkling, Manjit and her cousins begin the traditional baraat song about the groom leaving his parental home on the back of a horse: "Ni veer mera ghodi chadiya." The men clap along enthusiastically and the mood lifts. But only a couple of steps onto the front drive Ranjit stumbles over his sword which has swung between his legs. The collective gasp turns to relief as Amarpreet stretches out his arm and catches his son before he falls.

"Let's try that again! This time without the trip!" the videographer shouts. Everyone re-enters the house and waits for his signal.

This time the exit is perfect and the dhol player standing halfway down the driveway begins his beat exactly as the chorus of women start their song: "Ni veer mera ghodi chadiya. Ghodi chadiya ni saiyo ghodi chadiya."

The dhol beat echoes high into the hemlocks. *Dha nana nana dhadha na.*

Some neighbours have gathered at their gates while others look out from upstairs windows. Shoulder muscles twitch as those leading the parade begin to dance, and soon everyone's arms are held high and bouncing in the air. The dhol player bangs the two sides of the drum a little louder and the dancing gets more animated. *Dha nana nana dhadha na. Dha nana nana dhadha na.* Uncle Monty reaches out of his limousine window with a hundred-dollar banknote in his hand. Without missing a beat, the drummer bends his head low for the blessing while his assistant accepts the note and tucks it into a satchel. The windows of Uncle Monty's limousine remain open as the procession moves into the middle of the street, and everyone stops long enough to join hands and bow heads in his direction. He waves at Devinder, beckoning him to the car.

"Shaabaash, Devinder! That pagg. Vah-vah!"

Devinder beams proudly. His first responsibility of the day and Uncle Monty has given his approval. The schedule might be running late but receiving Monty's praise means everything.

Devinder hurries back to join the baraat as several guests queue behind him for Monty's blessing and acknowledgement. For a few minutes the scene morphs into a street party, complete with the occasional holler of, "O, bullé!" Men dance up to the dhol player and circle twenty-dollar notes around his head before handing them to his assistant. A few notes fall to the ground and are blown into the surrounding gardens. *Dha nana nana dhadha na. Dha nana nana dhadha na.*

Ranjit steps into the first of the three red-ribboned limousines parked at the end of the street, followed by Auntie Deepa, Amarpreet, Baljit, and Manjit. He rolls down the window and waves at the joyous baraat, his heavy gold kara glinting in the sun. Devinder shakes his right wrist, to see if his own gold bracelet is stuck beneath his shirt sleeve. He presses at his wrist to feel for the hard metal, but there is nothing there.

ACT III
DUPEHAR BAAD—AFTERNOON

EMILY SET DOWN the last of the boxes and was taking a rest after several trips up and down the stairs. While she was lying on the hardwood floor, her gaze landed on a grease stain above the stove. She silently cursed the previous tenants for not doing a better job of looking after *her* place. The thought of more repairs made her anxious. She took a deep breath. *It's okay, I only need to call the building supervisor and he'll make the arrangements.* It was a minor miracle that she'd managed to rent the same apartment where she'd once lived with her mother. It was like returning home after a long vacation. A very long and very gruelling vacation.

When they'd first arrived in Vancouver from Northern Ireland, Emily and her mother spent a few days in a motel on the Kingsway and then a month in a short-term rental in Kerrisdale. Once it was settled that Emily would attend school in Kitsilano, they began to look for a more permanent home. Luckily, the Coastline Apartments on Trafalgar Street had a two-bedroom place available. Even back then the complex was starting to show some wear and tear, and a two-flight climb was not ideal, but a location near the shore and a short walk from Emily's school was exactly what they were looking for.

"It's almost the same size as our Belfast home," her mother had boasted. "And aye, I hate those stairs, but if we weren't so high up, we wouldn't have this view. It's priceless!"

Emily poured herself a glass of water at the kitchen sink. The view from the window lifted her spirits immediately: the dramatic landscapes of mountains and ocean that had made her fall in love with this place in her youth. *Just get moved in*, she told herself, *there'll be plenty of time to worry about getting everything sorted later*. She touched the windowpane with her hand and soaked in its coolness. Examining the windowsill, she could make out the discoloured ring where Ma had placed the jar of soil she'd carried in her handbag across the ocean.

"If I die here," she'd instructed her daughter, "be sure to drop this wee bit of home on my coffin."

Emily's thoughts were interrupted by the sound of footsteps coming up the stairs, followed by a series of knocks: two loud raps spaced apart, followed by three quick taps. She shut her eyes tightly for a moment feeling a strange mix of anticipation and dread.

"It's open. Come on in."

There was the sound of shoes being removed and then Dev's head popped around the wall that divided the living space from the entryway. He had a grin on his face, one arm twisted behind his back.

"Aren't you supposed to be at school?"

His grin grew wider. "Just sent my students' grades in. Another year of teaching done!"

"Good work, Dev! Congratulations."

"I was driving home," he continued, "and thought I'd drop by to see how you're settling in."

As they embraced—Dev using only one arm—she couldn't help but think of their early moments of intimacy and fought back the urge to place her hand on his chest to feel his fast-beating heart.

"Ta-da!" he said, as he straightened his arm and revealed a jade plant. "Dr. Williams finally retired and left this behind in his office. I thought you might want something rescued for your new-old-new home."

Something discarded, something rescued. An old phrase from their days of scavenging the back laneways of Kitsilano for cast-aside records and books, plants, and small items of furniture for her apartment.

She dipped her finger into the clay pot before placing it in the sink and letting the tap water run onto the parched soil.

"You were always so good at reviving things and keeping them alive," he said. "I still have your monstera in my home office by the way."

"Aah," she uttered in surprise. She hadn't thought about the plant and its giant Swiss-cheese leaves in ages.

"Do you want it back?"

"Nah! I'm sure it looks swell at your place. It must be ginormous by now." She didn't mention that she worried about the questions that might be asked if the plant suddenly disappeared from his home. Or if the blue Turkish vase— which she would love to hold again—were to do the same.

Emily took a damp rag and wiped down two plastic chairs she'd borrowed earlier from the community garden. "Still classy, huh?" she joked, swiping a dry paper towel over the seats. She placed the chairs side by side at the far end of the room—where the settee used to sit—so they faced the kitchen window. It was the part of the day when the light in the apartment was brightest, the reflections from the buildings across the water gleaming yellow and orange.

Dev sat in one of the chairs and stared toward the window. She could tell he was revisiting the same memories. *Evenings when we'd talk and listen to music, discuss books, art, film, and politics into the wee hours and make love on the futon bed, fall asleep to the morning chorus of birds.*

After a while he pointed to the boxes stacked against the wall. "I see you've already got some things from the storage locker. Would you like help with the rest?"

Funny, she thought, he hasn't changed a bit. *He never misses an opportunity to lend a helping hand.*

"I've already picked up the essentials," she said as she washed and dried a pair of wineglasses.

"Remember these guys?" She held the goblets in front of her like trophies. Small metal charms dangled from their stems. "How much wine did we drink out of these?"

Dev laughed at seeing the old relics. "If I remember correctly, you were the sea horse and I was the starfish."

"There's a bottle of Piesporter in one of the boxes. It's well aged. I'll slip it into the freezer to cool for a bit."

While the refrigerator did its work, Emily took Dev on a little tour of the apartment to show him the progress she'd made. In the main bedroom a collection of dresses and sweaters hung in the closet. She ran her fingers over the floral prints and fine wool button-up cardigans; clothes she hadn't seen in years.

"It's a good thing I'm oblivious to fashion, hey?"

The smaller bedroom had a single foam mattress on the

floor which she'd borrowed from Sarah and slept on the previous two nights. In the corner sat boxes marked Art Supplies. The sight of them brought back her anxiety.

"Will this be your studio again, Em?"

She was hoping not to show her uncertainty, but the words toppled out before she could stop them. "I won't lie to you, Dev. I'm finding it rather unreal being back here. It's like I haven't completely woken from the nightmare of the last few years and could fall back into it at any time." Dev's hand on her back felt warm and reassuring.

"I tried painting while I was at Sarah's, hoping to find a way back in," she continued. "Instead, I spent hours staring at empty canvases."

"Be patient with yourself, Em. It's only the first week back in your own space. And given what you've been through, it's going to take time."

She had plenty of ideas for new projects, but they were merely concepts for now. "Some days I worry that I'll never paint again!"

"That sounds a little familiar, Em. When we first met, your mother had returned home to Belfast and you were feeling the same way. But a few months later you were painting up a storm."

At times she wondered if Dev's naivety was intentional.

"That's because I'd met you!"

They looked into each other's eyes until Emily broke the moment.

"If we're going to speak about my creative initiatives, or lack thereof, then we better have that glass of wine, hadn't we?"

Back in the living area she uncorked the chilled bottle and poured generous portions into the sea horse and the starfish. They moved the plastic chairs to sit across from each other and knocked their glasses together. Emily mouthed a *ting* sound. *Just like the old days.*

They reminisced about the simplicity of their student lives. Those first few years together, when no matter how full their days were, nothing ever seemed hurried or forced. They laughed about their breakups and their fights, her short fuse, and his stoicism.

"Fighting with you always felt like I was arguing with myself," she confessed.

To which he offered his standard reply, "Then don't fight!"

They could laugh about it now.

Emily told him of her visit to Emily Carr earlier in the week. "It's a long shot but I'd like to pick up my career where I left it."

"Are your friends still there?"

"I wouldn't call them 'friends' exactly, but yeah a couple of my old acquaintances are still around." A lot had changed over the past nine years; the school was now an institute rather than a college and was offering bachelor's degrees. "I did get a chance to walk through campus and the galleries on Granville Island. Everything seems familiar, but also a little distant and detached."

"Like I said, it's going to take some time, Em." Dev had always been encouraging and supportive. And even though his words could sometimes sound like platitudes, it was good to have him on her side again.

She asked about his work, and Dev revealed the struggles

he was having with one of his students. "He's my brightest pupil but lately he's been so disconnected. I asked him at the end of our final class if everything was all right with him. He nodded but left the room with tears in his eyes. I sent him an email telling him to contact me during the holidays if he needs to."

"I'm sure he'll reach out if he feels it's the right thing to do."

She was sure they had a version of this conversation years ago, maybe when he came to see her in Belfast. It was one of the differences between them. Dev was always pushing to help others while Emily figured if someone really wanted help, they'd ask for it. Dev was trusting and Emily was pragmatic. *Maybe it's the differences that made us such a good match,* she thought.

Dev's eyes wandered to a pile of boxes in the far corner. "Hey, is that my handwriting?"

A year into her stay in Belfast, Emily had reached out to Sarah to close out her apartment lease and move her furniture and other belongings into storage. It was an effort to complete over long distance with many faxes sent back and forth for signatures. "I don't think I'll be back any time soon," she'd said. "I'm sure Dev'll want to help, but you take the lead, please." Her disagreement with Dev during his visit to Belfast was still an open wound at the time.

Emily looked at the boxes that held her record collection and that strange mix of apprehension and excitement returned. And then, as though he'd just remembered, Dev pumped his fist in the air. "Oh wow! Your vinyl. Right on!"

Before she knew it, Dev had pulled open the flaps of the box marked *A–E* and was flipping through the albums with excitement. As each one was lifted out, Emily categorized them in her mind within the chronology of their relationship: the records that she owned prior to meeting him (including her da's collection); the records that she purchased because of Dev's influence; and the records they had bought and learned to love together.

Dev paused at the Cure's *Disintegration* and slowly read out the song titles while staring at Emily with raised eyebrows. Emily had bought the vinyl version of the album only to discover that the compact disc, which Dev owned, had two additional songs. He had teased her constantly about it when they were together. She tapped him lightly on his arm with her fist and moved her chair a little closer. "Too bad I haven't retrieved my turntable."

They began rummaging through the second box and Dev held up the twelve-inch single of "Love Will Tear Us Apart"— the monochrome image of the stone angel, eternally grieving, a portal to another time. Dev began to hum the melody. He stood and alternated between air acoustic guitar and air bass—low to the ground—while Emily held both hands in front of her and mimed playing the synthesizer parts. Their feet tapped the drumbeat. *No turntable required.* They could imagine the melody, the acoustic strum, the machine-like drums, and the moment when Ian Curtis began his lament. They took turns to speak out the lyrics. It felt as though they were in their early twenties once more.

They laughed out loud at their own silliness and collapsed on the floor in a heap, their strained breathing the only reminder of the intervening years. "When I shared my favourite songs with you, it was like hearing them again for the first time."

"Oh dear." She chuckled as she caught her breath. "We'd more energy then for sure."

Dev flipped onto his front and looked into her eyes. "We were hooked on sadness. Except when we were with each other."

THERE WAS A moment when either one of them could have chosen to pull back. But it was soon past and never acknowledged; not when he leaned in to kiss her, not when she put her open hand on his chest and stirred the bird wings beneath his ribs. And not when he pulled her T-shirt over her head. They knew their lives would be changed forever, that there was no going back from this. And they were fully aware of the other lives that would be changed, too. "Maybe we shouldn't," she said. Dev nodded in agreement while unbuttoning his shirt.

ON THEIR THIRD evening in Istanbul, they drank apple cinnamon tea on the rooftop of their hotel. Emily was content, filled with thoughts of a future life with Dev. They'd been together for the better part of six years and though there had been some ups and downs and a couple of months-long separations, they always found a way back to each other. She'd dated other men during their interludes, but those short-term affairs only left her questioning her reasons for breaking up with Dev in the first place.

The trip to Turkey had come together quickly. Emily's initial plan was to spend two weeks in Northern Ireland with her mother, her first visit back to the old country. Her flights to Belfast had been booked weeks before she and Dev rekindled their relationship following three months apart— an argument over Christmas plans. She was elated when he suggested that he join her in Northern Ireland and was certain that Ma would be over the moon to see him again.

Once he confirmed, they decided to add a few extra days to the trip. They wanted an opportunity for adventure, to immerse themselves in an unfamiliar culture. Emily had always wanted to know Dev in a different place, away from the entanglements of his family. They considered several destinations in Europe but eventually settled on the storied city of Istanbul. Emily had been studying Islamic art, architecture, and textiles. Dev was curious about the faith of his birth mother. Five days were added to their itinerary.

Then a couple of weeks before their planned departure, Dev closed on the purchase of his house in Kitsilano, and the owners insisted on a quick possession date. So, plans were changed for Dev to fly back to Canada from Istanbul and for Emily to visit her mother alone. Initially the change of plans annoyed her. For one thing the purchase of the house came as a surprise, and if he was serious about their future together, she should have been consulted. When she confronted him, he said it had come together so quickly that even he was surprised, that his family had helped him with the purchase—it had been listed as a "rare find" and they did not want him to miss his chance. He promised to do better.

THEY SAT SIDE by side on a divan, leaning their backs on a stack of cushions. In respect of local customs, they curbed their public affections, but here on the rooftop where there were few people around to see, they allowed their bodies to tilt into each other. Emily loosened the cotton scarf that she kept wrapped around her shoulders for walking the city streets and visiting the ancient sacred sites. She thought of Klimt's mosaic *The Fulfillment*, two lovers embracing, frozen in time, never kissing.

They timed their rooftop visits so they could hear the

evening calls to prayer from the surrounding mosques—
elegiac voices crackling through loudspeakers as though they
really were calling to the heavens. From their divan they had
a view of Hagia Sophia lit up against the darkening sky. Emily
sketched the domed roof of the museum—once a Byzantine
church, once an Ottoman mosque—four slender minarets
and a circle of windows around the main dome bathed in
orange and yellow.

That morning they'd woken up early to go for a meand-
ering walk through the ancient city—the cafés and restau-
rants not yet open and the streets empty but for labourers
waiting at trolley stops and the ubiquitous stray cats. They
climbed a secluded street far from the tourist hotels. The end
of the steep ascent led to an awe-inspiring view; the walled
perimeter of the old city, minarets and green domed roofs,
the wide Bosphorus Strait—bustling at this early hour—and
the newer, shinier districts connected across the water by the
Galata Bridge. The dawn light uncovered the panorama like
a blanket being drawn back.

They discussed how the Bosphorus marked the division
between the modern and ancient, the secular and the religious, East and West, Europe and Asia. Reminded of the
dividing walls and steel fences of Belfast, Emily was suddenly
nervous about her visit home.

On their walk back to the hotel, they stopped at a shop
near the Basilica Cistern selling Turkish ceramics. They'd
been meaning to visit the "art emporium" since they first
arrived, but the place was constantly filled with tourists.
Emily had been drawn to a cobalt-blue vase in the window,
tulip shaped with hand-painted flowers and vines. Holding it

in her hands, feeling its heft and examining the intricacy of the brush work up close, she decided to purchase it; a bit of an extravagance perhaps, but she had picked up extra courses for the following year of teaching, and surely, an indulgence now and then was allowed.

After some good-humoured haggling, Dev paid for the vase as an early birthday present. The salesman wrapped it in layers of newspaper so it would survive its journey to Belfast and then Vancouver, but they couldn't leave until they shared tea with him and answered his questions about where they were from, how they had met, and how many children they intended to have. Everywhere in this city they were seen as a novelty.

She was thinking of the blue vase as she sat next to Dev on the divan, imagining a place for it in his new home—in *their* new home—somewhere prominent so they could tell guests the story of its origins in Istanbul. The evening prayer was over and the air was still and silent but for the occasional car horn, the scratch of Emily's pencil on paper, and the sporadic buzz of moth wings. In this serenity the drawing came easy.

"Em, I've been thinking ..."

She looked up from her sketchbook and turned her head slightly toward him.

"When we're back in Vancouver, I'd like you to meet my brothers."

Emily put down her pencil. She'd been waiting for this moment since they'd met, it seemed. That Dev had voiced it as more than just a hypothetical scenario took her by surprise. She felt a mix of agitated disbelief and hopeful relief. She wanted desperately to trust that meeting his brothers was a necessary step toward meeting Auntie Deepa and Uncle Monty. *And then …* She fought the urge to get ahead of herself.

"Yeah?" she said, still a little surprised. "Of course, Dev. I'd love that!"

Prior to getting back together, she'd given him an ultimatum: "Either we take the next step in this relationship or we split for good." The last breakup had hurt her more than any of their previous pauses—*another Christmas alone while he's with his family*—and she was determined not to face another. She understood that Dev navigated a wider circle than she did, that he had to consider alliances and debts that only he fully grasped. In her childhood she had witnessed the power of unshakable allegiances and how badly they could end. Living through the Troubles, she longed for compromises, but Dev lived his life forever afraid to upset the balance.

She paused a moment, carefully weighing her words. "Why now? What's changed?"

"There's only one person I can see myself building a life with, Em. I've been sure of that for a long time." Dev turned his head to look at her directly. "It's just that I feel like everything's in place now. I've finished my master's. I have my teaching job. I'll have my own place soon."

"Dev, my love for you wouldn't be diminished if you didn't have those things."

"I know that. But this family, *my* family, has given me so much. They took me in when I had nothing. I don't want to let them down."

She wanted to interrogate his overwhelming need for

certainty. *Nothing is ever perfect!* she wanted to scream but was afraid he might clam up again. She'd accept this good news for the moment.

That night they were awoken by a persistent knock on the door of their hotel room. Emily rubbed her eyes as Dev staggered out of bed, wrapped a towel around his middle in the darkness, and answered.

"Sir, there is a call for Mrs. Gill."

"Thank you. We'll be right down."

They had only just closed their eyes and it took a few minutes to shake themselves awake. They dressed for the walk down the three flights of stairs to the lobby. Dev stood at a short distance to let her take the call.

"Hello?"

"Emily? It's your uncle Patrick. Sorry to ring you at such an ungodly hour."

Her heart dropped. "What's happened?"

"Aye, it's your ma, dear. She's had a bit of a mishap. Your aunt is with her in the hospital. We thought it best to let you know right away."

After hanging up, Emily had the hotel dial the Royal Victoria Hospital and learned that the "mishap" was an intracerebral hemorrhage on the left side of Ma's brain. Blood had escaped into her brain tissue. She had already been moved from A&E to the Neurology ICU and surgery was scheduled for the next morning. To relieve the swelling, a piece of skull would need to be removed.

In the morning, the hotel staff helped Emily make changes to her itinerary through a local travel agency. She bought a ticket on the first available flight to Heathrow that would connect her to Belfast. Dev asked if she wanted him to change his booking and accompany her. "I could probably make it for my closing if I can get flights to Vancouver for the following day," he proposed. Part of her wished he wouldn't need to ask, that he'd take the initiative himself. On the other hand, taking possession of the new house was extremely important and couldn't be delayed. Not to mention, the house was part of her hope for their future together.

"No, Dev. That's good of you but you go and do what you need to. I'll see you at home soon anyway."

She suddenly remembered the vase. "Can I leave it with you to take back?"

"Of course. That's the last thing you should be worried about."

She kissed Dev in the privacy of their hotel room before he carried her suitcase downstairs. She waved goodbye through the back window of the taxi as it pulled away.

AUNT DAWNEL AND Uncle Patrick were waiting for her at Arrivals. The Royal Ulster Constabulary checkpoint on the airport road was a brusque and painful reminder of what she'd left behind years earlier. Maybe it was a good thing that Dev wasn't with her. Each time she was asked how long she planned to stay, she replied, "Only a fortnight."

Dawnel and Patrick filled her in on more details during the drive to the hospital. It took a moment for Emily's ear to re-tune itself to her aunt's thick lilt. She hadn't realized how much her own accent had softened over the years. From what she could gather, her mother had been complaining about a headache the previous day and left work in the afternoon to go home and rest. When she didn't show up for her evening shift, Dawnel sent Patrick over to check on her. There was no answer, so he let himself in and found Ma passed out on the kitchen floor.

"We found your hotel details on a notepad by the phone."

Emily had spoken to her mother earlier in the week. She'd sounded excited about the upcoming visit, but there was clear disappointment in her voice when she learned that Dev would not be joining.

"I had the place cleaned all nice for him," she'd said.

At the hospital Emily was told that the surgery had been successful, but her mother was still comatose and intubated—a ventilator was connected to the intubation tube to deliver oxygen. She squeezed her mother's hand as hard as she could; there was no response. Emily advised Dawnel and Patrick that they should get back to the Auld Pheasant, knowing that as the publicans they couldn't be away too long, not on a Friday evening. They shared with her that the visceral fear had lifted somewhat lately and business was finally picking up.

Emily sat by her mother's bedside for the remainder of the day as various members of the clinical team checked in periodically. Late evening, tired after the restless sleep and still jet-lagged, she decided it was best to try to get some rest. She stopped at the pub to pick up the spare keys and made her way to her childhood home. The treeless street was deserted, and the rattle of suitcase wheels echoed off the pavement and brick. A strange mix of familiarity and concern made her breathe more heavily and walk a little faster than normal.

She didn't recall the house being so small, so musty, everything in a state of disrepair. *Why has Ma not refreshed the place with a coat of paint or new curtains at the very least?* The thought was immediately followed by the realization that this was what Ma had called "cleaned all nice" for Dev. *Bloody hell! What did it look like before?*

Every room flooded her with memories. Every door she pushed open, every creak in the floorboards reminded her of her childhood, of the time when her da was still around, years when the house was filled with love and laughter. Her parents would lock the front door, draw the curtains, and pretend they were the only three people in the world—that nothing could penetrate their fortress.

A familiar sign saying NO RELIGION. NO POLITICS. hung by the front door. Framed family photographs were still nailed to the living room walls or sat on the dusty mantelpiece. The furniture—the grey settee, the oval coffee table, the long wooden stereo cabinet—in the same place as in her childhood. Emily thought back to the days when her parents would crank up the volume on the amplifier, excitedly changing records on the turntable to dance with each other. Her early memories were soundtracked by the Rolling Stones, the Beatles, and Elvis Presley, with a dose of Van Morrison, the Clancy Brothers, and Tommy Makem thrown into the mix. A memory of Da surfaced, teasing her that as a toddler she'd jump up and down screaming "Getno," until he would throw on "Satisfaction" by the Stones.

In the dimly lit kitchen, she unwrapped the sandwich that

Dawnel had packed for her and ate to the sound of a buzz-ing light bulb and the gurgle of the plumbing. If Ma was still expecting Da to walk back into the house, wouldn't she have made some effort? Or did she finally give up hope? Was the realization that he wasn't coming back what pushed her over the edge?

Twice Emily tried dialing the hotel in Istanbul and was disappointed to hear the engaged signal.

Upstairs she found the mattress in her childhood bedroom had been stripped bare. A set of folded sheets sat on the dresser. Her cousin Sean, Dawnel and Patrick's son, had stayed in the house during Ma's years in Canada and Depeche Mode and Samantha Fox posters hung on the walls.

In her parents' bedroom, concealed behind the must of the wallpaper was another familiar smell. A nearly empty bottle of after shave, the kind Da wore, sat on the night table. She breathed in the sweet citrus-and-clove fragrance, imagined the cradle of his shoulder where she would rest her head. Too tired to make up her bed, she left her suitcase, still packed, in the corner and lay down on her parents' bed. The pillows gave off the less welcome odours of tobacco, malt vinegar, and fried food, the smells of the Auld Pheasant, but it was comforting to be enveloped in the same sheets her ma had slept in.

The next morning at the hospital the neurosurgeon assured Emily that the procedure had gone well. The bleed-ing had stopped, and the hematoma had been removed. "It's important that you're here when she wakes up, so she has a recognizable face to see. It'll lessen the confusion," he counselled.

She squeezed Ma's hand, gently this time, but still received no response.

That evening Dawnel dropped by the hospital with fish and chips, warm and vinegary, smelling of childhood trips to the seaside.

A few days on, Ma still unresponsive, Emily made an early morning excursion to Belfast City Cemetery and found her grandparents' graves. She hadn't prayed since the mandatory assemblies during her year in grammar school but found herself kneeling at the gravestone mouthing words that she thought might bring Ma comfort.

Then, finally, some good news. Emily was told that her mother was responding to vigorous stimulation and was now in what the surgeon described as a "semi-comatose state." He was "cautiously optimistic of a full recovery, though she might remain drowsy and inactive for some time." Looking at Ma lying in her bed, Emily could not discern any change.

One week later, Emily, at last, found a few hours to clean and tidy the house. Then she unpacked the contents of her suitcase into the bedroom dresser and called Emily Carr College to let them know she'd be delayed in returning to work because of a family emergency. That same day she walked toward Cupar Way fearing what she might see of the Peace Wall that had been constructed when she was five years of age. The barrier was now several metres higher, and more foreboding than she remembered. The visceral fear may have lifted but the physical reminders of the sectarian divide were still very much in evidence. She wanted to fall on her knees and weep but that kind of public weakness would be noticed. There was safety in anonymity and silence.

TWO MONTHS BEFORE Meena's expected birth they added the final items to the spare third-floor bedroom. The nursery, which had previously been filled with an assortment of odd furniture, was fitted with a new crib, a children's dresser, and a toy chest. Devinder had wanted them to take an old crib stocked away in Karanpreet and Kiran's garage, but Kuldip put her foot down and insisted they buy new.

They fitted the back seat of their suv with a new child-safety seat and bought a high-tech stroller with enormous wheels—Devinder called it the "Moon Buggy."

Kiran, Baljit, and Harpal gifted them a baby bath, night lights, a bassinet, and stacks of clothes. Although Auntie Deepa had forbidden them from receiving gifts prior to the baby's birth—another of her mother-in-law's superstitions—they snuck everything in under the guise of renovations.

The house took on new smells, lavender and rosewater, baby balms and lotions. Tiny clothes, blankets, and packs of diapers filled empty closets. Cans of baby formula took up half the pantry. A second crib was placed in their bedroom at Kiran's advice: "If the baby cries at night, you'll want to be nearby. Trust me!" Kuldip insisted that they also buy this crib new.

Kuldip went into labour three weeks earlier than expected. By the time they arrived at the hospital, Auntie Deepa and Kiran were already waiting. Six hours later as Kuldip was wheeled into the delivery room, Deepa tugged on Devinder's arm and told him it was "not a place for a man." He had faithfully attended the prenatal classes and Kuldip wished he was beside her, but that decision had been made for them.

AUNTIE DEEPA INSISTED that she move into their house to help them manage the first months of parenthood; she slept in a single bed beside Meena's crib in the nursery. She diligently changed her new granddaughter's diapers, fed her from the bottles of formula that were kept in the refrigerator, and calmed her during her bouts of crying. Deepa was proud to announce that she had cared for her other six grandchildren in the same way.

"What good is it having a dadiji if your dadiji doesn't look after you," she would say as she rocked Meena to sleep in her arms.

Kuldip had to admit that Deepa's ways with the newborn were masterful; she was an enormous help in those first weeks when Kuldip was recovering from the delivery. By the end of that first month, however, she was ready to take on the responsibilities she had waited so long for and convinced Deepa, with prodding from Devinder, that Uncle Monty needed her care more than her new granddaughter did.

Devinder was allowed a semester of paternity leave and together they muddled through the feeding, dressing, changing, and bathing routines. They consistently checked for any sign of a fever or illness and devised strategies to deal with the unpredictable bouts of crying. At night, they tag-teamed to get Meena back to sleep.

Despite the constant barrage of well-wishers at all hours, those first few months were the best time of Kuldip's life. She had an overwhelming sense of belonging when holding her daughter in her arms with Devinder by her side. The love she felt for Meena was crushing, deeper than anything she had ever thought possible. *A real blood connection. Nothing could compare.*

ONE AFTERNOON SHE stepped out after a long shower to find Devinder napping in their bed with Meena on his chest. She tiptoed around the room as she dressed before heading downstairs to begin preparations for dinner. An hour later Devinder came down with Meena in his arms.

"I'm sorry, I fell asleep."

"Why sorry, Ji? Maninder looked so lovely. I took a picture with the new camera."

Devinder placed Meena, who was still sleeping, on a blanket in the bassinet that now centred their living room. He was smiling as he walked back into the kitchen looking at the captured image on the digital camera.

"That's a keeper for sure."

Kuldip was confused by the expression. "Keeper?"

"It means this photograph is so beautiful, I'll keep it forever."

Forever! Devinder was always cautious with his words, but she liked the sound of "forever."

He nuzzled his face over Kuldip's shoulder and inhaled the aroma of the masala mixing in the large pan. She closed her eyes and stopped stirring, only continuing when she noticed the sizzle had slowed and the tadka was sticking to the bottom of the pan. *In the future, when you ask, "When did you know for sure that you loved Daddy?" this will be the moment I'll recall: here in this kitchen, with the steam from the pan and our bodies slack and untroubled, leaning against each other, and you asleep peacefully in the next room.*

"DO YOU THINK the boat will fit in here?" Emily jokes as Sarah reverses her boxy minivan into a parking spot close to the entrance of the gurdwara. It's tight but Sarah manages it with ease.

"Like a pro!" says Emily.

They inspect the invitation card and the "Program for Wedding Day"—they've reviewed it together several times leading up to today but one more time won't hurt. The ornate card, printed in embossed gold letters, reads Milni ~ *12:30 p.m.* but they can see through the metal fence that the parking lot on the grounds is more than half empty. It's already well past noon.

"Dev warned me that things tend to run late. We might as well head in before the crowd arrives."

Sarah senses a little tremor in Emily's voice and squeezes her knee for reassurance.

"When I asked him why, he said that everything has to be perfect, and perfection takes time. And a lot of retakes."

Sarah laughs. "That sounds like a Dev response."

They inhale deeply and nod to each other as if psyching themselves up for a strenuous hike. "Let's do this!"

Emily reaches into her bag for her oversized sunglasses.

They enter through tall gates toward a large white building with golden domes placed symmetrically on the roof to either side of the main entrance. At the top of the marble steps, the large double doors, elaborately engraved with Punjabi Gurmukhi script and a khanda, the crossed-sword symbol of the Sikh religion, are open wide. Sarah motions to Emily to pull her scarf over her head.

Emily turns to look at the gathering at the far end of the parking lot: men in suits standing with their arms crossed, women in colourful Punjabi outfits huddled in small groups, and a few children scampering between parked cars playing games of chase. To one side, a tall, thin man in a wrinkled brown suit paces nervously by himself. She surmises that this must be Rina's side of the wedding party waiting for Ranjit's family to arrive. *Punjabi Standard Time.* A part of her wishes she could remain outside for their arrival.

Once inside they are directed by a young man to a side room where they remove their shoes in accordance with gurdwara rules. They take note of the number scribbled inside the wooden cube into which they place both pairs, then wash their hands at the long communal sink.

In the New Great Hall a few people are already seated. A pathway of bare carpet runs down the middle toward a golden throne and domed canopy, raised off the ground, in which the Guru Granth Sahib sits beneath layers of shiny fabric. Dev has often talked to her about how much he admires the rituals of the temple, how the book of scripture is considered an earthly embodiment of the ten Gurus who founded the religion, that at the end of every evening it is kept in a special room and left to rest for the night, then carried in a procession the next morning to the prayer hall.

The remainder of the floor is covered in long white sheets; two young men in blue turbans move through the hall stretching each sheet to make sure there is no gap between them. The walls are bare and the lofty ceiling has a series of simple pot lights and two white fans that spin silently.

Ahead of them, an elderly woman, thin, unsteady, is led down the central path by a younger woman. They hold their hands in prayer pose as they walk slowly toward the Guru Granth Sahib. A man dressed in white with a blue turban sits cross-legged at the back of the throne and removes the layers of shiny fabric from the holy book. He mouths a prayer as he turns pages with both hands, almost in slow motion. Emily assumes he must be the Head Granthi. She admires the reverence in his actions: the gentleness with which his fingers touch the paper, how each page is turned precisely and then delicately pressed down. An assistant sits beside him and waves a ceremonial whisk of long white hair above the sacred text.

The elderly woman stops and remains standing with her hands held in prayer, head bowed. The younger woman bends down onto her knees, places her hands on the carpet in front of her, and touches her forehead to the ground. She takes a folded banknote and places it in the long metal donation box in front of the raised throne. The older woman reaches down with a closed hand and passes her donation, like a secret note. In one smooth motion the young woman stands while keeping her hands in prayer pose. She then takes her older companion by the arm and leads her to the back of the room—the left side for women, the right side for men, as Dev had primed her—where an elevated bench has been built against the wall for those too infirm to sit on the floor.

When it's their turn Emily lets Sarah go first and then copies her. They keep their hands in a prayer pose as they walk away, their bodies facing the dome for the first few steps. They move to the corner and take a spot where they can lean their backs against a wall.

"Like a pro," whispers Sarah.

Emily laughs. "I practised at home. Dev showed me awhile back but I'm glad you and the young woman were ahead of me."

Three gentlemen wearing simple white outfits have taken their places on a stage to the left of the golden throne behind a set of tabla drums and two harmoniums. They sit cross-legged in front of their instruments. The drums are tuned with light taps of a hammer on small wooden blocks tied against the curved body, followed by finger taps on the skin. After every slight adjustment, the drums are rotated a few degrees and the act is repeated. The harmonium players occasionally squeeze the bellows of their instruments with their left hand while pressing keys and adjusting levers with their right. Then they take turns playing notes, giving one another appreciative nods when all three instruments are in tune.

"I'm glad we're here early," Emily whispers to Sarah. "We get to hear the sound check."

The oldest of the three gentlemen begins to sing kirtan, the scriptures set to the tap-tap of the tabla and the hum of the harmoniums, the music lifting into the air. Emily closes her eyes and savours the sense of peace; her stress and uncertainty drain away. It's the musicality of the hymns, she reckons, that moves her, written and arranged in the melody of the classical Indian music she and Dev would sometimes listen to together.

EMILY'S FINGERS DANCE and tap lightly against each other as the singer's voice rises and falls, speeds up and slows down. The other players occasionally join in vocal harmony as phrases are repeated and accentuated. They have been sitting for almost an hour and still only a handful of guests have arrived. She feels a soft nudge in her side and opens her eyes. Sarah motions toward the entrance. A young girl is spinning; her bright shiny skirt petals around her. She spins faster and faster, stumbles when she finally stops and has to stretch her arms out wide to steady herself. When she is still, she takes a long look around the room before setting her sights on them. Her bangles clink as she tiptoes their way.

Emily would know her anywhere.

"Hello, Auntie Sarah," Teena exclaims, a little short of breath.

Sarah lifts her into her lap, removing her shoes. She takes one strand of her own scarf and pulls it over Teena's head.

"Oh, silly me. I forgot. Did you see me spinning? I went so fast!" Teena puts her hands on either side of Sarah's face as if to monopolize her attention. Sarah puts her finger to her lips to get Teena to speak more quietly.

"I did, sweetie. That looks like fun. Where are your mom and dad?"

Teena ignores the question, stares in Emily's direction, and says, "I haven't seen you before."

"My name is Em," she replies. She has only ever glimpsed Teena from a distance, in the neighbourhood with her sister and parents; each time she's changed direction to avoid them. She detects Dev's dark eyes and dimpled chin.

"That's funny. *M*! M like Meena." Sarah lifts her finger to her lips again. Teena sits up in Sarah's lap and stares at Emily with more intention and scrutiny.

"Where are your mom and dad, Teena?" Sarah whispers again.

"You know, it's Ranjit Bhaji's *actual* wedding day?" Teena replies as she turns her head back to look at Sarah.

"Yes, that's why we're here, sweetie."

"Did you know there's going to be a milni and my dad's going to lift a man into the air? Lift him way up! Come see!" Teena's voice rises as she gets more excited and pulls at Sarah's scarf, urging her to stand up.

"You two go. I'll wait here," Emily says.

"Noooo ... you come, too, Auntie M. Come see!" Teena squeezes Emily's upper arm and pouts her bottom lip. "Please!"

They are now getting looks from the other guests and Sarah nods at Emily to assure her it'll be okay. Teena leans her head back and gives a cheer as Emily rises.

In the front hallway they find their shoes in the cube where they'd left them. Sarah stoops down to help Teena. A tremble travels up Emily's spine as Teena, trying to keep her balance, reaches for her hand. She had anticipated the complexity of emotions in seeing Dev with his family. It's not regret exactly—she reserves regret for circumstances in which she could have done something to change an outcome—but a feeling that her life has been a series of near misses and close calls. Undone by Teena's touch, she worries about her own steadiness, a slight buckle in her legs and a tingling in her feet.

At the exit Emily puts on her sunglasses but waits in the doorway as Sarah walks into the sunshine. Teena seems to have forgotten about her earlier insistence; she drops Emily's hand and skips away. Looking out at the parking lot Emily can tell that both wedding parties are now gathered for the milni, what Dev had explained was the traditional exchange of gifts that's become a kind of genial jockeying for position between the two families. Amongst the throng of well-dressed men, she spots Dev. His designer suit looks made-to-measure, of course. Dev and the other men without turbans wear large saffron-coloured handkerchiefs, folded diagonally and knotted behind their heads. Ranjit stands tall and straight. His turban looks splendid. Everyone is engaged in casual conversation, relaxed and cheerful. Meena is at Dev's side, holding his hand. Observing the sea of bright-coloured women's outfits, Emily suddenly feels underdressed. *Maybe I should have worn the green leggings after all.*

At the piercing screech of car wheels all heads turn in the direction of the driveway, and she quickly sneaks back into the building.

"I'M ALL SHE has," she'd say to Dev whenever they managed to connect. She never mentioned that she feared the inverse was also true; all *she* had was her mother.

The first time he called from his new house she asked him to describe it in detail. "The kitchen's a good size. There's a new gas stove, an old-style dining nook. In the living room, two large windows face Hadden Park. You can see two enormous maple trees and a sliver of ocean. Original red oak floors throughout, with thick baseboards and window frames."

He described the back garden with its bleeding heart and hydrangea bushes. He told her about the den on the main floor that he was turning into an office and the two bedrooms upstairs, a front balcony off the main room that had the "best view" of the inlet, and two rooms on the middle level. "Empty for now."

Emily's imagination filled in the vacant spaces: a gathering of potted plants on the back deck, a painting on the wall between the two large windows in the living room, the blue Turkish vase on a shelf made from salvaged wood, and most encouragingly, a studio in one of the rooms on the middle floor filled with canvases and an easel by the window. She imagined Hadden Park and the silhouette of the West End and Stanley Park.

Emily snapped back into the present as Dev repeated his question, "Em, I asked if you're taking care of yourself." She looked at the peeling wallpaper in the hallway where the olive-green phone hung on the wall, the notepad with the number of the hotel in Istanbul curled at the edges like a leaf. She wondered who the NO RELIGION. NO POLITICS. sign had been meant for. After Ma's parents had both passed, there were never any visitors other than Dawnel and Patrick. The one time she recalled someone from the Council coming into the house, the sign had been taken down and hidden in an upstairs closet.

Emily gave her head a shake. "I have a sick mother to tend to, Dev. Honestly, I haven't thought much about myself lately."

***

AFTER SIX WEEKS in the ICU, a decision was made to move Margaret Rice to a care home. There were times when Emily squeezed her hand and thought she sensed a slight response but she couldn't be sure it was anything more than a reflex. Occasionally her mother would open her eyes, only to stare vacantly at the ceiling until the nurse gently closed them again. "It happens," the nurse informed Emily. "You think they're back, but they're not. Not really."

Emily met with the physical medicine and rehabilitation team to review treatments that would ensure Ma's joints remained mobile and slow the atrophy in her muscles.

Every day was the same, a recurring dream she could not wake from. She sat by Ma's bedside from morning to evening, sometimes assisting the nursing staff with the cycles of feeding and cleaning. Occasionally one of Ma's friends might visit or Aunt Dawnel would relieve her for a few hours. Time became meaningless. Days, weeks, months bled into one another—one long continuous coil.

In the house she searched without success for her father's boxes of books, which the university had sent to them a year after his disappearance. She did find Da's 45s, but there was no turntable to play them on. Besides, she wasn't sure she could handle the memories those songs would dredge up. In a closet beneath the stairs she found a stack of books that Ma had brought back from Canada. Emily took a couple of them to the care home and read out loud from the short story collections. She clung tightly to the hope that her mother could hear her voice, taking long pauses between sentences, waiting for a response.

***

THE MONTHS CONTINUED to drift by. Emily grew accustomed to the creaky floors, to the doors and drawers that didn't quite shut, to the misty windows and the rattling radiators. She could block out the clang and crack of the plumbing and tolerate the geyser that scarcely produced enough hot water to fill a bucket. With an extra sweater, the draft through the back-room window did not bite so hard. Breathing in the musty air was now a well-worn penance.

Dev's connecting flight had been delayed due to a snowstorm in Toronto and he'd arrived in Belfast a day later than planned. The wait had only increased her anxiety. Ten months had passed since they'd waved goodbye at the hotel in Istanbul. They spoke on the phone regularly, but a strange silence now crowded their conversations.

"It's all right, Em. It's good to see you." She'd been apologizing for the condition of the house and not being able to meet him at the airport. "Us spending time together, that's what matters."

He handed her the set of drawing pencils and sketch pad she'd left in Istanbul in her rush to get to Belfast. She flipped through the pages until she got to the drawing of Hagia Sophia, the dome and minarets, a starry sky, a half moon. Their time in Istanbul seemed like a fantasy world she'd conjured up in her head; a world she frequently wished she could click her heels and return to.

"What are the doctors saying about your mother's long-term prognosis?" Dev asked as he tenderly held Ma's hand the next afternoon at the care home.

"They say it's tough to predict. If we can keep her stable, there's always a chance that she'll recover."

The last trip Ma had made to Vancouver was during one of the breaks in their relationship and Emily had been annoyed that she kept asking about him. "He's such a lovely boy, love. Can't you patch things up?"

In the evening, Emily took Dev to the Auld Pheasant. Dawnel and Patrick greeted him warmly and told him Margaret had spoken about him often. They were grateful he'd come all this way to see "our Em."

Emily overheard Patrick telling Dev, "Aye, the sadness has been upon her. She could use a good friend 'bout now, so she could."

Later, back at home, Emily heated up the lamb stew that Dawnel had insisted they take with them. Dev made a comment about the thickness of her aunt's accent, and it felt good to laugh together. "I only just about understand her myself. You poor man. I'll be your interpreter next time."

The stew was thick and rich with carrots and potatoes— *hearty* was the word Dawnel had written on the chalkboard menu. Soaking up the gravy with Dawnel's homemade bread, Dev asked, "What are you doing to look after yourself?"

The question was meant well but it still managed to irritate her; just when they were enjoying a moment of lightness. This time she could not hold back.

"I'm by her side every day, Dev. Aunt Dawnel's busy with her business and Ma has no one else. Sure, there are a couple of friends, but they have their own lives to attend to. I stop at the Auld Pheasant a few evenings a week for a quick catch-up. Dawnel and Patrick are very good to me and it's a relief to sit at the bar and eat a warm meal. But each conversation is like a replay of our previous conversations. Some days it's easier to avoid the topic of Ma's health altogether. Talking about it only deepens this feeling that I've stepped into a dank peat bog and I'm never getting out."

Dev rubbed his open hand across her back as she stared

at the remainder of her dinner. His instinctive response in a moment of stress was to embrace her. Her instinct, in the moment, was to pull away.

"Mostly," she said, as she stood to refill her glass of water, "I feel fucking wrecked. My body, because I don't move most days. My mind, because it saps everything out of me. All I ever talk about, ever think about, fucking dream about, is Ma's condition."

Dev tried again to put his arm around her, but she moved away to put the kettle on.

"Tell me what's happening back home," she said once they were reseated at the kitchen table, hoping that might change her mood. Dev brought her up to speed on the changes he'd made to the house, which were minor, but consequential.

"Navpreet was upgrading his bedroom furniture, so I furnished the two spare rooms on the middle floor with his old stuff. Now whenever my nephew and nieces come to visit they have a place to sleep. It's not much but it fills the space."

There goes the fucking studio, she thought.

"It's so easy for me to get back and forth from work now," he continued. "I can spend my evenings exploring Kitsilano."

She was unsure that she wanted to hear any more about the neighbourhood she was desperately missing. "How is work, anyway?"

As always, Dev spoke of his students with admiration and regard.

"What do they make of the books you've assigned them?"

"One student recently wrote a paper on Canadian literature's obsession with countries of departure and the journeys taken to arrive in Canada. What they really want is to see more diverse characters who identify as Canadian."

It was more like one of their regular conversations and for a short while Emily forgot about Ma and the months apart from Dev. Then he asked her if she'd read anything lately.

"I found a stack of books Ma brought with her from Vancouver. I've been reading short stories to her. Carol Shields and Alice Munro, mostly. Their familiarity is comforting. There are days when reading aloud is the only conversation I have. I keep waiting for a response—a nod, a hum, a tick, the slightest tremble in her lip. Anything to validate that what I'm doing matters."

After they'd washed and dried the dishes and were back in the front room, Dev excused himself and returned with five mixed CDs he'd compiled for her; the songs listed in his neat handwriting.

"That's super sweet, but of course there's no CD player in the house," she remarked.

Dev said nothing as he placed his Sony Discman next to the stack of discs on the mantel above the unused fireplace.

"I come home from the hospital tired each evening, Dev. It's a struggle to feed myself and clean up afterward. My only indulgence is a hot bath and for that I'm at the whim of the geyser. Then I'm straight to bed. I haven't painted since I got here. I haven't switched on the TV or seen a movie in months. I'm not sure the TV even works. To be quite honest, music seems a luxury I no longer have time for."

Dev joined her on the sofa and they sat in silence for what seemed like an eternity, before he finally said, "I miss you, Em."

"I miss you, too, Dev. And you know, I'd love to see the

new house and spend time in our old 'hood, but as long as Ma's unwell, I need to be here."

LONG PERIODS OF silence filled the remainder of Dev's visit. Conversations that might have gone on for hours back in Vancouver now came to abrupt ends. Emily was at the care home most of the day. Dev stayed home grading student papers, joining her for a short while and then touring the streets with his handy pocket map. She'd circled the places that she thought might interest him—Queen's University, the Grand Opera House, Botanic Gardens—and cross-hatched the districts he "best avoid."

One evening he came home with ground spices he'd charmed away from the owners of the Empire Indian Restaurant close to Queen's; spoonfuls of cumin, turmeric, and coriander folded into paper packets. He cooked a chicken curry, served it with raw sliced red onion and lime pickle, and reheated the famous Empire naans. Emily wore the dress with red flowers—retrieved for her by Dev—and loosened her hair from the hairpins she had become accustomed to wearing.

"Deepa's been teaching me how to cook. After this meal you too will be a proper Punjabi."

Emily offered a polite "Thank you." She realized she was drained and unable to reciprocate either affection or attention. It was the first time he'd ever cooked for her, and the curry was first-rate. "I'm sorry, Dev. You're being so kind, and I'm ..." She hated that she always felt the need to apologize to him, as if he was the one always going out of his way.

Dev drew close and this time she let him hold her as she wept, more for the comfort of finally allowing herself to be vulnerable in another person's arms rather than any warm feeling for him in the moment.

"Do you want me to move out here, Em? Until things improve, I mean."

She was startled by the suggestion. She pulled away, wiped her eyes, and held up her hands. "We both know that doesn't make sense. What would you do here? This place is a bed of tinder sticks, and someone could light a match any day. And you've got your job, your house, your family. So, no! Thank you, but that's a terrible idea."

They fell into a deep stillness, the half-eaten meal left on their plates.

Dev spoke first. "I'll always wait for you, Em."

She was tired of fighting and constantly wondering if they still had a future together. But this was Dev, the only man she'd ever truly loved. "Promise?" she asked in an attempt to please him.

"Yes. I promise. When your ma's better and you're back home, it'll all be fine. Promise."

She let him hold her a little tighter.

"Will our kids have rhyming names?" she said between her tears, a hint of joy mixed with the sadness.

"Of course, now that you're a proper Punjabi." He laughed into her hair. "We don't have to give them Punjabi names though. We could call them Niamh and Steve." It was an old joke they often shared, but it had been Iqbal's creation. She laughed and leaned her chin on his shoulder.

"How is our friend Iqbal?"

Dev went quiet. "Mmm … He's back on the streets, I'm afraid," he finally said. "He was home for a short while, but then his mom was diagnosed with breast cancer. That news was hard enough but his father blamed him for her illness. Last month, I ran into him near Kits Beach. I didn't know that he wasn't living at home anymore. He had a shopping cart full of empty bottles and cans. Said he couldn't go back to the Lower East Side. Kept repeating, 'Too many leeches there, too many leeches!' I tried to give him some money, but he wasn't having it. I invited him home for a meal, but he was flighty and left our conversation mid-sentence. It'll be good if he stays in the neighbourhood and I can see him now and again, but I dread the day I'll get *that* call about him."

She knew how much Iqbal's friendship meant to Dev and squeezed his hand. When they were first together, he was always looking to Iqbal for approval and guidance. This latest news made her sad, but at least their conversation had found a familiar rhythm. They fell asleep in the living room wrapped in each other's arms.

The next morning, she slept in. She'd have to hurry to make her monthly meeting with Dr. Osbourne, Ma's newest doctor. Dev was trying to lend a hand by making her tea and toast, but she'd gotten used to her routine and his attempts at helping felt more like interruptions.

Back upstairs, she was pinning her hair into place as he was rummaging in his suitcase. He made a comment about how he couldn't wait for them to live together. Her words rolled out before she had time to think. "You'd plenty of years to do something about that, Dev. You never fucking did! I was always second to your family." Dev stopped rummaging. "And to be honest, I'm not convinced that'll ever change!"

She'd obviously stunned him with the force of her response and his eyes grew big and distant. His voice shook. "I'm sorry, Em. I didn't mean to upset you."

"That's the fucking problem, Dev. You never want to upset anyone!"

She ran downstairs, nearly falling as she tripped on the bottom step. On her way out she slammed the front door hard and was too flustered to turn back when she heard breaking glass—a cracked window was the least of her problems.

"WE BETTER NOT lose!" shouts Sam, one of Ranjit's cousins on his mother's side. Everyone snickers until Vaddé Maamaji reminds them, albeit with a slight grin, that this is a serious occasion. Along with Vaddé Maamaji, who has double duty as eldest maternal granduncle and substitute paternal grandfather, Devinder and his brothers make up the front row of milni greeters. Uncle Monty watches the proceedings from his limousine, the window rolled down and a wide furrow cut in the crowd to ensure his view is unobstructed. A couple of steps ahead stand Ranjit and Amarpreet. Though the mood is carefree, Devinder can tell the guests are anxious to get inside and out of the direct heat of the midday sun.

Devinder has spotted Sarah and Teena at the entrance to the gurdwara but is distracted by the yellow Mazda Miata entering the parking lot, the loud screech of its tires has caught everyone's attention. He must find Teena once the milni is over and make sure she is by his side for the remainder of the ceremonies. It was foolish of him to lose sight of her given her propensity for wandering.

The speeding car is another matter. The Miata belongs to Balraj Sharma, a young man that his brothers refer to as a "going concern." Or as Monty likes to say, "Bad news waiting to happen." Amarpreet and Ranjit glance at Devinder, their subtle way of reminding him that the responsibility falls upon him. Devinder will have to pull Balraj aside at some point during the day and have a stern talk. That kind of behaviour at an event like this, at a place of worship, where children are playing, is unacceptable. And while the Sandhu family tends to skirt potential conflicts, sometimes a line needs to be drawn.

Devinder is considering how he should approach Balraj when there is a familiar tug on his pant leg. He bends down to pick Teena up in his arms. "Hey, you. Where have you been?"

"Daddydaddy, I jussaw andysarah."

Devinder looks her in the eye and says, "Now tell me again, sweetheart, but slo-o-wly."

Teena counts each syllable with her fingers; "Dad! I! Saw! Aunt-ee! Sar-ah!" and this time she adds, "And! Aunt-ee! M!"

Devinder needs a moment to digest the news; his heart races a little faster. *This was not in the plan. No contact with Kuldip or the kids. That's always been understood!*

"Really, were you inside already, darling?" he asks as calmly as possible. "You know you have to stay close to Mommy or me all day, right? We've told you many times."

"Oh, Dad. It! Was! Fine! Aunt-ee! Sar-ah! Was! There!" She pouts her lower lip before she adds, "Mom is cross with me, too."

"Well, sweetie, she only gets cross when you make her worry about you. Now, you won't leave my side again, will you? Will you?"

He tries to sound stern and has to wait a moment before Teena responds with a huff. "Okay, Daddy!" She kisses Devinder on the cheek and rests her head on his shoulder.

He bends down to pick up Meena in his other arm. "Okay, girls, I'm going to need some good luck, so give me the tightest hugs you can." They grit their teeth, tense their arms, and squeeze him tight.

The junior Granthi arrives to facilitate the milni and both parties stand to attention, hands folded and heads bowed, for the recital of the ardaas, the daily prayer. There is a sense of lightness and excitement once the ardaas is completed, in anticipation of the exchanges to begin.

Devinder finds the whole lighthearted and competitive nature of the ceremony bizarre and a little out of date—an act of theatre where the women are largely quiet spectators.

Baljit, who has been speaking with Kuldip and her other sisters-in-law, makes her way over to take her position beside her husband and son.

The Granthi reads the first set of names from a scrunched piece of paper in his hand—the men from the two families are paired based on like-for-like relations—and Vaddé Maamaji greets Rina's paternal grandfather. They exchange marigold garlands and Vaddé Maamaji is presented with a wool blanket on top of which sits a hundred-dollar banknote and an out-of-circulation one-dollar note; the extra dollar Iqbal used to refer to as the "plus one," given as a symbol of good luck. Vaddé Maamaji accepts the blanket and the money is returned after some animated and affected banter—except for the "plus one." The photographer snaps a shot of the two men embracing. Vaddé Maamaji joins his hands and bows in the general direction of the limousine. Devinder wells up again. Teena traces the tear with her finger as it runs down his cheek.

Since there are no maternal grandparents, the next pairing is the two fathers. Amarpreet walks toward Rina's father, with whom he has developed a friendship during the months of preparation. They've even golfed together a few times. Amarpreet stands almost a foot taller and is probably twice his weight. He could lift Rina's father easily if he wanted to, but the father-to-father milni is not the time to break decorum. They exchange garlands and Amarpreet returns the hundred dollars and tucks the "plus one" into his trouser pocket. The two men shake hands, embrace, and pose for the photographer before they walk away.

Then it's time for the uncle-to-uncle meetings. Navpreet's round is incident free with both parties somewhat hesitant. A draw. The round with Karanpreet is when the serious rankling begins. Because Rina has only one first uncle on her father's side, her family has recruited two spare uncles to even up the numbers. Karanpreet's match is a retired wrestler who has appeared many times on *All-Star Wrestling*. A ringer! His professional name had been the Star of Amritsar and he was famous for his toned upper body, muscular thighs, and thin ankles that made him look like a cartoon Hercules. On TV his body would gleam under the lights from a generous application of mustard oil, which made him hard to pin down. The Star was a minor celebrity, well-loved in the Punjabi community, and though he is only a distant third uncle, he's been recruited to give Rina's side a chance of victory. The excitement is palpable and the bride's side are clearly expecting an easy round. The Sandhu party holds their breath, slightly awed by the celebrity wrestler and fearful that Karanpreet will be easily hoisted into the air, though he's no lightweight either. The men exchange garlands and as they are about to pose for a photograph the Star wraps his arms around Karanpreet's thighs and tries to lift him. Karanpreet sees the move coming and bends down low, spreading his knees wide, so the grip becomes awkward. His feet remain firmly rooted to the ground. The Star tries again, but to no avail. They walk away smiling after their photograph has been taken. Another draw, but a win of sorts for the groom's side.

Devinder walks forward and lets Meena and Teena down from his arms. He performs a few stretches to draw a reaction and is rewarded with whistles and hollers, the loudest of which seem to be coming from Ranjit's sister, Manjit, and the other cousin-sisters doing their best to play a role in this all-male drama. As he collects a new marigold garland, Devinder hears Teena shout, "Go, Daddy!" and turns around to wave at her. He has done his homework and has a tactic in mind. Rina's family's second choice for a spare uncle goes by the nickname Vadhu. They call him Uncle, but those from Rina's generation are not sure how he is connected to their family, though he's always been around. This spare uncle is tall and gaunt, slightly gauche in his creased brown linen suit.

Now that they're standing only a few feet apart, Devinder reckons his chances are good. After they've traded garlands, he moves swiftly to bend down and place his arms above Vadhu's knees. He links the fingers of his hands firmly, and when he's sure he has a sound grip he lifts using both his legs. Uncle Vadhu has been immobilized and Devinder easily lifts him into the air, his arms flailing helplessly. A loud cheer erupts from the Sandhu party as Devinder lets the luckless man down slowly. *He'll be ribbed for the remainder of the day for sure.* They shake hands as the photographer documents their exchange and they walk back to their respective parties. Devinder quickly removes the garland and flicks his hands over the lapels of his jacket. From the limousine, he hears, "Shaabaash!" His brothers offer him high-fives. There are a few more milni greetings left but the contest is essentially over. Devinder's victory will be remembered and recalled long after today.

His daughters clap enthusiastically as he lifts them both into his arms. "You won, Daddy. You won!"

WHEN EMILY THINKS of her past life in Vancouver, Dev and Sarah always come to mind first, followed by the creature comforts of her apartment, her art studio, her hiking routes and the neighbourhood parks and beaches, and morning swims in the ocean. But perhaps what she misses most of all is that version of herself: adventurous, confident, resourceful, and creative. She'd give anything to have that Emily back.

Dev's visit to Belfast had not gone as planned, but they continued to speak regularly once he was home, and she was hopeful that a visit to Vancouver over the Christmas break might get them back on track. But then her mother caught a cold and the visit had to be cancelled. The medical team had warned Emily that in her weakened state Mrs. Rice would be more susceptible to infections. In the back of her mind, the words of the neurologist still haunted her: "There might come a time when we have to make a quick decision." The last thing she wanted was for someone else to have to make the call on Ma's care. Though Aunt Dawnel would be consulted, the final decision rested with Emily and no one else.

On the phone with Dev, she sensed his disappointment at the change of plans. "You're so lucky to have siblings. If something ever happened to Deepa and Monty it wouldn't be all on you." There was a heavy silence on the other end before she realized her mistake. "I'm so sorry, Dev. That was insensitive." She had not meant to downplay the deaths of Dev's birth parents. At every turn, she and Dev seemed to miscommunicate.

Uneasy interludes began to fill their conversations over the long-distance line. From speaking every couple of days, they shifted to weekly calls. Then weeks would go by and there'd be no communication at all. When they did speak Dev always closed with, "I love you, Em. I'll always wait for you," but that pledge sounded more hopeless each time it was spoken.

Finally one day Emily cut him off. "Please stop saying that, Dev. I'm not sure how long I'll be here and your promise only makes me feel guilty." Of course she knew she was not to blame for her mother's turn, but something in Dev's insistence made her feel she should be elsewhere. "I don't have a choice, Dev! This is my lot for now!"

More silence. More drift.

EMILY'S CARE HOME visits always began with a short recap from Nurse Ciara on Ma's overnight health. Even if Emily was a little late, Ciara would wait to see her before closing out her shift. But there were only so many ways for her to say "No change." At first these morning updates had been welcome, but the longer Ma remained semi-comatose the more Emily longed to hear Ciara deliver real news.

In her handbag Emily kept a small sketchbook and every day she would draw as she sat in her mother's room: the flowers that she ritually replaced in the vase on the window-sill; the view from the window of the shipyards and smoke-stacks with the rolling hills in the distance; her mother's hands folded and resting on her stomach. Mostly she drew the side view of Ma's face until she could sketch it from memory—the sharp peak of the tip of her nose, the ravine-like divot above her lips, the plain contour of her eyelids, and the fine wrinkles ridged on her forehead. Her mother's profile became a line on the horizon.

"You look tired, dear," Ciara said to her one morning. Emily's sleep had been particularly restless the previous night. "You know you don't need to be here every day. We'll look after your ma. Someone as young and beautiful as you … you need to be living your life, dear."

Emily looked at herself in the mirror of the care home restroom. Ma used to call her "delicate of feature," but the skin beneath her eyes was sagging and her cheeks had lost their flush. She hadn't cut her hair since she'd left Vancouver and had given up on pinning it back. She ran her fingers through the limp mop that hung over her shoulders. It was not the first time Ciara had given her this advice. *Maybe it's finally time to listen.*

She went home early that day and slept through the afternoon and evening. The next morning she asked Aunt Dawnel if she could help around the Auld Pheasant and was given a couple of evening shifts to wait on tables.

Emily allowed herself to take the occasional day off. She bought a swimsuit and a membership at the local recreation centre. Leaning over the bathtub, she cut until her hair was back to the length she'd kept it in Vancouver, though she lacked the inclination to tackle the budding grey.

One afternoon, after Emily had taken a leisurely morning swim, she arrived at the lobby vending machines at the same time as the junior doctor who'd recently arrived at the care home. He was hard to miss with his thick-framed glasses and Brylcreemed ginger hair combed into a perfect coif. At that awkward juncture he stepped back to allow Emily to feed the coffee machine ahead of him.

"Please. You first."

She watched the paper cup fill with milky liquid and then offered it to the young doctor, and he in turn fed the machine and did the same.

Emily took a sip and made a dismayed face. "Every day I know exactly how bad this'll taste and every day I come back for more. Why?"

The doctor gave a nervous laugh. "I ask myself that, too."

"Oh, thank you by the way," Emily said.

"Oh, you're welcome. Thank you," he replied as he raised his cup.

"No, no, not for the coffee. Well, yeah, thanks for that, too. But I meant thank you for doing what you do here."

It took a few seconds before he nodded in response. "Aah, you're Mrs. Rice's daughter, right?" She was impressed. Ma was not one of his patients, but he knew of her nevertheless. He put out his hand and said, "I'm Paul Watts. I'm just up from London for a couple of years."

"Oh, lucky you!"

The nervous laugh again.

He was fidgety, frequently scratching his head and the back of his neck. He told her he'd recently completed his five years of medical school at King's College in London. He'd been born near Derry, but then his family had relocated to England while he was still an infant. "So, when I saw this posting come up in Belfast, I thought it might be a way to reconnect with the old country."

"I moved away when I was young, too. To Vancouver, Canada."

"That explains why you're drinking coffee instead of tea then. You kept your accent though," he commented.

"Aye, the accent had faded somewhat, but I'm proud to say it's come back pretty *t'ick*. I've been back four years now."

Four years! It was strange to say it out loud. *Four years of this nightmare and who knows how many more.*

Without realizing it, she spoke the words again, "Four years!"

Paul looked confused. "Pardon?"

Emily shook her head. "Sorry. That was supposed to be my inside voice."

He fidgeted with his shirt collar and tie. "I hear grand things about Vancouver."

Emily settled herself back into the conversation and added with an enthusiasm she hadn't heard in herself for a while, "On a clear day it's the most spectacular place. The ocean, the mountains, the sky. The forests and the giant trees."

"And I guess you were used to the rain having grown up here?"

His glasses warped the space around his eyes, making it difficult to read him.

"Well, both places have their share of days when it's lashing out the heavens, but Ma found the rain in Vancouver particularly hard to take. 'Relentless,' she called it. That's one of the reasons she moved back here."

She dared not get into a conversation about her father's disappearance, and though she never did buy into Ma's justification for her return, it would have to suffice for now.

They walked over to a row of connected vinyl chairs in the waiting area. Emily was glad to have a real conversation, even if it was only about the weather in Vancouver.

Paul told her what it was like to grow up near Richmond Park and how he spent one summer living on a riverboat on the Thames. When there was a lull she asked him, "So do you have friends and family here?"

"No, I can't say that I do. I have a couple of cousins in Derry, but I haven't seen them in decades." After a long pause he asked, "You?"

"I have my aunt Dawnel, Ma's sister, and her husband, Patrick. They own a pub nearby. The Auld Pheasant. I work there a couple of evenings each week. And if I'm not working, I'll often stop there to grab a bite on my way home. If you're ever hankering for a warm meal you should drop by. Dawnel pulls a mean pint of Guinness." She tore a strip of paper from one of the lobby magazines, pulled a pen from the pocket of his white doctor's coat, and wrote down the address.

A WEEK LATER, Emily stopped by the Auld Pheasant in the late evening and took her regular seat at the end of the long bar. Without waiting for Emily to say anything, Dawnel placed a glass beneath the Guinness tap and let the thick stout pour out. She shouted, "Roast!" through the swinging door into the kitchen.

Emily was halfway through her drink and mopping up the remaining gravy from her plate with a slice of soda bread when she noticed Paul in the gilded mirror behind the bar. He looked a bit lost, trying to figure out where to sit. She turned and waved him over.

"You—you can sit here if you want, Dr. Watts," she stammered, and pointed at the empty seat next to her.

He held out his hand a little awkwardly. "Call me Paul, please."

"Are you okay sitting at the bar, Paul? I could get us a table. I have connections, you know. Or are you meeting someone? Sorry to assume."

"No, no, this is good. I was hoping to see *you*, actually." Hearing that made her feel better after her stumbling introduction. He wasn't the only one who was nervous.

Paul took off his navy overcoat and draped it over the back of the empty stool next to him before he sat down. Emily wished he would take off his glasses so she could see his eyes properly.

"So, you found the place then?"

"I've walked past here before but never stepped inside. It's nice."

Emily looked around the room. The woodwork had seen better days, the floors were scuffed, the tables were beer stained, the chairs groaned under the slightest weight, the green fabric on the benches in the booths was faded, and cigarette smoke had yellowed the walls and ceiling. The whole place needed some serious rejuvenation. But there were newcomers mixed in with the regulars who'd been coming here for decades. These days, the hope for peace seemed less outlandish and people were starting to venture out again. *Paul's right. It is nice!*

She introduced him to Dawnel, who nodded in his direction and said, "Guinness?" Before he'd even had a chance to say "sure," she was pouring him a pint.

Paul shuffled on his stool as he loosened his tie and unbuttoned his shirt collar. He looked bemused as he stared at the dark liquid in the tulip-shaped glass. Emily asked, "I take it you're not a Guinness man then, Paul?"

He gave a slight laugh. "I'm more of a lager man myself. But when in Rome, you know."

Paul talked of his day at the hospital and then suddenly looked a little anxious. "I hope you don't mind." He looked at her as though he was uncertain if he should continue. "I took a look at your ma's file."

She emptied her glass quicker than she'd planned.

Paul explained that his training involved transit between the Royal Victoria and the care home, so he saw patients at both facilities. "Your mother's condition isn't unusual." His voice took on a more formal tone. "Often, after an intracerebral hemorrhage the patient might be in a minimally conscious state for some time. What's worrying and less normal is how her condition isn't changing." He explained the Glasgow Coma Scale and how Ma's score had not budged since a few days post-surgery.

Emily appreciated the open and honest analysis and Paul's way of cutting through the medical jargon. *Why haven't any of the other doctors talked to me this way?* She noted how much more confident Paul was when he was in "doctor mode."

"IS THERE ANYTHING on the menu that you'd recommend?" he asked.

"Definitely the roast with mashed potatoes!" Emily replied without hesitation.

As they waited for his meal, Paul asked her to tell him more about her time in Vancouver. She shared her love of the temperate rain forests, Lighthouse Park, and Lynn Canyon, and riffed on the names of the mountains on the North Shore. He perked up when she mentioned the West Coast Trail and hikes with her "best friend" Sarah. Then he asked her what she did for work in Vancouver.

"Well, Paul, that's a subject that might get me as sad as talking about Ma's health. I'm an artist and a fledgling college art instructor. Well, a lapsed artist if I'm being honest." She took a moment to reflect before continuing. "Maybe not lapsed exactly. I draw, most days. Sometimes as I'm sitting with Ma and sometimes just out and about. Maybe I'm in a rut, and that's why I draw the same things over and over again. If I talk about it, I won't be good company."

He was saved from having to respond by the arrival of his dinner and as he unfurled the cloth napkin and picked up his cutlery he murmered, "It's okay, Emily." It was good to hear him call her by name.

At the end of the evening, after they had both downed one more pint of Guinness, Paul asked, "I wondered if you might be interested in joining me for a drive someday. On a weekend when I'm not on call." His voice cracked with uneasiness as he reached his hand down to the pager on his belt.

"A drive? You mean like sightseeing and stuff?" Emily grinned as she spoke.

Paul was quick to catch on that she was just having a laugh.

"Well, yeah, 'sightseeing' is I guess what you'd call it."

"Won't your supervisors think poorly of you for fraternizing with a patient's daughter?" she teased.

"Well, your ma isn't technically my patient."

She was craving company and if things got complicated, she'd deal with it.

"That'd be nice. To be honest, when I was growing up here there wasn't much appetite for sightseeing. Not sure that there is even now."

THEY MET THREE more times at the Auld Pheasant over the next fortnight.

For their first trip out of town Paul drove the little Vauxhall Astra he'd brought with him from London north on the Causeway Coastal Route toward the Giant's Causeway. It was a blustery day and spray from the Irish Sea washed onto the roadway. Emily held tight to the handlebar above the passenger door as Paul kept both hands firmly on the steering wheel. She could barely make out the coastline of limestone, castles, and harbours that she recalled from her childhood.

An hour into the drive Emily said, "I remember doing this trip once when my grandparents were alive." She had to raise her voice to be heard over the wind and rain lashing against the windshield. "I was six or seven, I think. I sat in the back seat between them. Granma told me about hedge schools in the years after Partition and wild fables about fairies living inside hawthorn trees. We had a Thermos of tea and Granma's scones to warm us up when we stopped."

Paul took the hint. "Let's get something warm inside us then."

Minutes later they pulled into a side street in a village off the Causeway Route. The inside of the tavern smelled like the sea. Paul took off his glasses and dried them with the sleeve of his shirt. *Finally,* she thought. His eyes were almost cobalt. Close set. He seemed embarrassed when she told him how fine he looked without the cover of thick lenses. She also liked how the rain had flattened his hair; he looked less put together.

"I swear, becoming a doctor ruined my eyesight. I could see fine until medical school."

She prodded him to tell her more about his path to becoming a doctor and he spoke lovingly of his uncle Tim, a cardiologist, who he'd admired since he was a child. It was Tim who had encouraged him to pursue medicine.

"He must be so proud of you."

"Unfortunately, he passed away last year. He was only sixty. He looked after other people's hearts but forgot to look after his own. A massive myocardial infarction while he was doing his rounds. They say he was probably dead before he hit the ground." He wiped at his eyes.

"I'm sorry to hear that, Paul."

He nodded appreciatively and they sat in silence as they read the menu.

"WAS THERE SOMEONE who inspired you to become an artist?" Emily noticed a hint of hesitation in his voice. "We don't have to talk about that if it's private."

"It's all right. I'll give it a shot," she said, while formulating a response in her head.

"I don't think there was any one person. I loved drawing when I was young and was cheered on by my parents, my teachers, and friends. Ma and Da were always buying me colouring pencils, sketch pads, and pinning my scribbles on the wall. I drew all the time. Once I was in Canada, I began to take a sketch pad with me everywhere, and it became something more, almost something I had to do to keep myself healthy."

"Mmm … that's interesting. Like it feeds a need inside you, you mean?"

That's a good question, thought Emily. She wanted to reach across the table and touch his hands.

"It's like the world slips away and it's just me and the blank surface calling me to make that first brush stroke and see where it leads." She spoke excitedly about paint and canvas, light and shadow, how each brushstroke was a decision. Listening to herself she realized how much she missed it. *What I'd give to have that back*, she thought. *To get truly lost in something.*

For the rest of their lunch, Emily let Paul do most of the talking, afraid to reveal anything that would give way to the tears barely contained beneath her eyelids; the weight of hopelessness pulling her under. There were days she wished her mother would live forever, and others when she wished for a quick end. She listened to Paul's stories, glad to have his company, to be away from the tedious bedside conversations with the hospital staff. Her own life was suspended in motion and would stay that way until Ma either recovered or passed away. *Like those ancient insects caught in amber.*

By the time they got back on the road, the weather had deteriorated further. Thankfully the drive was more inland and less precarious. They parked in the empty lot of the Causeway Inn and began the trek down to the shore and the rock columns that stepped into the sea. The wind made hard work of the hike, and they were only able to view the series of hexagonal pillars from a distance, the wet and cold sank into their bones and the wind howled and stung their faces. They could see a pair of intrepid backpackers stepping onto the wet rocks—their footing unsure—and then retreating from the waves. Getting any closer would be foolish.

"Maybe another day!" shouted Paul, and put his arm around Emily as the wind pushed them uphill toward the car.

By the time they arrived back in the city the dampness of her clothes burned against her skin. At his apartment Paul ran a hot bath, leaving an oversized sweatshirt and a pair of soccer shorts for her on the vanity. When she emerged a half hour later, he'd changed into a bright blue tracksuit. He poured her a dram of Bushmills and heated up a can of cream of mushroom soup, which he served with thick slices of toasted bread slathered with butter. The rain tapped hard against the windowpanes, but she was warm and comfortable.

An hour later, after some awkward half hearted good night gestures they kissed and stumbled onto Paul's bed. It was comforting to be held and to hold someone back after so long.

TWO DAYS LATER when she arrived at the care home there was a new sketch pad on the table beside Ma's bed, a selection of drawing pencils, a map with a few routes highlighted in yellow marker, and a brand-new expensive-looking umbrella.

THE LIGHT TOUCH of Sarah's hand on her shoulder startles her. She moves her handbag, which she'd placed beside her to save the space. When Emily had first re-entered the prayer hall, the thought of leaving, of skipping the ceremony altogether, was heavy on her mind, but listening to the musical hymns has convinced her to stay.

As though anticipating what she might be thinking, Sarah whispers, "Well, let's hope there are no more surprises," and presses her hand. She's holding two colourful printed cards, the same style as the invitation, and passes one to Emily. "They're handing these out now."

The front reads *Ranjit and Rina's Anand Karaj*. Listed on the inside are the wedding events:

Baraat—Groom's Arrival
Milni and Tea—The Two Families Meet
Kirtan—Pre-Wedding Hymns
Ardaas—The First Prayer
Palla—The Father Giving Away the Bride
The Four Lawaan—The Union of Two Souls
Ardaas—The Final Prayer
Karah Prashad—Sacred Sweet Offering

There is a column with detailed descriptions next to each item and a glossary of Punjabi terms is on the back. Seeing the detailed program calms Emily's nerves—there is an order to the day.

She closes her eyes and lets the kirtan wash over her, still convinced that being here is the best way to bring closure to her relationship with Dev. *A peek into the life I never had and then a new beginning.*

TWENTY MINUTES LATER the congregation starts to enter the hall in larger numbers and each attendee kneels and bows to the Guru Granth Sahib—hands in prayer pose, forehead to ground, an offering to the donation box. The adherence to this ritual, its repetition, is both soothing and uplifting.

Soon there is a lineup on the carpeted pathway. Emily shifts a little closer to Sarah to make room for an elderly woman searching for a section of wall to lean against. Each member of the congregation—the sangat—sits in silence, cross-legged, with heads covered. The kirtan has picked up in volume and enthusiasm.

It's another fifteen minutes until Dev's family begins to enter. Sarah whispers their names in Emily's ear. "That's Navpreet with his wife, Harpal." A minute later. "That's Karanpreet with his wife, Kiran, and their daughters."

Emily could have picked out Dev's brothers herself, of course; the matching suits are a dead giveaway. The young men that Emily had seen in photographs many years ago are now distinctly middle-aged: heavyset with laboured gaits.

These men could have been her brothers-in-law. Their wives, her sisters-in-law. *If ifs and ands …*

"And that's Auntie Deepa walking in with Ranjit's sister, Manjit." Deepa looks exactly as Emily had imagined: elegant, small, kind. She's dressed in a rich cream-coloured fabric and stands upright and straight with an inimitable look of pride. Unlike her daughters-in-law, there is no elaborate embroidery on Deepa's clothes. Her plain white chuni is pulled over her head, wrapped around her shoulders, but does not completely cover the thick white braid that hangs down her back. A steady stream of guests bow in her direction and bid her "Sat Sri Akaal." They bend down to touch her feet. She places her hand on top of each lowered head.

In all the years that Emily's known him, Dev has never uttered a bad word about Deepa. He has expressed many times that Deepa's poise and grace is what holds the family together across the generations and shared his fear that without her things might fall apart. The unreserved respect and commitment that Dev, his brothers, and the extended family practised for each other was largely for her sake. "She's our lodestar," he'd often say.

Sarah chooses to stay silent when Kuldip enters the New Great Hall with Dev by her side, their daughters on either side of them. *No introduction required this time.* Kuldip's complexion is as smooth as marble, her smile radiant and her dazzling salwar kameez fits her like a glove. She blends in and out of conversations, projecting warmth and gratitude. Meena looks like a miniature version of her mother.

Kuldip walks both girls along the central pathway and demonstrates to them the kneeling ritual in front of the Guru Granth Sahib, before helping them to place coins in the donation box. She adjusts their dupattas to completely cover their heads and takes a seat beside Harpal and Kiran.

And then all heads turn toward the entrance as Ranjit enters with his parents. He is resplendent in his red-and-gold sherwani, burgundy turban, and a neatly cropped beard. He looks nothing like the jeans-and-T-shirt-wearing student Emily has gotten to know and love over the previous two years. He makes his way up the strip of carpet, bows, then sits cross-legged in front of the book of scripture. Baljit takes her place behind him alongside her sisters-in-law.

It is another ten long minutes before Rina is led in by her parents, dressed in a rich, deep crimson kameez with gold-embroidered edges. Her head is covered by a dupatta that veils her face—held up by her elaborately henna-painted left hand. Though her feet are invisible beneath her long pleated skirt, the jangle of ankle bracelets scores every measured step. Her head is bowed, and her shoulders slightly hunched from what Emily assumes must be the weight of her ornate outfit. A soft murmur of adoration builds as she floats across the hall before her mother assists her in taking her seat next to Ranjit, completing the symmetry of the arrangement.

Emily's gaze shifts back to Kuldip. Over the years Dev has shared snippets of information about her, that she was abandoned as a newborn and left a difficult arrangement in New Delhi to come to Canada. The tenderness that Kuldip projects is easy to admire. Not to mention her striking beauty: Emily notes that her eyes are hazel. She tries to imagine herself in Kuldip's place, sitting with her sisters-in-law, in green-and-turquoise; she even dares to invent a couple of young children beside her. *If ifs and ands ...*

Regret? Maybe that is what she's feeling after all, at the back of this huge room, with her face hidden in her scarf, imagining a life that never happened. A life that *can* never happen. *That life is Kuldip's now.* Emily shakes her head to clear those thoughts. But the feelings do not recede.

And then she's hit by another wave of emotion. This time more guilt than regret—for the life of duplicity she's been living these past years. Being here has eradicated any lingering doubt for what needs to be done. *I have no right to be with him. The sooner I break it off, the better.*

Emily is so absorbed in herself that the opening announcements barely register. She is frozen in place, unable to be in the moment. And leaving now would only draw attention. It's only when Ranjit and Rina stand for the opening prayer that she snaps back into the present and shifts closer to Sarah, glad to have her friend by her side.

EACH LAWAAN PRAYER is sung loudly and exuberantly as Ranjit and Rina stand to walk a clockwise circle around the Guru Granth Sahib. Ranjit in front, Rina behind, tethered by the long gold-laced red scarf, the end of which Rina grasps in her hands. Four young men take turns holding Rina by the arm and accompany her as the couple complete each lawaan.

The urge to leave gets stronger. Sarah, sensing Emily's discomfort, reaches into her purse and produces a bottle of pills. She drops a tablet into Emily's hand.

"Here, put this under your tongue," she whispers.

Emily tastes ginger and the pit in her stomach starts to shrink.

WITH BOTH GIRLS in grade school and Devinder working longer hours at the university, the loneliness that had gripped Kuldip during her first months in Canada returned like an annoying monsoon mosquito. It didn't help that autumn had been particularly dark and dreary, and then the few inches of snow in early January turned to ice, making the steep sidewalks in Kitsilano extra foreboding. It was such a letdown after what Meena had wistfully called "the best summer ever!"

All through July and August, Kuldip had spent entire days outdoors with her daughters, sometimes walking to Jericho Beach and Spanish Banks or to Granville Island and False Creek. Teena was always eager to be the first to spot a monkey puzzle tree or a bird of prey overhead, and Kuldip had to be diligent to make sure her younger daughter never wandered too far ahead. On days when it was too hot for long walks, they'd go swimming at Kitsilano Pool, where they got to put into practise what Devinder had taught them over the previous months. But the days the girls looked forward to the most were when they took the small ferry across to Sunset Beach and meandered past English Bay into Stanley Park. They loved the trek around Lost Lagoon, the mother mallards with their packs of trailing ducklings, the calm majesty of the blue herons standing solo in the water, and the hysterical honking of the marauding gaggle of geese. Walking the seawall, Teena screamed with delight whenever a wave sprayed onto the path, at the crunch of empty mussel shells beneath her shoes.

AFTER DROPPING HER daughters at school, Kuldip resisted the shortest path home. A bench between two weeping willows offered an uninterrupted view of Kitsilano Beach. The willows in winter seemed almost spectral amongst the clusters of naked elms and maples, the yellow branches hanging straight like the hair of an elderly woman. From the bench, she could observe crows gathered in the huge linden tree and seagulls scrounging around sand and driftwood for the previous day's scraps. On days when the tide was out, explorers with metal detectors, headsets over their toques, would search the ocean bed for lost treasure, digging clam shovels into the wet sand in the hope of good fortune. Some days, bundled in winter layers, she would lose track of time, unaware of how long she sat at the bench.

One cold and windy morning in late January, a fierce wind was blowing waves over the seawall, and though she had only just sat down, she figured it was not a day to linger. The ocean roiled brown and murky, and menacing dark clouds arced over the North Shore. Three unmoored boats floated precariously at a distance, looking as though the next wave might take them under.

She had been in Vancouver for nearly a decade and knew her winter sadness was largely due to the lack of sunlight. Certainly, she was thankful her life at Lytton House was a distant memory—the heartlessness of Mr. Sethi rarely entered her thoughts anymore. She worried about Mrs. Sethi, though. A package from New Delhi had arrived after Meena was born containing an assortment of dolls dressed in dowdy Victorian outfits similar to those she had been given after her arrival at Lytton House. Since then, Kuldip's handwritten letters had gone unanswered. She mailed photographs of the newborn Teena but there was no reply. Uncle Monty and Auntie Deepa had broken off all communication with the Sethis at the behest of their sons, still upset by the slippery practises and deception of Mr. Sethi—it did not help that the car service business that he had convinced them was doomed to fail without additional investment was supposedly thriving. Kuldip would have liked to invite Mrs. Sethi to Ranjit's wedding, but inviting one without the other would have been an affront to the sacredness of the family unit.

What she would have really loved was to invite Ehani, for Meena and Teena to hear her full-throated laugh and unfiltered wisdom, but that seemed even more improbable.

Motherhood had been the greatest of gifts, and though there were times when she felt she would drown under the weight of responsibility, she also knew she could not live without her brilliant daughters. They were the last thing on her mind before she fell asleep and her first thought when she awoke. It was reassuring to know that they were also loved by the extended family. In the worst-case scenarios she sometimes imagined, they were always looked after, secure and cared for by grandparents, uncles, aunts, and cousins.

Lately she had been haunted by thoughts of her birth mother. *Did she ever wonder what became of the newborn she left by a shrine? Could she imagine that her child had travelled so far from that place?*

But those other thoughts were only fleeting. If she was to be honest with herself, her present persistent sadness had more to do with the state of her marriage. At the weekly Tiger Team meeting the previous weekend—what Devinder called the "T-minus-six-months summit"—Amarpreet had printed off the initial invitation list for Pinky. It was meant to serve as Pinky's guide to calculate the number of tables required for the reception at the Royal King Palace Banquet Hall and Convention Centre—shortened to RKP by the team. As with most Punjabi receptions it was impossible to give a number with any certainty; each invited family was free to bring as many members as they deemed appropriate, and there were always those that took advantage. The Tiger Team had agreed that for now it was best to confirm eighty tables of ten guests each, and then added four more tables to be safe.

They discussed the decorations for the ballroom and the timing for the evening's events. Amarpreet shared the early blueprint for a fifteen-foot-tall, mirrored gateway with a ten-foot archway that Patel and Sons Inc. had generously offered to build at the entrance to the reception hall. "Trust me," Sonny Patel had said, "this will be the talk of the town."

Once the meeting was over, Pinky, Bubbly, and Pippi left with their event files. Devinder, Amarpreet, and Ranjit descended to the "man cave" to watch sports, and Baljit moved to the kitchen to prepare lunch. Meena and Teena were with Manjit at the tiny beach at the bottom of the bluff behind the house. Kuldip was clearing the clutter of glasses and empty cups of chaah when she noticed Pinky's invitation list. She ran to the front door, but Pinky's car was already backing onto the street.

Back in the living room she was flipping through the list nonchalantly when she noticed *her* name; halfway down page 8, between the Randhawas and the Roys: *Mrs. Emily Rice and Family.*

Seeing *her* name on the list had been jolting but she'd reminded herself that Emily was Ranjit's art instructor— he had proudly shown her a beautiful woodcut of Uncle Monty and talked about how much he had learned from his instructor, Miss Rice. Kuldip convinced herself that Emily would not attend. The invitations had not been sent out yet, and surely Devinder would scratch her off the list when he noticed.

If it had not been for those blissful early years of marriage, perhaps his indiscretions would be easier to accept? If he was a ne'er-do-well like Mr. Sethi, then others would acknowledge him as such. Even Kiran, her closest ally, refused to address the matter. If Kuldip hinted at Devinder's infidelity, Kiran switched subjects or shut her down by reminding her of the good she had in her life. "Think about your daughters," she would say. "Do you really want to upset their happy lives?" On the subject of Devinder's adultery, Kuldip was alone. In fact, all three sisters-in-law would often remind her that "a mother's job is to raise and protect her children. Nothing else matters!"

She observed and admired in Devinder what others admired in him, too: his kindness, generosity, and absence of judgment. Whether it was with friends, family, or strangers, he was always benevolent. He had a ready smile and a hello for the street people and weekend canvassers on West 4th Avenue and could never pass them by without an acknowledgement and often a conversation. At the university he had a similar reputation, never too busy to see a student in need, never short on advice, always available to write a letter of reference.

Early in their marriage he had told her about Pete, a graduate student in the department whose brother had just passed away. Pete was torn up that he was unable to afford the flight home to Halifax for the funeral. Devinder discussed the situation with Kuldip and suggested that they should give Pete the money he needed.

"It's his brother's funeral," he said. "How can we not help him? And of course his daughter will need a ticket, too."

Kuldip had objected. "Ji, why doesn't someone from his own family buy him the tickets? What if we never see the money again?"

"So what? Raab sabnunh dindain hai," he replied.

She was amused by his use of the phrase that she had learned from Swarno Kaur and often recited herself—"God provides for everyone."

There were many reasons that those around her chose to ignore Devinder's indiscretions, but perhaps the most obvious was that wilful ignorance was much easier than conflict. An expression she had overheard once between quarrelling lovers came to mind—"Don't make waves unless you can live with the consequences." But she was tired of her own excuses and feared her past silence had been misread as acceptance.

That frosty January morning, so lost in contemplation that she temporarily blocked out the cold, an exceptionally strong gust of wind forced Kuldip to turn her head to the side. By the seawall, where the beach ended, a small crowd, a disturbance. At the centre was what looked like the body of a bright blue creature. She was not sure why, but she felt compelled to walk in the direction of the commotion, fighting against the wind.

As she got close, she realized that the blue creature was only a tarp covering a shopping cart. And leaning over the cart was a figure wearing a matching rain jacket. He was in distress, breathing erratically, his head buried in the tarp, and his arms folded around the cart's metal frame. Someone shouted, "Look man, we're trying to help you. Let us help!"

She made her way through the gathering and placed her hand on the back of the jacket, moving it in gentle circles. She moved her lips close to his ear and said, "It's me, Kuldip, Devinder's wife."

At first he just stared at her blankly. She repeated, "It's Kuldip. Dev's wife."

Iqbal relaxed his body but continued to cling to the shopping cart, his knuckles white from gripping with such force.

"It's okay," she said. "These kind people will not take anything. Come sit with me." She unclenched his fingers one by one until his hands were free. As she led him away to the bench beneath the weeping willows, she could hear a shovel shifting sand from around the cart's wheels.

She rubbed his hands and soon they began to warm and soften. Ten minutes later, a couple of the good Samaritans wheeled the shopping cart to where they sat. They gave her a thumbs-up as though to say, *Good luck!* and Kuldip held her hands up in gratitude.

She sat with Iqbal, hardly saying a word, until his breathing steadied. The wind died down and there was a hint of sunshine above the snow-capped peaks across the water. She checked her watch. There was laundry piled up and the house needed tidying before she picked up Meena and Teena from school.

"Bhaji, I need to go now. Will you be okay?"

Iqbal nodded to say yes, but his hands still held on to hers.

"Tomorrow I'll be at this bench at the same time. Will you come to meet me?"

He nodded again, the faintest of grins on his face.

As she walked away, she could hear the rusty wheels of the cart as it moved in the opposite direction.

WHENEVER THEY MET at their bench, she would bring him a Tupperware of food. She noticed very quickly that his gums bled easily and decided she would stick to soft dhals and porridge. The first time she brought him khichdi, the yellow-lentil-and-rice dish that Ehani would make for her when she was unwell, she noticed how glum he looked as he mixed in the dahi.

"My mother used to make khichdi," Iqbal cried after a few bites. "Any time I had a cold or fever. Sometimes I'd pretend to be sick to stay home from school." He put the container down and pulled a weathered photograph from his pocket. A young woman dressed in stylish clothes with a baby in her arms and a young boy standing beside her. Iqbal's mother was still celebrated in the community, but Kuldip had never seen her likeness before. She struggled to keep her poise. Iqbal's hands shook as he spooned out the last few grains of rice.

At future meetings he revealed more and more, and soon he was confiding in her like a long-lost friend.

"I miss my sister so much. I've never met her kids," he confessed one day. After a few minutes of reflection he added, "I want to be an uncle. A proper uncle. There's nothing I want more."

"What if I speak with Devinder? He can get a message to Rupi," she suggested.

"No, Kuldip. Devinder and Rupi mustn't know. If they know, then my father will find out." His face took on a fearful look every time he mentioned Mr. Rai.

"But how can I help you, Bhaji?" She was at a loss as to what she could do without assistance from others.

"I don't know," he said. "But something good will happen. I can feel it when I'm with you."

Kuldip was not sure either. Before they parted that day, he said, "I have one other thing to ask of you, Kuldip."

"What is it, Bhaji?"

He laughed as he replied, "Please stop calling me Bhaji. There's no need for formalities between us. Call me what Dev calls me: Iqqi. We're friends now, you and me."

THEY SCHEDULED THEIR meetings for Tuesday and Thursday mornings, and she would always make sure she had the housework done, so as not to rush their time together. After each meal he would shout, "Compliments to the chef!" flip his head back, and laugh out loud. In fact, his mood seemed to improve with each visit. He remembered every word they exchanged and sometimes had to remind her of where their previous conversation had left off. He could also recall detailed memories of his time in school with Devinder. Her friendship with Kiran was the best she had ever known, but it did not compare to what Iqbal described of his companionship with his "little brother."

"We used to get up to all sorts of shenanigans," he said, stumbling over the long word, but she knew what he meant. "We kept a notebook with funny lists and sayings. We'd crack ourselves up. The Top Ten Superstitions of Punjabi Moms. The Top Ten Reasons to Get Married According to Punjabi Parents. The Top Ten Things to Know When Visiting Your Punjabi Friend's Home." He could recite these lists from memory, laughing so hard from deep in his belly that he would double over on the bench. Then he might suddenly turn sad.

When she asked what else she could do for him he mentioned his days as a DJ, and the next time they met she handed him Devinder's old Sony Walkman, which had been stored in one of their living room drawers. She randomly selected five cassette tapes from the hundreds packed in a box in his home office.

A month into their visits he was biting into an omelette sandwich when she noticed his gums were bleeding again.

"Does it hurt very much?" she asked while making a mental note to cut the crusts in future.

"Some days are okay. Others not."

When she suggested he should have a doctor examine his gums, he looked back at her with disbelief and shook his head. "Who'll give their time to a tramp like me?"

SHE WAS UNCERTAIN what she was searching for but made inquiries at dental offices in the neighbourhood. It felt good to be doing something, but each clinic asked about Iqbal's supplemental dental insurance, a barrier she did not think she could overcome. And then one of the kind dentists on West Broadway told her about the Public Health Dental Centre and wrote down the name of a prosthodontist, Dr. Shapiro, who worked with the city's poor and addicted, people who had fallen off the public grid. An initial phone call got her an appointment for a consultation. The clinic was outside her neighbourhood and getting there and back within the narrow window of time she had available would require a high level of coordination. Iqbal was ecstatic when she told him, and she knew she must find a way to make this happen. She left the first consultation feeling dejected, having learned that the cost for the premium dentures—the quality Iqbal deserved—was significant and only partially subsidized. Of course she and Devinder had ample money but how could she access such an amount without raising suspicion?

Then she remembered the roll of money that Mrs. Sethi had given her when she departed New Delhi. There had never been any need for it until now—Raab sabnunh dindain hai.

At the next consultation Dr. Shapiro examined Iqbal's mouth before her assistant ran the X-rays. Iqbal was prescribed antibiotics to reduce the swelling in his mouth prior to the surgery. Kuldip helped him fill the prescription and then had to rush to pick up Meena and Teena from school.

Two weeks later Dr. Shapiro extracted Iqbal's few remaining teeth. That afternoon, it was difficult to leave him, and she asked multiple times if he wanted to sleep at their home— his cheeks bulged like those of a snake charmer playing a wooden flute—but he simply shook his head.

She was relieved to find him sleeping on the grass by their regular meeting spot the next morning and stirred him awake to offer up a small tub of ice cream. The swelling had come down slightly but the gauze he removed from his cheeks was soaked in blood. Dr. Shapiro thought it best to allow two months for the bone and gums to heal and the next appointment, to take an impression of his gums for the dentures, would not be until the middle of April. Then there would be a series of appointments for the first and second try-ins, for the teeth to be set in wax, and then a final visit when the wax would be replaced with acrylic. Even after all those appointments he would need to return if any denture sores developed. It would be too much for her to juggle between school drop-offs and pickups and her household duties. She would need to get Iqbal healthy enough to get to the clinic on his own.

***

THE WEEPING WILLOWS had replaced their yellow winter coats with green and silver that shimmered in the light breeze. Any other day his lateness would not be of much concern—she had gotten used to Iqbal's erratic timing—but there was a final important visit to the clinic remaining. Devinder would be on his summer break soon and her meetings with Iqbal would need to end, or at least be put on hold.

A few successive days of sunshine had renewed Kuldip's confidence and lifted her mood, and she was allowing herself to feel pride in the good deed she had done. What a difference she had seen in Iqbal over the last few months. Most of all she was delighted at how happy he looked when they met, although she still had not plucked up the courage to address him as Iqqi—that did not seem proper.

At the beginning of the previous week Dr. Shapiro had appraised the wax dentures—"Aesthetics, phonetics, and bite are the determinants of success," she disclosed. All that remained was to pick up the acrylic devices when they were ready. Hopefully, if adjustments were required, they would be minimal. The clinic staff were amused when Kuldip uncurled the old Canadian banknotes, passing them around to one another with a look of nostalgia over how young the Queen looked. "Money is money," Dr. Shapiro told them. "If the bank still takes the notes, we're good."

"I'm so sorry to be late, Kuldip."

His voice startled her. He was out of breath, like he had been sprinting.

"I slept the whole night," he said proudly. He had confessed earlier that on days when he failed to show it was often because he did not want her to see him fatigued. *That he can get any sleep at all out here is remarkable*, she thought.

From the pocket of his rain jacket, he pulled a bouquet of bluebells, a little crumpled but still beautiful, their stems wrapped in an elastic band. "For you, Madam!" He curtsied as he presented them to her. "Thank you for everything, Kuldip." He seemed to have an extra bounce in his step today. "Dev's a lucky man," he added. "I hope he knows how truly lucky he is."

"The pleasure has been all mine, Bhaji."

Then he surprised her with a series of questions about Ranjit's wedding: the date, the time, the location.

"I had an idea," he said excitedly. He wanted to surprise Rupi at the reception. All he needed was something suitable to wear. Each time he mentioned the possibility of meeting his nephews his eyes lit up.

On the one hand, Kuldip knew that Iqbal's presence would not be appreciated by everyone, while on the other, she figured she had nothing to lose. Maybe a little shakeup of the *perfect* day might not be such a bad thing. She just needed to figure out how to get him the clothes. After months of Tiger Team meetings, she knew the details by heart and wrote down the address of the RKP in the little notebook he had started carrying with him.

"How will you get there?" she asked.

"I'll find a way," he said with his roguish gummy smile.

EMILY ARRIVED TO find her mother's room filled with a medical emergency team. A clinician she'd never seen before was telling everyone to stand clear as she jolted Ma's body with a defibrillator. The bedside monitor bleeped a constant alarm. The clinician tried one more time. The alarm continued.

Nurse Ciara pulled Emily aside.

"Her heart lost its rhythm and then gave out, dear. We called you but you must have already been on your way here. It happened so quickly."

In the place where Emily should have held sorrow, there was only emptiness. She'd known this day would come but had imagined something more dramatic. There was no agony of waiting, no pacing the hallway, no critical decision to make at a moment's notice. Her mother's body had found its own way of bringing its extended epilogue to a close. The resident priest hadn't even arrived in time to administer the last rites.

Emily was allowed time to sit alone with Ma, the bleeps and neon numbers of the monitor finally muted.

A couple of hours later, when she went to deliver the news to Dawnel and Patrick, they were preparing to open the pub for lunch, taking chairs down from tables and straightening the wooden stools at the bar. As soon as Emily told them, Dawnel wrote a note in black marker, CLOSED FOR THE DAY, and taped it to the front door. They insisted that Emily stay with them while Paul was at work.

When Paul heard the news he called the pub and promised her he'd finish early so they could be together that evening.

"Just let yourself in," he said. "I'll be there as soon as I can."

She felt a pull to be alone.

Dawnel advised her that it would be best to take the day to let Ma's passing sink in. "Aye, there'll be time to make arrangements soon enough," Patrick added. "We'll be with you all the way, of course."

Emily was appreciative of the offer. They wanted her to stay longer, but she told them she needed air and let her feet take her where they willed. The slopes and plateaus of Divis and Black Mountain sparkled silver after a brief sprinkle of rain and she wandered in their direction not knowing how far she would climb or when she'd turn around.

By the time she returned home it was late evening and the place seemed darker than usual. The answering machine flashed amber. She delayed returning Paul's calls. Looking at the dull walls and ceilings, cracked windows, peeling wallpaper, she reckoned it was finally time to begin those renovations. The roof and the upstairs would be a good place to start. Rain had leaked into the attic and there was mould in the bathroom and in the seams of the textured paper on the ceilings. And of course, a new geyser was unavoidable.

She'd only been home for ten minutes before the phone purred itself awake. Paul was upset that she hadn't let him know where she was all day. "I left the hospital early hoping to see you," he said.

"Sorry. I didn't know myself where the day would take me."

"I'd feel much better if you were here. Let me come and pick you up," he pleaded.

"Paul, right now I need my bed. I'll be by tomorrow, I promise."

She hung up and made a list of what had to be done in the house, assigning duties to Dawnel and Patrick. But then it occurred to her that her aunt had the grief of losing her only sibling and she scratched over their names.

MARGARET RICE WAS buried in a plot next to her parents. Emily selected a black dress from Ma's closet. There was a sense of relief in knowing her wish to be buried in Irish soil was made real, and Emily thought about the jar of earth that was seven thousand kilometres away, in a box inside a storage locker in Vancouver.

Nurse Ciara had come straight from her shift to be by Emily's side, and her cousin Sean made the trip from Dublin. Paul held her hand through the verse from Ecclesiastes that Dawnel had chosen for Father Casey to read: "For everything there is a season, and a time for every matter under heaven: a time to be born, and a time to die; a time to plant, and a time to pluck up what is planted ..."

Aunt Catherine, Da's youngest sibling, drove in from Lisburn with her two teenage daughters. It was the first time Emily had seen them, or anyone from Da's side, since she'd been back in Ireland. She greeted them warmly. *They're family; this is a funeral. But why didn't they visit when Ma was ill?* Lisburn was less than an hour's drive. It became apparent from Catherine's awkward questions after the burial that her attendance was not entirely noble. Emily figured she'd drawn the short straw amongst her siblings to inquire if they had any claim on the Belfast home.

DAWNEL ASKED IF she wanted to work full-time at the Auld Pheasant, but Emily's priority was to get the house fixed up. Finding contractors was easier than she'd feared, and the planning and supervision of repairs proved a welcome distraction from her grief. It was rewarding to take on a project that required creativity and design skills.

Before the contractors could start, she had to empty the house of its contents. The bed and dressers were moved downstairs, and she kept only a few essentials, like towels and sheets. The rest of the furniture and housewares were either given away or sent to the rubbish dump. While the upstairs bathroom was under construction, she bathed and washed her hair at the kitchen sink. There was still a functional loo at the back of the garden.

Organizing and packing her mother's belongings proved to be quite simple and only took a day—the essential keepsakes and documents fit inside a single box.

One morning, at the bottom of a dresser drawer, she chanced upon the stack of CDs that Dev had left behind years earlier. The batteries in the Discman were dead, so she took the AAs from the flashlight. It was not noon yet, but the contractors had the day off and she opened a bottle of red wine she'd taken from the Auld Pheasant. She selected a CD at random and within minutes she was lost in memories of Vancouver. Although most of the tracks were new to her, the mix could only have been made by Dev—melancholy and introspective, mostly minor key.

He had reached out to her when he got married to Kuldip and again when Meena was born, but two years had now passed since they'd last spoken. She'd been so engrossed in the details of the funeral, the estate, and the house repairs that she hadn't thought to ring him to let him know of Ma's passing.

At the end of the second CD, as Pearl Jam's "Black" came to its plaintive close, she found herself dialing his number, impressed she could still recall it from memory.

"Hello," said a woman's voice. She sounded half asleep.

"Oh, hello. I'm sorry …" It dawned on Emily that it was still very early in Vancouver, and she cursed herself for not thinking before she dialed.

"Hold on," said the voice on the other end.

She could hear the rustle of bedsheets.

"Hello?"

"Dev, it's Emily."

"Oh, hi." Dev suddenly became alert. "Gimme a minute." More rustling, a door opening, and then a tapping sound.

"Sorry about that. I had to move the phone."

"No, I'm sorry to call so early. I was thinking of you, and honestly, I forgot about the time difference. We can talk later."

He must have picked up on the worry in her voice and asked, "Has something happened?"

"I should've called to tell you earlier ..." She struggled to complete the sentence. "Ma passed away last month."

Dev took a moment to respond. "Oh, I'm so sorry, Em."

"I don't know what I wanted to say exactly, Dev."

"I'm glad you called. How are you coping?"

It was a new version of a familiar question. But it was good to hear it again after so long.

"I waited all these years for Ma to take her final breath, dreading the day. And now that it's happened, I feel as much relief as I do sadness. And then I feel guilty for feeling relieved."

"There's no one right way of feeling. Give yourself permission to experience all those contradictions, Em."

The tension left her shoulders. His words of comfort were exactly what she needed to hear.

"Thanks for that." She realized her voice was getting unsteady and thought she should end the call. "I won't keep you long. Thank you. Again, I'm sorry I called so early."

"It's no bother. I'll be here if you need someone to talk to."

"I know I haven't been in touch much these last couple of years and I should have called you sooner. I've just ... I've spent the last month drowning myself in work."

"Oh, you're painting again?" She was warmed by the sound of genuine excitement in his voice.

"I guess you could say that. I'm having the house done up. The roof, the plumbing, the heating, the chimneys. There'll be some painting once the renos are complete. You remember what the place was like? Well, it's even more decrepit now." It suddenly struck home that it had been seven years since his visit. She looked at the small window beside the front door and the thick Sellotape holding it together.

"All this time," she continued, "I think I was waiting for Ma to tell me what she wanted done to her house, and now that she's gone it's all up to me."

"I'll message you tomorrow, Em. Maybe we can talk again soon. By the way, how's Paul?"

"Yeah, Paul's well." It was an automatic response. *Paul did seem well*, she thought. They spent most evenings together but their relationship was finding a new equilibrium; a complication Emily was not going to get into. *Not in this moment. Not with Dev.*

"It'd be nice to have a longer chat, to get caught up properly." She was about to say goodbye and then remembered his daughter. "How's Meena?"

"She's good. Pretty excited to have a little sister."

Right on cue, she heard a cry in the background.

"Oh, wow! You have a new baby. How wonderful! What's her name?"

"Tejinder, or Teena as we call her." She could picture the grin on his face as he spoke those words.

"Aah, Maninder and Tejinder. Meena and Teena." They both laughed.

"We had to keep the tradition alive."

KULDIP HAD ONLY just fallen asleep after feeding Teena when the loud ringing woke her. On the other end, an unfamiliar voice. A woman's voice. She passed the receiver across the bed. Devinder shook himself awake and rested the hard plastic against his ear. There was a slight but audible gasp as he threw the covers off. The coiled cord tapped loudly against the door frame as he moved farther into the hall, and Teena, who had been sound asleep suddenly rustled in her crib.

When the phone rings in the night, it's never good news. Good news can wait till morning, but bad news needs to be delivered immediately.

The conversation was short and difficult to decipher, though she could hear him sharing his new cellphone number. She was rocking Teena in her arms when Devinder returned to the bedroom and fumbled to place the receiver back in its cradle. She asked him who it was and what had happened.

"An old friend," he whispered. "Her mother passed away after a long illness."

"Oh, I'm sorry. Is it someone I've met?"

He mumbled, "Umm … No."

Kuldip sensed that the call had unnerved Devinder and decided not to ask more questions for now. Of course she had quickly figured out who the old friend was. After she placed Teena in the crib and lay back in bed, she put her arm around him, but his body offered nothing in return.

***

OVER THE NEXT year, caring for their daughters remained Kuldip's only priority. There was a sense of security in knowing that she was needed by them. They never spoke of the phone call again. She told herself it had been a singular event, that a wide ocean separated Devinder from his former lover. *Besides, she's with someone else now, and he's with me.*

Devinder continued to be his kind and generous self, but his everyday behaviour shifted in small ways. He became quieter, more private. His gaze frequently turned downward. At other times he appeared distracted, but always had an explanation at hand when she asked what was wrong: "Work's been stressful lately. My brothers want my opinion on a new development project."

What did not shift was the love that Devinder poured into their daughters. He was home every evening so that they ate meals together. He helped feed and bathe them. He took them out—Teena in the Moon Buggy and Meena holding his hand—to give Kuldip time alone, in which she would do her yoga and qigong exercises, or perhaps indulge in a hot bath. He shared the responsibility to get up during the night to rock Teena back to sleep. Meena pouted and cried when he kissed her goodbye in the morning and jumped to grab his legs when he returned.

THE SANGAT STANDS for the closing prayer, repeating the phrases "Waheguru" and "Sat Naam" in response to the Head Granthi's call. After another round of kneeling and touching foreheads to the ground, the sangat sits and he addresses Ranjit and Rina directly.

"What this passage of scripture says is that if you go toward someone you really want to go toward, then that person will move toward you. If you ever need reminding of why you chose to move toward each other, look into each other's eyes. In fact, look into each other's eyes often and enjoy those moments of being together, of oneness. Life is short. Life gets busy. So, enjoy those special moments. I would ask everyone here to look into your children's eyes, your parents', your grandparents'. Hold that gaze. Looking into each other's eyes and holding that gaze says more about your devotion than words ever could."

After a long passage in Punjabi he reverts to English and announces that everyone should stay seated for a short speech by Ranjit's uncle. "And you must stay to receive the sacred karah prashad," the sweet offering—a mix of ghee, sugar, and flour—that will be distributed to every member of the congregation.

Emily senses another shift in mood, a sense of completion and accomplishment. A low murmur spreads across the hall, hushed salutations and congratulatory embraces. A few men stand and move toward the bride's and groom's fathers and uncles to shake their hands or pat them on their shoulders. On the women's side, the congratulations are more muted and reserved, a nod of the head or the raising of a hand. Soon everyone is passing good wishes to each other. Emily struggles for words and can only offer a quiet "thank you" in return for the congratulations offered by the women around her.

The Granthi asks everyone to sit, sounding a little annoyed that his instructions were ignored. Once the hall is quiet, a well-dressed man in thick glasses, grey Nehru suit, and black turban steps up to the microphone beside the central throne. He introduces himself as Professor Balbir Singh, the elder brother of Auntie Deepa.

"Most of you know me as Vaddé Maamaji, but in my other life I am simply called Sir." Clearly enjoying the spotlight, he repeats the line a little louder this time. He switches fluently between Punjabi and English, and his face takes on a stern look as he addresses the newlywed couple. "The scriptures say that 'They are not said to be husband and wife who merely sit together. Rather they alone are called husband and wife who have one soul in two bodies.' Today you, Ranjit, and you, Rina, have made the most important promise that you will ever make: the promise to support each other for your remaining days no matter what comes." He fixes his gaze on Ranjit and Rina to let his words sink in. Then he turns to face the sangat. "And as we are gathered to witness the souls of these two beautiful young people become one in front of God, it is my duty not only to welcome Rina and her family into ours but to remind each of you of your responsibility to make sure that this union is everlasting. If you've been invited to the ceremony today it is because of your importance and commitment to the future success of Ranjit and Rina's marriage, to stand beside them and remind them that you were here as witnesses and will hold them to their promise.

"As witnesses you are responsible for reminding them that though there will be times when they have difficulties, times when stress and hardship might overwhelm them, they must remember their lawaan. Anyone who completes the lawaan must never break their pledge to God. So, on behalf of both families I would like to thank you for being here today and being witness to this special union."

Two older men move around the room holding large stainless steel basins. As they step from person to person, they dip one hand into the basin and roll a bite-sized ball of karah prashad. Sarah signals to Emily to hold her hands out in front of her, fingers of one hand folded over the other, to accept the offering in the hollow of her joined palms. Emily looks around her as the sangat accepts the prashad, raising hands to foreheads and devouring the sweet.

She is surprised by the heat of the prashad and passes it from palm to palm until it is cool enough to eat.

Sarah reaches into her purse and pulls out a couple of hand wipes to clean the ghee left on their fingers and palms.

In the meantime, the room has grown loud with conversation. A rush of guests form a line behind the newly married couple. This is the moment Emily and Sarah have been waiting for, the sagan, a chance for the congregation to bless Ranjit and Rina as a newly married couple.

By the time they stand, their limbs stiff from sitting for over three hours, the sagan line has already reached the back of the hall.

"How long do you think we'll have to wait?" whispers Emily.

Sarah studies the queue. "It's hard to say. Thirty minutes?"

That's probably accurate but not what Emily wanted to hear. *Thirty minutes of standing on display. Thirty minutes of opportunities to be noticed.*

Sarah senses her discomfort. "Maybe we should just go now," she offers.

"But our entire reason for being here was to congratulate Ranjit and Rina in person. I don't want to disappoint them."

They're caught in this state of uncertainty when they're interrupted by Auntie Deepa who has suddenly appeared by their side.

"Sarah, dear. How lovely to see you! Thank you for joining us today."

Sarah joins her hands in salutation and offers a small bow.

"I'm so glad to be here, Auntie. It was a lovely ceremony. You must be very proud."

"Yes, yes. So true," replies Deepa. "We are happy Ranjit has found himself a partner to share his life."

Emily shifts from foot to foot.

"How is Uncle?" asks Sarah.

"Aah. Uncle's health is in God's hands. We are grateful he is still with us for this auspicious day." She joins her hands and turns slightly toward the Guru Granth Sahib.

"How are your boys, Sarah? Will I see them at the reception?" As Sarah is replying that her boys are well, Auntie Deepa turns to Emily. "And you are?"

"Umm … Emily. My name is Emily," she answers tentatively.

"Aah! Ranjit has spoken of you. You are his teacher, no."

Emily is unsure if this is a question or a statement of fact.

"Yes, that's me. Congratulations, Auntie. Ranjit is a wonderful young man. He and Rina are perfect for each other."

"Aah, so true! Perfect for each other? Yes, I think so."

Emily has a sense that Auntie Deepa knows very well who she is, and that this encounter has been planned.

Deepa takes Emily's hand and looks directly into her eyes. Her gaze is hypnotic, not unfriendly but quizzical, as though trying to solve a riddle in her mind.

"Emily, dear. Will we see *you* at the reception?" It comes across as a question seeking confirmation of the opposite.

Sarah interjects. "Actually, Auntie, Emily has another function to attend. We were hoping to give our sagan to Ranjit and Rina, but since the queue is so long, could we ask you to pass on our congratulations and blessings to them, please?"

"Tsk! Tsk! Tsk!" Deepa shakes her head vigorously and wags her finger to chide them. "You cannot leave before you have had a chance to give your sagan. That is bad luck! Come with me."

Deepa leads Sarah and Emily by their hands like little children and walks them past the long line of guests. When they get close to the front of the queue a spot opens for them.

"There you go, dears!" Deepa continues to look at them with speculation and distrust.

They kneel behind Ranjit and Rina, who are still sitting cross-legged on the floor.

Emily says in a hushed voice, "Congratulations, you two! We're glad to be here for the ceremony." She and Sarah each drop a twenty-dollar note into the palla, which is now spread in front of the newlyweds, and overflowing with a jumbled mess of paper money, a plate of Punjabi sweets and two coconuts. Sarah adds a slim envelope with a gift certificate to a spa in Coal Harbour.

"Oh, Miss and … Sarah." She detects surprise in Ranjit's voice as he says their names together. "Thanks so much for being here."

Rina turns her head slightly and smiles broadly at Emily.

Sarah offers them her congratulations and apologizes that Douglas and her boys were unable to make it.

"It looks like you've got quite the bounty there," jokes Emily.

Ranjit whispers out of the side of his mouth, while keeping one eye on his grandmother. "Don't tell anyone, Miss, but if we weren't dressed up in this armour, we'd make a run for it." Rina lets out a short laugh before she catches herself.

Deepa looks unamused and kneels next to the palla. As her hands move dexterously and expertly to stack the banknotes the same side up, she gives quick guarded glances at Emily.

"I'm afraid I've another function to get to. I have a gift, but I'll wait until you return from your honeymoon to get it to you. I'm sorry I'll not see you at the reception."

Ranjit lets out a visible sigh. "Oh, I'm sorry to hear that, Miss."

Once they've said their goodbyes, Deepa walks Emily and Sarah to the entrance, her hands pressed into their lower backs. She offers them both a hushed blessing as they exit.

They retrieve their shoes and wash their hands in the long communal sink. Once outside they make their way down the marble stairs and along the path leading back to the street. When they are far enough away from the building, Sarah whispers, "Well, that wasn't subtle, was it?"

"Very 'here's your hat, what's your hurry'!"

"So true!" Sarah responds.

Emily wants to scream at the top of her lungs and cannot wait to be in the minivan. "Oh, I so need a drink."

Douglas has taken the kids to Playland for the day and Sarah offers that they're free to go wherever Emily's heart desires. They decide a glass of wine at Seasons might be the ticket; at least, for once, they can be sure that Dev and his brothers will not be there.

Only steps from Sarah's minivan, and out of listening distance from the other guests, Emily is about to continue their discussion when a white limousine with heavily tinted windows pulls up in the middle of the street next to them. The driver-side door opens and out steps a well-muscled man.

"Excuse me, please. Is one of you ladies with the good name of Miss Em-uh-lee?"

He speaks her name as though he's been rehearsing for this moment. Though she's never met Pehalvan Singh, she clues in immediately that he is Uncle Monty's driver and caretaker; Dev has made mention of him over the years.

"Yes, I'm Emily."

"Please, Madam. Mr. Mohan Singh Sandhu has requested

that I ask if you might have time to meet with him?" He beckons in the direction of the limousine.

Emily and Sarah look at each other in disbelief. This certainly wasn't something they'd anticipated.

"My friend and I have to be somewhere else. Is it okay if I could meet him some other time?"

"Mr. Mohan Singh says it would be best if you could meet today. A few minutes, please." And then after an awkward silence. "You will talk while I drive." Upon noticing the confusion on Sarah's face, Pehalvan adds, "And Miss Sarah will follow."

Emily reluctantly agrees. She understands now what Dev has always called the tacit commands that he'd grown up with; even second-hand the invitation is impossible to contest.

Pehalvan holds the door open as she ducks her head and climbs into the air-conditioned limousine.

An enthusiastic yet tired-sounding voice greets her. "Emily. Thank you, thank you, thank you!" He reaches out his hand and she leans forward to shake it. His skin is fine, papery, soft like a child's. The gold-framed glasses and gold watch seem in discord with the austerity of his raw cotton outfit. As does the luxurious interior of the car—white leather seats and neon track lighting around the perimeter. A gold pin in the shape of a curved knife adorns his breast pocket. In his other hand, he holds a handkerchief with which he intermittently wipes sweat from his face. Behind the rims of his glasses, she can see purple bags beneath his eyes, as though he hasn't slept in a very long time. Resting in the seat beside him is a briefcase.

"Thank you for being here for my grandson's wedding. He tells me that you've helped him greatly with his education."

"I've worked with him for the last two years, Mr. Sandhu."

"Please call me Uncle. Uncle Monty, if you like. I'm sure you've heard of me, have you not?" His laughter catches in his throat, and he coughs loudly into the handkerchief.

Emily completes what she was going to say. "It's a pleasure to work with Ranjit. He speaks of you all the time, Uncle."

"Thank you! Thank you, Emily! You are too kind."

She offers up her congratulations and mentions what a good match Ranjit and Rina make, still at a loss for why she's been asked to this meeting.

"Yes, yes. Rina is a top-notch girl. A good addition to our family! She will fit right in."

Is this a commentary on my own unsuitability? She decides to let it slide.

Monty continues. "You know my dear Ranjit will be working in the family business soon, doing what he has always been meant to do. Someday he'll lead Sandhu Properties, and he'll be training one of his own sons to follow him. This was always Ranjit's destiny." He coughs loudly into his handkerchief but continues before Emily can say a word. "He'll be able to keep doing his hobby. We've prepared a studio for him. Maybe you'll see it when it's complete?"

"Yes, I hope so," she says, trying not to sound terse.

Before Emily can say any more, Monty picks up a pile of paper from the briefcase, an impressive stack bound together by a thin metal coil. On the cover is a woodcut print of the young Monty in his army uniform: Ranjit's first assignment.

"I was wondering," he says hesitantly. "Might you have a

few more minutes for this old man? There's something I'd like to share."

Emily is racking her brain for a way to make an elegant exit and devises the excuse that she needs to text Sarah to check on something.

As she types a message on her phone, the door opens and Pehalvan delivers a carafe of tea and two lidded mugs. She remembers another one of Dev's family rules: if someone offers you chaah it is rude not to accept it.

No getting out now!

The car rolls forward. The chaah is almost too hot to sip but the warm mug and the smell of cardamom and ginger offer her some comfort.

ACT IV
SHAAM—EVENING

ONCE THE GUESTS had left, Devinder retrieved the carrom board from the closet in his bedroom. Karanpreet joked, "I'm only playing because it's your birthday. Consider this another gift." Devinder flicked the disc with ease and was well on his way to clearing the board when they were interrupted by Uncle Monty.

"Son, will you come to the garage, please?"

Captured by the excitement of the day, Devinder thought that perhaps there was another gift that they had held back. He followed Monty to the five-car garage, which was filled with furniture from the previous house: plastic-covered couches, bedroom sets, and the battered Formica dining table. Unpacked boxes were stacked high against the walls. The party guests had been given tours of the sprawling mansion, allowed ample opportunity to admire and praise each room and the extravagant new furnishings—including rosewood bed frames, enormous leather storage trunks, and a porch swing built for two shipped by sea from Rajasthan—but were kept well away from the disorganized garage. In the ten years Devinder had been part of the family they had moved four times, each house larger than the previous.

Monty would renovate or make additions to each home and then sell at a significant profit. Harmony Estates was the culmination of this pattern, a transition from a life of building and saving to one of settling. An emblem of their growing wealth. A dream fulfilled.

The afternoon had been full of laughter. Initially, he had not wanted a sixteenth-birthday party. He had to admit, though, that today had been a happy day—"an auspicious day."

At times they could drive him crazy with their rules and expectations; in the Sandhu household there was a right way and a wrong way for everything, and no one was ever clear on the reasons why. Though there were occasions when he felt out of place, an intruder, he realized it was his own sadness and insecurity at play, and not anything they intended. What they had given him was incalculable.

He dressed in the new pair of Lee jeans and a striped Pierre Cardin dress shirt that Amarpreet had bought for him the previous week during their annual birthday visit to the downtown Woodward's. They invited close friends of the family, including Devinder's closest friend, Iqbal, and his parents and younger sister. Iqbal gave him a copy of Joy Division's *Unknown Pleasures*, holding the record up to the light to show him the red tinge of the vinyl.

"It's a collector's edition, man. I had to order it special from London," he bragged.

"Right on, Iqqi! I can't wait to play it." He fully trusted Iqbal's recommendations. "You know, Uncle Monty and Auntie Deepa got me an SL-3200 for my bedroom."

Iqbal seemed impressed. "Vah-vah-vah! Oh man, a Technics record player for your bedroom! Shantih!"

MONTY DRAGGED TWO tattered pvc dining room chairs—now replaced with full-grain Italian leather—and placed them across from each other. Taking a seat on one, he motioned at Devinder to sit across from him. Devinder noted the pensive look on his face—the look he knew always preceded serious or difficult conversations.

"After your parents had their accident ..."—he took a moment to compose himself—"your auntie and I had to clean up the basement where you'd lived." The metal frame of the dining chair creaked under his weight. "Your parents didn't have much, but they had saved enough for a down payment on a new home. We placed that money in a trust in your name. It's time now for you to have it, son. Do with it what you want. Just know that we will continue to ..." Monty cleared his throat. "That we will always ... support you. No matter what."

Devinder hesitated, thinking back to the days of the basement apartment. He wasn't sure how he should respond. "I don't know how I can ever thank you enough ... for what you and Auntieji have done for me."

"Son, you've been a blessing on us all!"

It was the first time Devinder had seen Uncle Monty with tears in his eyes, and he stood to give him a hug—his arms unable to completely enwrap his father's ever-growing girth.

"There's something else." Monty motioned for Devinder to sit, his voice shakier than before. Twice he opened his mouth to speak and then stopped himself. Finally he stood and announced, "Narinder and Mira also had some personal belongings."

Hearing his birth parents' names spoken out loud was

disconcerting. Though Devinder thought of them often and could recall every detail of their being, their given names were only abstractions. He couldn't remember the last time he'd heard either Deepa or Monty mention them by name.

Monty continued, "We've been waiting for the right time to pass those belongings to you."

He walked to the side of the garage and brought over a cardboard box, placed it on the empty chair. Devinder imagined the box being moved from the basement apartment to the series of houses they'd lived in since—all these years he'd been oblivious to its existence and its contents.

"I'm going to help your auntie clean up."

Monty struggled with the sloped ramp that led back into the house and held the banister tightly as he moved up step by careful step.

A few minutes passed before Devinder shifted his chair closer to the box, studied his parents' names scrawled with a thick marker on the side, and spoke them out loud like a chant: "Narinder and Mira. Narinder and Mira ..."

The recessed pot lights above suddenly seemed overbright. He took a deep breath before he ripped off the discoloured tape and lifted the flaps. The contents had been shaken over the years. If there had been any order to the original packing, that order was long gone. At the top of the box were a few trinkets, lying flat or wedged in the edges: a small stone statue of Guru Nanak Dev Ji, words written in calligraphy on strips of thin silk, wooden prayer beads, an elaborate jewellery box engraved with a crescent moon and star.

The years with his birth parents were marked by an absence of religious imagery. They never betrayed any

affiliation or conviction. In the Sandhu house the symbols of
Sikhism were everywhere: the framed posters of the first and
last Gurus; a brass replica of the Golden Temple displayed on
a shelf; books on Sikh history; the steel karas worn around
the wrists, and the kesh, Monty's and Deepa's uncut locks of
hair; the memory of his brothers' first haircuts imprinted in
his mind. Monty wore a lapel pin in the shape of a kirpan,
a curved metal blade, on the left collar of his suit jackets.
At Harmony Estates Auntie Deepa began her mornings by
burning incense and listening to kirtan on a cassette player
in a tiny room near the kitchen.

The jewellery box contained only a pair of gold earrings,
but he could not recall his mother ever wearing them, or any
other jewellery for that matter. He put the trinkets on the
ground beside his chair to see what further clues he might
uncover. Inside a large brown envelope he discovered a handful of photographs, faded and creased. The first was a family
portrait, which Devinder scrutinized. *The younger man with a
beard and turban must be Pappa*, he thought. *Yes*, he recalled the
dark-framed glasses and behind them, even in that pocket-
sized picture, he could identify his father's eyes, their kindness
not forgotten. A closer inspection confirmed his father's smile.
At the centre of the portrait, an elegantly dressed older couple
sat on a rope bed. Devinder turned the photograph around
and found an inscription—a listing of names in tidy cursive.
The two elders were identified as Charan Singh and Amrik
Kaur. *Are these my paternal grandparents—my dadaji and dadiji?*
To their left stood his father and to their right stood a young
girl identified as Parminder Kaur. *This could be my puaji, Pappa's
sister*, he considered. In the back stood two gentlemen, Daljit

Singh and Harpal Singh. *Older than Pappa, so most likely they are my thaiajis, Pappa's older brothers.* The men in the photograph wore turbans and beards, sleeveless sweaters over striped collared shirts. His dadiji and puaji had their heads covered with chunis. Behind them was a simple brick house with peeling paint and tiny windows with metal grates.

The next photograph was a dulled likeness of his father, slightly younger, with a patchy beard, standing in front of a desk piled with books. The inscription confirmed *Narinder Singh, Chandigarh, May 1960.* And then a portrait of the gentlemen he assumed were his uncles as they stood over a group of workers cutting sugar cane with large scythes.

The only coloured snapshot was of his presumed dadaji standing in front of a mustard field, the yellow flowers bleached by time. He was dressed in a simple turban, a collarless shirt, a dhoti wrapped around his waist, thin sandals on his feet. From the look on his face and the confident pose, Devinder surmised that this must be land that his father's family had farmed and possibly owned.

Under the envelope of photographs were his parents' passports. Devinder noticed the altered surname on his mother's document: *Hussein* crossed out and *Gill* handwritten in its place. A *Government of India* stamp was placed next to the change. But the unabbreviated first name was also a revelation: *Samira.* He had only ever heard Pappa call her "Mira."

Folded into the passports he found boarding passes and immigration papers. From these he pieced together that he'd been born only five months after his parents landed in Canada. He checked the paperwork and found that his mother had been a late addition, that his father was originally scheduled to travel alone, and it was only in the month before their departure that Samira Gill had been added to the document.

In the remaining papers he found his father's degree certificate from the Punjab Engineering College, Chandigarh. *Had this degree been what had qualified him to immigrate?* All of Monty's friends had worked in sawmills and factories when they initially arrived here, but not Narinder Gill. An image of his father in his suit holding a briefcase flashed in Devinder's mind. There was also a marriage certificate dated a few weeks before their flight to Canada, with a poorly focused photograph attached with a paper clip. He imagined it was taken on the day of his parents' wedding; a young couple standing outside what could be a courthouse, his mother's hands folded over her belly, the swell of her kameez showing she was pregnant. Their eyes pointed down, away from the gaze of the lens.

Tucked in a bottom corner of the box was his father's Citizen watch. Devinder wound the crown a few turns, tapped the face with his finger, and the hands miraculously came to life. He slipped the stretchy silver metal band over his hand and onto his wrist.

Inside the final envelope—stamped with a *Government of British Columbia* seal on its top right corner—were his parents' death certificates. *Date of Death: Friday, January 15th, 1971. Birthplace: Punjab, India.* Devinder held the two certificates, turned them over hoping for additional clues, any details about the accident. Nothing.

He considered the circumstances of his parents' departure from India. *Their love was never accepted by my father's family.* And then there was the fact that his mother had been pregnant on their wedding day. *Another reason for their flight away from their homeland?* Devinder had always wondered why his parents had chosen to live their lives hidden away, devoid of religion, friends, or family. He understood now that it was a response to a past they could never reconcile, an attempt to bury their pain from the eyes of the world.

But what of my mother's family? The box offered no traces of them. *What was their role in my parents' exile? Did they also shun their daughter?*

He understood that his parents' anonymity and loneliness were never a choice, but a necessity. However far away they travelled, they were never able to escape their sense of loss and shame. He was angry that his parents were rejected by the people who were supposed to be there for them without condition, to accept them wholeheartedly. He recalled their moments of tenderness: the long embrace each morning as Pappa left for work, their arms around each other's shoulders as he sat between them on the bus.

Was I the one joyful outcome of their love? Or was I their unfortunate accident? An unwanted pregnancy that exposed their secret and made exile compulsory? Did the misfortune of my existence stop them from having another child?

Wedged against one side of the box were the two framed photographs that Devinder remembered from his childhood: the proofs of the portrait from his first year of school and the snapshot of the family taken at Queen Elizabeth Park. As he reached into the box a jagged piece of broken glass grazed his hand. It took all his strength to keep from screaming out loud as he pressed hard into the meat of his palm to stop the bleeding.

"HAVE THE GIRLS eaten anything?"

"Not enough."

"Let's get MJ to make a plate for them when we get to the hall."

"Of course."

"Are you okay?"

"Why wouldn't I be?"

Kuldip knows that her clipped responses will be seen by Devinder as being out of character, but she cannot act like nothing is wrong. When they had first agreed to arrive at the reception early, she worried they might miss out on the sagan; now it seemed a convenient excuse to get away. As soon as the ceremony had concluded, she and Devinder exchanged some hurried congratulations, gathered Meena and Teena, and made their way outside. The sagan line reached the prayer hall entrance and she tried her best to avoid glancing in *her* direction.

She has not been able to look at Devinder directly since she sighted Emily in the doorway of the temple. *To be a woman is to be an expert in forgiveness. But there must be limits.* She convinces herself that Emily will not be at the reception—*Surely not in a place that would offer no anonymity*—but that is of little comfort.

As they reach the parking lot of RKP—still new but already the most in-demand wedding venue in Surrey—she notices that several cars have taken the spots closest to the entrance. Though the invitation says the event will begin at six o'clock, a few eager guests have arrived early. *Not a surprise.* There is no time to waste. Once the girls are fed, she will have to put on her best party face and fulfil her responsibilities for the evening. *No getting out of it.*

Kuldip hopes that seeing the reception hall after all the months of hard planning will help her to shake off the resentment that is burning inside her.

At the entrance to the ballroom on the second level, they are met by Pinky Brar. She holds a clipboard, wears a headpiece connected to her smartphone, and looks both anxious and glad to see them. *Poor Pinky. Decades of experience as a wedding planner but here she is shaking like a leaf—that's what this family does to outsiders.* Not only have Pinky and her team been supervised at every stage by the Tiger Team, but Deepa and Amarpreet had insisted that someone from the family should arrive early to check on things. *To check on Pinky's work.*

"Hey Pinky. Everything okay?" asks Devinder.

"Oh, yes. The flowers arrived on time and are where you wanted them." Pinky does not need to be prodded to continue. "Everything's good. But there is one small problem. I tried calling you earlier, Mr. Sandhu. There's an issue with the bar inventory."

It's strange how many people mistake Devinder for a Sandhu, though the story of his adoption, the selflessness of Monty and

Deepa, are legendary in the community.

Devinder looks surprised, as though the bar inventory is not what he was expecting. "It's okay, Pinky. We'll get that sorted out right away. Not to worry." Devinder is as calm as always, but it bothers her—more than it normally would—that he has not corrected Pinky on his name.

"It's Mr. Gill!" Kuldip says more firmly than she had intended. Pinky looks defeated and apologizes profusely; Kuldip immediately regrets her overreaction.

In all their years of marriage, she has not once heard Devinder raise his voice with anyone, in any situation. That was why the family depended on him to smooth down the rough edges. Even with business matters, to this day, he is called in for guidance whenever a thorny problem needs sorting out, especially if it is with a major business partner. "Mr. Fix-It," she heard Baljit call him once—she had no idea at the time what that meant.

If only Devinder could quiet her mind right now.

While waiting in the parking lot for the milni to begin, Kuldip had felt blessed to have the companionship of her sisters-in-law. They understood the trials and tribulations of an outsider entering Deepa and Monty's clan and what it took to manage and negotiate both the explicit and tacit rules of engagement. They had joked about the rituals and traditions of their family events, and this week's wedding proceedings in particular; though they clearly grasped that as outdated as those traditions might sometimes seem, when it came time for their own children to get married, they would probably follow the same path. The tug and weight of tradition would be too much for them to resist.

Kuldip had set aside her dismay at being lectured earlier by Deepa on how lehengas were not appropriate attire for her daughters to wear at the gurdwara. Though she half expected it, the reprimand seemed overblown. *The girls look gorgeous and it's their choice*, she had wanted to say, but instead stayed quiet, as was expected of her.

Caught up in the lighthearted banter with her sisters-in-law, she had forgotten that she had seen Emily's name on the initial invitation list, but then there she was in the doorway to the gurdwara. And it was not simply the sight of Emily; it was the fact that Teena was in the same frame. How Devinder thought it was a good idea for her to be invited in the first place was beyond her. One word from him and Emily could have been stricken from the list, no matter how important she might be to Ranjit. He would have listened to his favourite uncle. *But that would have meant speaking the secret out loud. And speaking anything out loud made it real.* No one in this family wanted to scratch the veneer of perfection that cocooned them; reputation and status were far more important than truth.

Kuldip grips her daughters' hands a little tighter, knowing how distracted they will be by the spectacle of the ballroom decorations. Her main concern is to get them fed and comfortable for the long evening ahead. Meena has refused to eat anything since breakfast, and Kuldip was hardly able to get a bite down herself at the hurried post-milni chaah service. She was busy chasing Teena, who was more interested in exploring the kitchen and chatting with the parishioners on sewa duty than eating from the thali Kuldip had prepared for her.

They follow Pinky through the glass doors and the girls shriek with wonder at the mirrored gateway that obscures the rest of the room. Every arriving guest will have to walk through its ten-foot archway. The Tiger Team had seen a preview of the immense construction a couple of weeks earlier, but now that every square inch of its plywood surface has been covered with little mirror shards, she truly appreciates that Sonny Patel had not been wrong when he promised it would be "the talk of the town." *It certainly will*, Kuldip thinks, and affords herself a smile. Teena and Meena laugh at their splintered reflections in the dome above them. Devinder gives a soft knock to the mirrored surface and makes a swiping motion at his brow to signal his relief that the structure has not collapsed. He looks at Kuldip but she does not offer him anything back. She will not give him that easy satisfaction. *Not today.*

On the other side of the archway, still on the strip of red carpet that runs from the hallway, through the gateway, and into the ballroom, they are greeted by a cameraman who will be photographing guests in front of a printed screen with the new couple's initials scripted inside large red hearts. A souvenir photograph will be printed and ready for guests to take home with them as they leave, along with the more traditional box of ladoos and a generous slice of wedding cake. The photographer insists that they have their red-carpet Hollywood glamour shot taken right away, though they tell him they are in a hurry. The photo is taken with Devinder and Kuldip standing some distance apart with Teena and Meena between them.

The plan had been for the new co-parents-in-law to form a greeting line beyond the photo booth, but obviously everything is behind schedule. Maybe, once the girls have eaten, she and Devinder will act as a temporary greeting line. *That much I can do.*

She must admit that walking into the reception area through the gateway does make the first view of the hall more spectacular. Enormous chandeliers, eight feet in circumference, hang in two parallel rows, and there are dozens of smaller chandeliers spread along each side of the remarkably high ceiling. The elaborate crystal fixtures had been the clincher when the Tiger Team was reviewing the short list of banquet halls. In the daylight it is difficult to appreciate their true magnificence but later, when it is dark and the lights start to refract off each individual Swarovski crystal, the room will shimmer in a breathtaking show of coloured light. During the tour of the hall, wisely scheduled by RKP for a late spring evening, Amarpreet had joked to Baljit, "Well, that sure beats the disco ball we had at our reception!"

Auntie Deepa had been delighted that the marriage would begin in such a fanciful display: "To brighten the way for Ranjit and all future generations of our family."

Each of the eighty-four round tables spread across the floor is covered in a perfectly pressed white satin tablecloth with a huge bouquet of white roses in a crystal vase at its centre. The chairs are also covered in satin cloth, pulled tight over their backs and seats, making them look like ghosts in an animated TV show. There are nine tables marked RESERVED between the dance floor and the head table, three for the immediate family, two for the staff of accountants, lawyers, and marketers who run the day-to-day business, and

four for business partners of Sandhu Properties (contractors, builders, engineers, two municipal clerks responsible
for building permits) and VIP guests. A tenth table has been
reserved for Mr. Vikram Sohal, the recently elected Member
of Parliament. Mr. Sohal and his entourage, a pack of young
community leaders aspiring to reach the heights of their
mentor, have not confirmed their attendance, but a table has
been set aside just in case they decide to show up.

The head table, framed by a canopy of white hydrangeas,
is centred along the back wall and elevated on a platform one
foot off the ground, which will become a performance stage
later in the evening.

The arrangement to meet the florists and oversee the
distribution of flowers has been foiled due to the delay of
events, but Pinky, Bubbly, and Pippi have done an excellent
job making sure everything is as requested. The smell of
roses and hydrangeas, sweet fruit with a hint of anise and
jasmine, fills the room. Kuldip points at the centrepieces and
gives Pinky a thumbs-up. Pinky looks relieved.

Around the perimeter, shimmering red streamers hang
from the ceiling. Red and gold helium balloon bouquets sit
in silver buckets across the side wall and several coordinated projectors are displaying a slide show of classic family
photographs.

Meena and Teena hardly know which direction to look.
"Who's that, Mom?" asks Meena as an image of a young
couple on-board a ship is cast on the wall above the head
table. "That's Dadaji and Dadiji, sweetheart. That's when
they first came to Canada."

"On a ship?" Teena asks in bewilderment.

"Yes, sweetie. On a ship."

Both daughters scream, "Wow!"

Everything is as grand as Kuldip imagined.

One of the children's entertainers, wearing a polka-dot jacket, walks up to Meena and offers her a balloon peacock which she accepts enthusiastically. Of course Teena wants one, too, and they stop for a few minutes as the entertainer pulls balloons from his breast pocket, blows them into long cylinders, and then twists and ties them together to shape another blue-and-green bird. The girls laugh hysterically as he acts exhausted from the exertion and slumps into a chair.

Kuldip casts her eyes up to the ceiling directly above the dance floor where hundreds of red and gold balloons are held in a net. *What a vision it will be when they are released at midnight as Makhan Singh takes the stage.* The midnight balloon drop had been Kuldip's idea.

They continue the long walk across the room and she waves at guests who have already staked out the best tables. Mr. and Mrs. Sekhon, family friends, now in their nineties, have taken up chairs at one of the reserved tables, and as she looks across at Devinder she can tell he has already noted their error.

Devinder and Pinky stop at the main bar while Kuldip corrals Teena and Meena toward a table in the back corner, close to the kitchen. She waves over one of the facility staff and asks if she can speak with Manoj Jain, MJ, the executive chef. In the meantime, she takes a Ziploc bag of sliced bell peppers and a Tupperware container of hummus from her bag and puts them on a napkin in front of the girls. They tuck into the snack right away.

Kuldip's head is quieter now and the voices she imagined whispering around her have finally fallen silent.

"How can I be of service, Madam?"

"Hello MJ. My girls haven't eaten since breakfast. Do you think you could put together a plate of snacks to get them through to dinner, please?"

"Anything is possible, Madam." The Tiger Team had worked to finalize the menu with MJ's guidance. Kuldip likes her no-nonsense efficiency.

"Also, a couple of plates for Mr. Gill and myself, please. Whatever you have prepared will do."

"Madam, please allow me a few minutes to prepare the rice. Then I will bring you the plates."

Before long Meena and Teena are devouring fish pakoras smothered in tamarind sauce and gulping down tall glasses of cool buttermilk that had been thoughtfully added to Kuldip's request. MJ had promised them a jalebi each if they emptied their plates. Pakoras and jalebis were not typically allowed, but for this week Kuldip had made an exception. "What's a wedding week without too much fried food and sugar, anyway?" Kiran had asked. "It'll be good to take a few days off from being the sugar police!"

The girls amuse each other with their buttermilk moustaches. *They are good eaters when they are hungry and comfortable.*

Before she takes a single spoonful from her own plate, Kuldip confirms that another plate has been sent to the bar for Devinder. Her anger, a little dulled from earlier, does not preclude her wanting everything to run smoothly. The dhal makhani and malai kofta are excellent; MJ's mix of whole and ground spices provides the perfect mix of flavour and colour.

Meena inquires, "Mom, when can we play outside? You said we could play."

"Yeah, Mom," adds Teena.

It will probably be good for the girls to get some time in the sunshine, she thinks. *And it will give them a chance to be children for a while.* Earlier, she had spotted a playground area with swings and slides at the far end of the parking lot. *Once Alexis arrives maybe she can take them out—this whole week they have been missing their regular visits to the park.*

"You have to finish up your food first. Then you can change outfits if you like," she says. Meena lets out a sigh of relief, as if it hadn't been her idea to wear the lehenga this morning in the first place.

"And you can only play outside if Alexis is with you. You got that, Teena?" She looks directly at her younger daughter, who is licking tamarind sauce from her fingers.

Once the girls have finished eating, Kuldip takes them to the restroom. She scrubs the sticky sauce and jalebi syrup from their hands and faces before she asks them to choose what they want to wear. They both opt for brightly coloured cotton dresses, pink for Meena and yellow for Teena. Meena is only too glad to be out of her itchy choli.

Kuldip takes a couple of pills from her purse and swallows them down with a big gulp of water.

"Are you okay, Mommy?" Meena asks.

"Mommy has a headache, sweetie. But I'm fine." She softly pinches Meena's cheek.

The girls skip out of the restroom and Kuldip walks them to the centre of the hall. At the dance floor she suggests, "Why don't you practise your special dance for tonight. Just make sure you're not in anyone's way, okay?" Teena immediately lifts her arms in the air and starts spinning in the empty space. Meena watches hesitantly but soon joins her sister.

Kuldip has seen them rehearse the routine that they will perform with their cousin-sisters during the evening's formal program and cannot wait to see them in the spotlight. Their cousins have been characteristically encouraging and supportive, though her daughters lack the attention to master the choreography. Teena takes it upon herself to lecture her older sister, "Meena, you're doing it wrong. Like this. Watch!" She rotates her hips, shuffles her feet, and puts her right hand to her chin like her cousins have taught her.

As DJ Bijliwallah completes his sound check, Teena repeats "testing-one-two-three," and laughs out loud to herself.

The video team is also checking their equipment, and an image of Meena and Teena appears on the large screens at either side of the head table.

"Mom! Look, look! Mom!" they shout together.

In their loose dresses they are moving far more freely. Kuldip has changed their shoes, too: sneakers for playing and dancing. No uncomfortable dress shoes—another departure from the expected etiquette of the day.

The DJ tries out the smoke machine and a cloud of smoke wafts onto the floor. Teena runs hard and fast into the cloud with Meena following cautiously behind. *Such little characters they've become.* Kuldip is momentarily lost in a vision of her daughters as young women.

DEVINDER'S K-WAY WINDBREAKER pressed tight against his body. Past Kitsilano Pool and the Yacht Club, he paused to shake the water from his hood before attempting the steep stairway. Through the mist he could just make out the sawn-off log at the water's edge—the scene of his first kiss and countless summer evenings with Emily. On a clear day, they could take in the wide panorama of the ocean and the layered profile of the North Shore. Today was like standing inside a cloud. He was near the top of the steps when the sole of his running shoe met a fine layer of moss and he lost his footing. His body tumbled backward, arms flailing, hands failing to grab the metal banister. In an instant his head hit concrete.

When he awoke, he had no idea how long he'd been unconscious. The rain fell hard around him and the metallic taste of blood diluted with rain filled his mouth. He had a feeling of drowning and snapped his head to the side to clear the liquid from the back of his throat. His limbs were heavy and stiff, and he struggled to untwist his body. He stayed motionless for a few minutes, his head pounding, his heart beating furiously. The exertion required to stand and then drag his aching legs up the remaining steps drained him.

There was no one on the street, no one to flag for help, so he stumbled the hundred metres to Emily's. The wet, mulched leaves on the sidewalk were as slick as ice and the wooden steps, so familiar, were something to be feared. His vision was blurred and he fumbled to find the key beneath the planter. Once inside, he shouted Emily's name as he leaned against the door, unable to find the strength to go on.

***

WHEN EMILY REGISTERED Dev's voice her first response was to reach behind her. Finding only empty space she thought for a moment that it had been a dream. She'd been back in Vancouver for six months and Dev's morning visits, at first occasional, were now routine. He visited her a couple of times a week, at least.

There it was again—an agonized shout, almost tortured. She sprang out of bed and rushed toward the cry.

In the hallway she found Dev collapsed on the floor. She dialed for an ambulance and grabbed a towel to press against the cut on his chin. She sat with Dev's head in her lap and gently stroked his hair until the paramedics arrived and took Dev's vitals, placing an oxygen mask over his face and hoisting him onto a gurney. On her way out she grabbed her handbag and her white cotton raincoat from the rack near the front door. She held Dev's hand for the ride to Vancouver General Hospital, whispering assurances into his ear.

The paramedics asked for his health card, which Emily

was not able to provide. And they asked her what had happened. She told them he had shown up like this. "Just friends," was the best answer she could muster when asked how they knew each other. His blood marked her coat as she leaned over him.

Before he disappeared into the emergency ward, she touched Dev's face, tracing his hairline with her finger. There was a gash beneath his lip the shape of a tooth bite.

Standing at the check-in counter, alone and stunned, Emily looked for a pay phone. She pressed the keys slowly, trying her best to sound official and detached, but unable to mask the quiver of worry and apology in her voice.

"Dev had a fall during his run. He's in emergency at VGH."

Kuldip sounded confused and mistrustful. "How badly is he hurt?" she asked.

"They can't say for sure just yet."

Emily had not said her name, nor provided any more details—no mention of Dev's scream for help or how he'd gotten to the hospital. She'd simply hung up once Kuldip said she'd be on her way soon.

Emily asked at the registration desk for an update and was told that he was still delirious. They'd been able to suture the gash under his lip but were waiting to send him for X-rays to determine the extent of his other injuries. She thought it best to remain in the waiting room in case there was any change in his condition and took a seat in the back corner, holding a tattered copy of *People* magazine.

***

THOUGH ALMOST TWO years had passed since the mysterious call in the middle of the night, the voice had been unmistakable. Thirty minutes after hanging up, Kuldip entered the emergency department with Meena stumbling half-asleep by her side and Teena, still a toddler, in her arms. After some discussion with the nurses—Kuldip had to explain that she was the patient's wife and produce her driver's licence and Devinder's health card—she was given permission to see him.

Before leaving the registration area, she turned to look around the room and their eyes connected.

***

EMILY FELT THE air leave her lungs. Kuldip stood there for only a moment, but it felt like an eternity. Emily could sense the fury behind her eyes. But then Kuldip nodded, almost imperceptibly, but a nod for sure.

As the oxygen returned, Emily nodded back—timid, uncertain—and watched Kuldip lift Meena onto her free hip, push open the swinging door, and walk into the ward.

***

IT IS WITH *me that he shares a home and the responsibility of raising our children. It is our bed that he spends each night in. It is me he wakes up next to. It is with me that he plans our daughters' lives, their futures. It is our daughters that wake him with their bad dreams, their fevers, their need to be held; that tell him their days' stories, their spills and accidents; make him laugh with their funny phrases and made-up words; fill pages with drawings and scribbles of animals and kites that we stick proudly on our fridge. And these young girls still fall asleep on his stomach, curl their chubby fingers around his, still call for Daddy when they wake in the night.*

I've seen the notes that you send; the I "heart" Us and the Miss-yous, the mwah kisses and the When can I see you agains. I know where and when you meet. I know the art openings, the book launches, the concerts you've attended with him. I can smell you on his clothes and in his hair when you've been together. I know when you are working with acrylic and when with oil. I can tell from how he carries his shoulders or angles his head, how quickly he walks past me, whether you've been with him that morning or not.

There is a proper order to things, and my place is here on this side of the waiting room, waiting to be with him, to take him home. Yours is on the opposite, waiting to leave. He may share with you intimacies that he will never share with me, but this life of commitment is ours, these children are ours, mine and his. And the children will always be ours, and as long as I have them, I can stand anything.

***

EMILY STEPPED OUT onto the street and flagged down a cab. The rain diffused the bloodstains on her coat into enormous crimson flowers.

***

HE HAD A faint memory of waking up to the rain falling on his face, his body twisted out of shape. Then he was in the hospital with Kuldip by his side, holding his hand, tears on her face. Meena and Teena sat on the edge of the bed. His lips and chin were sore, his legs heavy, and there was a throbbing ache behind his eyes.

"What's happened?" It took effort to get the words out.

"Ji, you're awake. Meena, Teena, look. Daddy's awake."

Devinder asked again, "What happened?"

"You're at VGH. You had an accident while running in the rain."

Devinder winced as he tried to move his legs to sit up.

"Ji, no! The doctor says you need to rest."

Kuldip shifted Teena's body so he could see her face. She was fidgety and wanted to climb into his arms. "No, sweetie! Daddy's hurt. He has an owee."

"Owee," repeated Teena as she pointed a finger at her father's face.

"Where did you hurt, Daddy?" asked Meena.

"All over, sweetie." Devinder grimaced.

FOUR DAYS LATER when he telephoned Emily, he thought she'd be concerned because he hadn't been in touch.

"I had an accident. I'm okay but it'll take time to recover."

"It's good to hear from you, Dev. I've been worried sick."

"I'll be fine, love. I'm on the mend." He felt awful that he hadn't called her sooner.

"You looked a proper mess. How's your face?"

Dev was momentarily stunned. He ran his finger along the arc of stitches below his lip.

"You already knew?" He could hear the panic in his own voice.

"You showed up at my place and passed out. I called an ambulance and was with you for the ride to VGH."

An image of Emily leaning over him flashed in his mind.

"And, umm … Dev, she probably told you this, but because you had no ID on you, I called your home to let Kuldip know."

A cold sweat covered his body.

"She hasn't said anything. She was there when I woke up in the hospital."

"That's what I'm trying to tell you, Dev. Listen. She was there because I called her."

There was a moment of hesitation before Emily continued. "She saw me in the waiting room when she arrived."

Dev couldn't believe what he'd heard. "You were at the hospital at the same time?"

"Yes, Dev. She knows that you came to my place after you fell and that I took you to emerg."

He could sense his heart beating faster and his hands clamming up. For once he had no idea what he should do. He was still in considerable pain and would be convalescing for a while yet. Whatever he decided, it would be best to wait until he was fully recovered.

"THIS IS THE big one, bro!"

Devinder and Pete greet each other with a warm hug. Although they don't see each other often anymore, Devinder always enjoys Pete's company. His optimism and humility can lighten the toughest of days. There is also something comforting about playing the role of head bartender again. Devinder had volunteered himself for the role at an early Tiger Team meeting. "It's the biggest family function we've ever had. Why not have someone from the family manage it?"

Amarpreet had agreed once Pete was secured to assist Devinder, but there was one caveat: "You need to enjoy the party, Dev! We can't have you behind the bar all evening!"

Pete was practically a part of the family. Shortly after Devinder and Kuldip had provided him with tickets home to Nova Scotia for his brother's funeral, he had dropped out of school to focus on raising his daughter, Alexis. Devinder spoke to Amarpreet who in turn offered Pete bartending duties at Sandhu Properties functions. Within a year he'd been promoted to Manager, Major Events. From seasonal staff parties to the launch of new developments, Pete was always present.

"Your girls are getting so big," he says as he hands Devinder a printout of the bar inventory. "And Kuldip. What a beauty she is, bro! You certainly got lucky there."

Devinder looks to the back of the room where Kuldip is sitting with Meena and Teena, talking to MJ. The bewildered young woman he'd married was now refined and confident, her intelligence and enthusiasm much admired by the family. And she is an amazing mother. *I am lucky to have her.*

But it's inevitable that Kuldip will question him about Emily—she must know by now that Teena met her inside the gurdwara. That's the only explanation for her curt responses and cold shoulder. He is certain that she will not say anything to him today, or in the next few days as wedding events wind down. *She would never create a scene. No, she'll wait for a private moment when it's just the two of us.* He accepts that it's his own fault; he should have had Teena's wandering on the list of wild cards that might throw off the day. The rest of the plan has fallen into place well enough. Emily had stayed out of the way and was hardly noticed at the back of the prayer hall. He is eager to hear Emily's thoughts on the ceremony when they next see each other.

AS WELL AS the main bar there are three smaller bars, one at each end of the ballroom and one on the outdoor lounge deck, which will be opened after dinner for those wishing for fresh air, or a quiet moment while the dance floor is at its busiest and the music at its loudest. Devinder and Pete walk across the room to check the stock against the list.

"How's Alexis?"

Pete's daughter is heading into her final year of an economics degree at UBC and has plans for law school.

"Fine. She's here in fact. She's out taking a walk right now. As you know, she's not always comfortable in these large gatherings but she wanted to see your girls and is looking forward to babysitting them later if she's needed."

Babysitting? This is a surprise to Devinder. Alexis has been an occasional sitter for Meena and Teena, but he wasn't aware of any plans for later this evening. *Perhaps Kuldip forgot to mention it?*

Pete asks Devinder for advice on Alexis's application for law school. And then in his usual self-deprecating way says, "I don't know where she gets her brains from. Not from me. That's for sure!"

Devinder muses over the fact that almost every guest in attendance today would give anything to have a child at university with a perfect GPA, and the one attendee who does never mentions it. He assures Pete that he'll investigate and get back to him soon.

Returning to the main bar, Devinder confirms with Pinky that she was correct; they are short eight bottles of the Dalmore twelve-year-old. It's only eight bottles, but a deal is a deal and the embarrassment of running out of whisky is not something he wants to experience, even if the odds are extremely low—one hundred bottles had been ordered. Devinder could easily guess the guests who'll be the most upset if the worst were to happen. Putting together the required inventory had been one of his responsibilities; the selection and quantities carefully curated. Pinky was correct to alert him.

On the phone, the supplier is insistent that the ordered quantities were delivered that afternoon and Devinder resorts to the one argument he most dislikes. He firmly presses the supplier, "How much money has our family spent with you over the past few years?" The supplier, thrown off by Devinder's strategy, agrees to replace the missing bottles. Devinder feels a tinge of guilt as he tucks his BlackBerry into his jacket. He reassures himself, *There was no time to waste, and that was the fastest way to resolve the matter.*

More guests have arrived in the hall, and a few are hanging out close to the bars, looking eager for them to open. Pete gathers the bar staff so Devinder can deliver an abbreviated version of his customary pep talk. He recognizes certain team members from previous functions. For the sake of the newcomers he reviews the family's expectations: they are to be courteous to all guests no matter how busy their station might get; Pete is their main contact, but if anything extra challenging should come up they are to find Dev, or as backup, Nav or Kaz; if there are any problem guests with unreasonable demands such as insisting they be allowed to take full bottles of liquor back to their tables, they should find him immediately. "Let me have the difficult chats," he says reassuringly.

He closes by explaining that there is a car service available to any guest who should require a ride home. "They'll be lined up outside the main doors after ten o'clock. Please, please encourage people to take them." He looks around the group and sees heads nodding in agreement. Pete gives him the all-clear signal.

"Any other questions, team?" More nodding of heads but no one speaks. "In that case, let's get this party started!"

The staff give each other high-fives and take their places behind the bars. Within minutes there is a lineup at each station. Devinder thinks it's curious that Uncle Tarlochan and his regular cohort of drinking buddies—the sharabi uncles—are not in line even though they arrived early and staked out a table in a back corner. He looks in their direction and sees Tarlochan taking a swig from a red plastic cup he holds beneath the table. He notices red cups in the hands of each of Tarlochan's tablemates. He counts the number of sharabi uncles and knows now where the eight bottles of Dalmore 12 have disappeared to.

"I'M SORRY WE'VE never had a chance to speak before, Emily."

At last, a sign that he knows more about me than he's let on.

"I know what a busy man you are, Uncle."

"It's not only that, Emily. You are an old friend of our son Devinder. He's such an important part of this family, loved by everyone. He's never disappointed us."

Monty coughs loud and hard into his handkerchief and clears his throat. The car is now on a main road and Emily checks over Monty's shoulder to make sure Sarah is following. She is.

After a couple of minutes of further praise for Dev, Monty lowers his head, places his hand on his lapel pin, and recites a short prayer under his breath.

"My health is not so good, you know," he continues. "I'm not sure how much longer I have in this body. I love Devinder as much as I love my other three sons. He has brought so much light into this family. A wonderful son. And a wonderful brother to our boys. Thirty-four years he's been with us, and we cannot imagine our lives without him."

He taps the stack of papers and hands them to her with one hand as he coughs into the handkerchief in the other.

She flips through the manuscript and sees hundreds of pages of neatly typed prose separated by plastic dividers marked *The Early Years*, *The Middle Years*, and *The Later Years*. At the back, there is a collection of original artwork clearly made by Ranjit and a series of scanned pictures. She studies the photographs marked with captions containing locations and dates: A young couple on a ship (*Mohan Singh Sandhu w/ Pardeep Kaur Sandhu, in transit, June 1954*); a young family standing outside a wooden building with a pointed roof (*Mohan Singh Sandhu, Pardeep Kaur Sandhu w/ sons Amarpreet, Navpreet, and Karanpreet, Second Avenue Gurdwara, March 1967*); a copper-coloured medal in the shape of a six-pointed star with GRI VI in large script at its centre (*The Burma Star, 1945*).

So, he wanted to show me his memoir. But why me? Curiously, the copy that Emily holds in her hand is dedicated to *My Deareast Son, Devinder.*

Monty explains, "This is something to leave our grandchildren and their children and so on. To make sure they do not forget where they came from and the sacrifices made along the way." He takes a moment to gather his thoughts before he continues. "Though I've never met you, I feel I can trust you, Emily. There's a part of Devinder's story that I've kept to myself, which I have not shared with anyone. Not even with Deepa. It would break her heart if she ever found out."

The limousine pulls onto a highway, and though Emily's mug is empty, she continues to grip it tight.

TWO HOURS IN the back of the limousine and she's still no closer to understanding why she's here. As compelling as Monty's story is, she still doesn't know what it has to do with her or why it was so important that they meet today. Monty's speech is rambling, flitting from story to story as though he's randomly turning pages in a book. Emily still holds the manuscript in her hands, afraid to put it down in case she offends him.

"People ask me all the time, 'How is it, Monty, that you've raised such smart and successful sons? Such perfect gentlemen and never a bad word between them.' They tell me, 'Your family is an example to us all.'"

Occasionally he refers to a page number, encouraging her to look at a photograph or an illustration. "See that wooden building? That's the West 2nd Avenue Gurdwara. It's where Deepa and I started our Canadian journey. Most people don't know that there was a temple there once! And that's a drawing of the False Creek sawmill where I once worked. I described it to Ranjit, and he immediately started moving his pencil over the paper. He got it just right. Such a talented boy! But you know that already."

Dev has often fretted about Monty's cognitive decline, yet there are long stretches during which he is clear and lucid; he can recite entire sections of the memoir word for word and knows the captions beside each photograph and illustration. At other times he seems confused and disoriented, leaving Emily to wonder if he knows himself why he's asked her to meet with him.

Either way, she can hardly get a word in edgewise. When he does take a break, it's only to hold his handkerchief to his mouth to cough—persistent and fierce, from deep in the lungs. Once or twice, when the cough has become particularly harsh, she's contemplated getting Pehalvan's attention, but each time she motions in that direction, as though reading her intentions, Monty raises his left hand to signal that he's okay.

Through the tinted windows of the limousine, it's hard to tell where they're parked—behind a strip mall it seems, but she has no sense of the exact location. They had driven around for almost ninety minutes before stopping here. The air conditioning is on full blast, her scarf still wrapped around her head and shoulders. She's been receiving texts from Sarah and knows she's somewhere nearby waiting. *The patience of a saint, that one.*

After one particularly rambling moment, Monty seems to momentarily forget Emily's name and apologizes. "As you get closer to death," he says, "you wish more and more that it was possible to let go of your mistakes, to scatter them to the wind. But the past hasn't gone anywhere. No, sir! In fact, your past mistakes, especially the ones you've kept to yourself, will eat at your insides to remind you they're still there—no matter how much good you might have done in this world, it's the blunders, the miscalculations, the slip-ups, things you've kept bottled inside, that will haunt you as you prepare to leave this life. The only cure is to release them. I worry that if I don't share my secrets in this world, they will find me in the next.

"And I often wonder why God has kept me around this long, in such poor health, while he has taken so many others, younger, healthier, than me. When I heard you would be at Ranjit's wedding, it finally made sense to me that God wants me to release this burden. I believe it is God's will that you are here today."

Emily is hopeful that she might finally understand what is so important for her to hear, but instead he sidetracks into a story about how he was the first amongst his group of friends to buy a home, that they called him crazy and warned him about being forever in debt to the bank. Then he's off on another tangent, flipping pages in his head. Emily's patience and generosity are waning with each passing moment.

DEVINDER IS GLAD to see that Amarpreet is taking things in stride. Though the newlyweds have yet to arrive and the party is already well under way, his brother has shown no signs of panic. The three beers on an empty stomach have probably helped. He considers reminding him that the initial delay in the schedule was his fault—if only he'd waited for Devinder to take care of Ranjit's turban they might not have fallen so far off track. Instead Devinder says, "Well, you did say you didn't want the wedding and the reception on the same day, didn't you, Amar?"

"Yeah, but I didn't think they'd overlap!"

Amarpreet laughs and takes another sip of West Coast IPA.

Ranjit and Rina have been keeping them updated on their post-wedding delays. First there'd been a problem with the honeymoon suite at their downtown hotel—damage from the previous night's guests—and then they discovered that one of Rina's bags had disappeared. After a brief period of panic—the bag contained Rina's jewellery for the reception—it was found pushed deep inside the trunk of their limousine. Now they are stuck in the Saturday-evening traffic waiting to cross Granville Street Bridge.

Once the bar had opened, Devinder and Kuldip assumed the temporary responsibility of greeting the guests, leaving Meena and Teena with Alexis, who was more than happy to take them to the playground. Kuldip was still distant and cool, but he doubted the arriving guests picked up on her ill temper as they shook hands and embraced her. Even the obligatory small talk had been easy and did not betray any tension.

By the time Amarpreet, Baljit, Auntie Deepa, and Rina's parents arrived—the intended receiving line—the hall was more than two-thirds full and buzzing with boisterous conversation. It only took two enthusiastic young women, overcome by the beat of a classic bhangra hit playing low on the sound system, for the dancing to get started. Amarpreet signaled to DJ Bijliwallah to turn it up. Devinder was impressed.

"A year of planning." Amarpreet laughs again. Then raising his voice, he adds, "And nothing has happened on time."

In Devinder's experience, a memorable party trumps everything else. Long after today, it will not be the speeches and formalities that guests will remember, or what time the couple arrived. It'll be the party. In any case, this won't be the first wedding where the married couple miss out on the opening of their reception. Though the community of Punjabi Sikhs might live their daily lives under strict rules of behaviour, those rules become very relaxed when it's time to celebrate. The newlyweds' absence is merely a minor inconvenience.

Devinder and Amarpreet are joined by Navpreet and Karanpreet, both a little out of breath from dancing.

Navpreet insists it's time for the first brothers' toast of the evening and they raise their bottles in the air. With a mischievous grin, Karanpreet shouts, "Cheers to perfect turbans and milni victories!" and they all look in Devinder's direction. "If you hadn't lifted Vadhu, I swear I was ready to recruit Pehalvan as a brother-for-the-day." They roar with laughter and click their bottles together before huddling for a group hug. A roaming photographer captures the moment.

"Can you guys believe it? Our little Ranjit is married!" says Navpreet as they turn their gaze in the direction of Amarpreet who is glowing with fatherly pride.

"And look at this party!" adds Karanpreet as he gestures toward the sea of raised arms on the dance floor.

Amarpreet lifts his drink for another toast. "This is probably going to make me cry, but I have to say it. Thanks for all you've done for my kid. He wouldn't be the man he is today without his three brilliant chachas!" A tear streaks down Amarpreet's cheek.

They shout "cheers" and hug, this time a little tighter and longer.

Still sniffling and wiping away tears, Amarpreet says, "I better go do my job, guys. Biji's staring at me." He heads back to the receiving line, and Navpreet and Karanpreet walk in opposite directions so they can move around the hall and mingle—what Karanpreet calls their "official duty."

Back at the bar the staff is struggling to keep up and Devinder removes his jacket, folds it inside out, and places it carefully on a shelf beneath the back sink. The plate that MJ had sent for him is sitting untouched on a lower shelf. He immediately assumes the task of mixing cocktails, and is soon measuring, shaking, and pouring drinks into martini glasses and tumblers, which is met with loud applause from the thirsty guests in line. He juggles a couple of empty martini shakers for effect.

From behind the bar, he has a view across the length and breadth of the room. The tables reserved for business partners are full. He knows that most of these guests will remain seated for the evening except to get food at the buffet tables. For many it's their first time at a Punjabi wedding reception, and the dazzle of colour and sound has them entranced. Devinder had been amused by the look of eye-popping bewilderment as they first walked through the archway and grasped the size and splendour of the ballroom. Now they're happy to watch the dance floor action on the large screens, like an evening at home in front of their TVs.

Mr. Vikram Sohal, MP, and his entourage have not made an appearance and their table sits empty. Thirty more minutes and then Devinder will offer the table up to Mr. and Mrs. Sekhon and their friends, who he is sure will be glad to recover the prime seats they had given up earlier.

The visiting family members have staked out their seats, leaving jackets and purses beside chairs as they devour appetizers and socialize with one another. Vaddé Maamaji is busy working his way across the room, shaking hands and chatting with guests who are, no doubt, offering congratulations and praise for his post-ceremony speech.

There is a back section filled with unmarried young adults who have chosen to be near their friends, away from the restrictive gaze of their parents. For some it's a way of avoiding their parents' constant search for potential suitors—this evening offers a smorgasbord of options, it's a matchmaker's dream—and for others it's a rare opportunity to laugh, drink, and celebrate with their peers without judgment. A couple of underage guests come to the bar and bashfully ask for drinks. Devinder turns them down but creates a colourful mocktail instead. "That's as close as you're going to get to a drink tonight, kids!" They're disappointed but leave the bar smiling anyway.

To one side is a table of aunties who have been abandoned for the evening by their husbands, the sharabi uncles led by Uncle Tarlochan. Devinder had decided to let the uncles be, to let them think for now that they have outsmarted the bar staff. *No point in creating a scene.* Besides, if he did approach them to take away the pilfered bottles of whisky, they'd only protest the food, the lighting, or any other little matter. *Best they keep to themselves and not disrupt the celebration.* Uncle Tarlochan is one of the wealthiest people in the room and approaching eighty years of age but still resorts to this juvenile behaviour. Never mind that it's an open bar and there are perfectly good glasses to drink from. At one of the initial Tiger Team meetings, they'd discussed removing him from the guest list altogether, but the fear of offending an old business partner overrode the consequences of potentially bad behaviour. For now, Devinder will keep the knowledge of the stolen bottles to himself, but he'll have a word with Amarpreet later. He also needs to phone the liquor supplier and apologize, but that can wait, too.

Devinder is looking forward to seeing the moment when one of the abandoned wives sends a child into the group of sharabi uncles with a request for something banal and unimportant to gleefully interrupt their session. The abandoned aunties need their amusement, too.

DJ Bijliwallah has turned up the music and the dancing is now overflowing the boundaries of the dance floor. Ranjit's cousins, anxious to fulfil their "official duty" have assumed their expected roles. Surinder, Navpreet's eldest daughter, nicknamed Amy, is walking table to table pulling unsuspecting guests into the fray. She invites the newcomers in, dances briefly with them, and then excuses herself to find more recruits. Paramdeep, nicknamed Pam, Karanpreet's youngest daughter, has a reputation as the best dancer of the group and has taken her place at the centre of the floor. Those unsure of their own skills stand in a circle around her, clapping along as rhythmically as they can. Pam has mastered all the latest bhangra and Bollywood moves and combines the two seamlessly, along with the classical dance choreography she has learned over her years of training. Her hands and facial expressions act out a melodramatic story with theatrical twists of her elbows and wrists—unrequited love, tragic deaths, forlorn widows—as one foot angles up and the other taps flat against the floor. It is Pam who will lead the rehearsed cousin-sisters' dance later in the program.

The only dancers who rival Pam in reputation are Aunties Jothi and Seema. They're the exception to the rule and welcome to take full bottles of liquor from the bar—Devinder gladly handed them two unopened bottles of GREY GOOSE vodka earlier. Now he stands on his tiptoes to watch them, though the large screens are also showing their performance. The floor clears around them. They begin, as they always do, by balancing the GREY GOOSE on their heads, acting as though the glass bottles might slip and crash to the ground. Those familiar with their routine know this mock panic is part of the act. Once they've set the bottles on the sweet spot, the flat middle of their heads, they commence their frantic dance, circling each other slowly at first, clapping their hands one over the other. They gradually pick up speed until their chunis are flying around them. They twirl and pirouette as the lights flicker and pulse to the beat. Before long they are circling each other so fast that the clapping of the audience can hardly keep up. They make a rasping sound with their mouths to increase the drama. And of course, the bottles remain firmly in place.

Jothi and Seema are a fixture at weddings these days. Loud cheering, wolf whistles, and applause, as well as the appreciative refrain of "chak de phattay," accompanies their dance. Once they've finished, they take a bow and return to the bar with the two bottles of vodka still intact. Devinder places them in a safe spot knowing they'll return later for several encores. *They're only just getting warmed up.* The exuberance of their performance has raised the energy in the room and the bass beneath Devinder's feet gets a smidge heavier.

IT HAD TAKEN Kuldip many years to understand that the debts paid off by their hastily arranged marriage were not only those owed by Uncle Monty and Sandhu Properties to Mr. Sethi. There was also the debt that Devinder believed he owed to his adoptive parents.

But it wasn't only a transaction, was it? There was a time when he truly loved me, wasn't there? He was never generous with his emotions, seldom talkative, but our moments of tenderness were real. I'm certain of it. It was only when she re-emerged in his life that our marriage began to fall apart. Even then, our daughters should have been reason enough for him to remain faithful. I deserve better and our daughters do, too!

Divorce was unspeakable. When she had married it was not simply a covenant with Devinder but with the entire extended family, the community at large, generations of tradition. And who would take her side against the much loved and admired son? She would be blamed and shunned, even by those who know of Devinder's affair. *No, a divorce would mean exile.* Besides, a part of her still loved him and wanted to win him back.

***

"YOU'VE REALLY DONE an incredible job, Kuldip. Congratulations!"

Kuldip and Kiran have their arms around each other's shoulders and are taking a minute away from the dance floor. "How is it," Kiran teased, "that you and Devinder got to be on the Tiger Team and not me and Karanpreet?" Kuldip laughs for what feels like the first time today. "I guess we know who Monty and Deepa's favourite son and daughter-in-law are, don't we?" Kiran adds with a slight raise of her brow and a nudge of her elbow.

Kuldip looks around the reception hall and tries to shake off the residue of negative thoughts. Even in Ranjit and Rina's absence the reception is already a success. Many guests have congratulated her on how splendid the hall looks. And the appetizers have had to be refreshed more than once. The fish pakoras were a huge hit—a last-minute addition to the menu on Kuldip's advice—and the cocktail-sized samosas, fried paneer squares, and curried spring rolls were perfect for those who preferred to stand and mingle.

In fact, the party is such a success that it will be difficult to get the guests to sit down later for the formal program. She can imagine the groans of protest when the bhangra beats are turned off. The democracy of the busy dance floor has always appealed to her: couples, groups or singles, men and women, young and old can dance together without judgment of their ability. It is also a place where past discrepancies can be forgotten or forgiven. Earlier she had seen Uncle Vadhu step out and heard Rina's family cheer him on like a hero.

Kuldip and Kiran's conversation turns to the children, as it often does, and she remembers that she will have to bring Meena and Teena back in from the playground soon. "I'm so glad Alexis is here. My girls needed some proper playtime. They really love her." Thinking of Alexis, she is reminded of the disparaging comments she has heard whispered about the young woman's piercings and tattoos, her black lipstick and pink hair.

"People can be so judgmental, you know. Let the poor girl dress how she wants!"

Kuldip did not mean to speak the words out loud, but Kiran nods in agreement before adding, "I hear she has a perfect GPA."

"Speaking of perfect," Kuldip says, "your Pam! Wow! Those classical moves. You must be so proud!"

Kiran beams at the compliment and clinks her flute of orange juice against Kuldip's glass of sparkling water. "I'm not sure where she gets her talent from. Not from me and obviously not from her dad. Karanpreet has as much rhythm as a wet J Cloth. The only boy in this family who has any moves is Devinder." Another nudge of the elbow. "I expect to see you drag him onto the dance floor soon. He can't hide behind the bar all evening."

Kuldip reckons this is a good opening. No matter how hard she tries, she cannot shake the image of Teena walking out of the gurdwara with Emily framed in the doorway behind her. She's sure she will find supportive words from her closest ally.

"Did you notice Devinder's friend at the—" she whispers.

"That's your problem to deal with!" Kiran says loudly before Kuldip can finish her sentence. "It's up to the two of you to sort it out. Not anyone else. Don't bring me into it!"

Kiran's response is a brutal reminder that though her sisters-in-law have their own particular challenges in their respective marriages, they would never dream of jeopardizing their outwardly perfect lives and those of their children. But she had still hoped for some sympathy. In the matter of Devinder's infidelity she is more alone than ever.

Not wanting to show her tears, she walks toward the empty corner across from the main entrance. Next to the floor-to-ceiling windows she has an unobstructed view of the parking lot and the playground. If anyone tracks her here, she can make the excuse that she is checking on her daughters.

She practises her calming exercises as discreetly as possible: she clicks her teeth, back, middle, and front; circles her navel with both hands, first clockwise, then counterclockwise; and hugs her upper body with slow hand movements up and down her arms. She repeats the routine for another round. And then another. She drops her head into her chest to ease the tension in the back of her neck.

Guests are still trickling in and the parking lot is jammed full. A couple of latecomers are driving around trying to find a spot close to the entrance. Past the rows of shiny parked vehicles, Kuldip spots the bright pink- and yellow-flowered dresses of her daughters in the playground. Her body relaxes. *No matter what happens, I will always have them. No one can ever take them away from me.* Alexis is easy to spot with her burst of spiky pink hair. She sits on a swing not far from them. A few other children and a couple of young mothers are also in the playground, and Kuldip is reassured that Meena and Teena are in good hands. *They are the centre*, she reminds herself. *Nothing else matters.*

Teena is swaying fearlessly from rung to rung on the monkey bars while Meena is playing patty cake with one of the other girls. She'll give them ten more minutes. With them beside her, she will be able to keep her emotions in check. And she wants them to experience the reception with their cousins. Once the wedding festivities are over, she is hopeful they can have the kinds of adventures they had the previous summer. But first she needs to regain her party face.

Out of the corner of her eye she spots a figure walking down the main driveway toward the hall. She is convinced that he is standing more upright than he was months earlier, a far cry from the hunched wreck she had encountered on Kitsilano Beach, frozen with fear. She was not certain Iqbal would make it here today and the tension in her neck muscles drains away.

***

TWO WEEKS BEFORE the wedding, Kuldip had called the dental clinic and was overjoyed to hear that the dentures for Mr. Iqbal Singh Rai had been picked up. She felt a tinge of guilt in checking up on him, but those months of sneaking around and carefully managing her schedule should not be wasted.

She had a package of clothes ready to deliver to him, pieced together from Devinder's stash of unwanted family gifts—shirts and trousers that had never been touched during their years of marriage. She was sure they would not be missed. The shoes she had found in a plastic bag amongst the pile of garments Devinder planned to donate to the Salvation Army. The pile had sat in their garage for years.

On the Thursday morning before the wedding, she told Devinder that she needed to get more fruit from Apple Farm Market. He looked puzzled but never questioned her. She took a detour to the bench under the willow trees. Though it was a little later than nine thirty, their regular meeting time, she was hopeful he would show up. Her leg twitched of its own accord, a mix of excitement and apprehension. The typical parade of runners and dog owners passed by, and the beach was already a hive of activity. After twenty minutes, he had not shown up and she feared that she would not see him again until after the wedding, perhaps not until the girls were back in school in September.

As she was about to leave for the market, she opened the package and tucked the last of the dated Canadian banknotes into the trouser pocket before wedging the plastic bag between two of the bench's wooden slats. *What harm could there be? Even if someone else picked it up. So what? Perhaps they would make good use of the clothes and money.* Raab sabnunh dindain hai.

* * *

A BURST OF pride fills her as she watches Iqbal walk toward the banquet hall. Her other concerns have momentarily drained away. His stories and laughter were a warm balm that had soothed her winter despair. His words of appreciation and his humour—"Compliments to the chef!"—always brightened the most miserable of days.

Even from a distance his face looks fuller, less hollow. His beard has been trimmed and his hair is cut short. He walks with conviction and a steady pace, his head held high, confident and proud. She is amused that he has his blue jacket zipped all the way up to his throat. The grey trousers are a little short, but the shoes seem to fit well. If a stranger were to look at him, they would not guess that this handsome man has lived on the streets for almost two decades.

She cannot wait to see the look on Rupi's face when her brother walks in with his new set of teeth, all dressed up. Or the look on Iqbal's face when he meets his nephews. She even dares to think that someday her good deed will be celebrated as having been the necessary step to reunite Iqbal with his family.

Her eyes refocus on her reflection in the window; the touch of mascara she had applied this morning is smudged down her cheeks. She takes out a Wet Wipe and removes the makeup from her face.

AT LAST THE lineups have shortened. Devinder presses the martini shakers into the glasswasher and then leaves them upside down on a towel to dry. He signals to Pete that he'll be taking a break, opens another beer, and walks out from behind the bar. *Time to mingle.*

Ranjit and Rina have still not arrived, but the room is buzzing with laughter and conversation, and the dance floor is only getting busier. Amy and Pam are playing their parts and even Auntie Deepa had stepped onto the dance floor for a minute, her grandchildren taking turns to twirl around her as she stood in place and clapped.

As Devinder moves across the room he is greeted warmly and embraced tightly, a constant stream of "Vadhayian!" and "Congratulations!" Guests, both business and personal, are eager to greet Monty and Deepa's youngest son. If ever there was a day that proved his place in this family, then this is it. He is loved and appreciated, an essential slice of the Sandhu mythology, the prime illustration of their benevolence and self-sacrifice.

Though he'll never forget Narinder and Mira, his position is now well established in *this* family. The boy rescued from the basement—welcomed with open arms. And he has never once let them down, never done anything that might make them feel shame, or regret their decision to take him in. Any youthful doubt has long dissipated. In fact, since his marriage to Kuldip and the births of their daughters, his stature has only become more elevated. Marriage and fatherhood have legitimized him with his family and the wider community in a way that an unmarried man without children could never hope for.

There are some, he knows, that see him as the family's *lucky charm* and that's okay. They speak of how their fortunes grew exponentially after his adoption. *Let them think that.* He was witness to the industry and enterprise of Uncle Monty and his brothers and knows what it took to build their business empire. And Auntie Deepa is the backbone of it all. *Some people would rather claim chance or fortune than credit others for their hard work and sacrifice. There are worse things than to be seen as a real-life four-leaf clover.*

At the sight of the children's entertainers—an endless supply of balloons in their breast pockets—he is reminded that he must check up on Meena and Teena soon. He scans the crowded room to find Kuldip to tell her he'll step outside and bring them in.

He does a double take. With her back to him and her mane of wavy hair he almost didn't recognize her. She is on the side of the dance floor speaking to Kiran. *Matching suits and matching hair. Closer than sisters, those two.* He's glad they have each other and is reassured that Kuldip is finally having a good time. No doubt they're plotting when to get back on the dance floor.

At least Kuldip has put aside her antagonism for now.

Everything will be fine, he tells himself. Kuldip knows that Emily is Ranjit's teacher. That said, he decides to keep his morning visits with Emily short for the next few weeks. *And perhaps it would be best to postpone our walk in Lighthouse Park until after the dust settles.*

As he begins to move toward Kuldip, Devinder's path is obstructed by Mr. Sharma, who shakes his hand vigorously and offers congratulations on the day. "Oh, and great work at the milni, Devinder. Shaabaash, my boy, shaabaash!" Mr. Sharma gives him a wink as he starts to walk away.

Aah, the milni. Thinking now's as good a time as any to let Mr. Sharma know about his displeasure with his grandson Balraj, Devinder grabs him by the arm and walks him to an empty table nearby for a private chat. He eases into the conversation before broaching the difficult matter.

"Uncleji. One thing though. This is not easy to say but …" There is worry on Mr. Sharma's face, as though he knows what's coming. "It's about Balraj."

The words have barely left Devinder's mouth when he is interrupted by a loud noise, like the rumble of thunder before a great storm, and then a shimmering symphony of breaking glass. Even over the blaring music, the crackle and shatter can be heard throughout the ballroom. The shower of glass seems to last an eternity and Devinder, unsure of exactly where the sound is coming from, puts his arms over Mr. Sharma to protect the older gentleman. And then the ominous sound of creaking wood, like a barn door being opened in a horror movie.

When he straightens up again, the room has come to a standstill and all heads are turned toward the entrance.

The dancing has come to a stop though the music is still pounding.

Dha nana nana dhadha na. Dha nana nana dhadha na.

Even the sharabi uncles have put down their red cups and stare in the direction of the commotion. Over the sea of heads, Devinder can see that the mirrored gateway is askew and missing large chunks of its mirrored surface, the tacky plywood frame exposed.

Mr. Sharma looks shaken and Devinder squeezes his shoulder before he takes his leave. He hurriedly winds his way in and out of the gawking crowd and when he's twenty metres from the entrance he notices a flash of blue—the same shade of blue he had looked for earlier that day. *Oh fuck!* He'd forgotten to tell Rupi about his morning encounter with her brother.

Dha nana nana dhadha na.

Iqbal kneels with his head in his hands. Rupi is holding him, rubbing her hand across his back. Above them looms Mr. Rai, shouting a stream of profanities, spittle at the corners of his mouth, his open hand held in the air, angled as though he is about to strike again.

Dha nana na—

The music stops abruptly. The lights get brighter.

Mr. Rai's fury is now unfiltered. "How dare you show your face here! Have you no shame? Wasn't causing your mother's sickness enough for you?"

Rupi pleads, "Please, Pappa, stop! Stop, Pappa!" She curls an arm around Iqbal to shelter him but Mr. Rai ignores her pleas.

The floor around them is sprinkled with broken glass that glitters under the bright lights. Amarpreet and Navpreet arrive and place themselves between Mr. Rai and his children, and for a moment the older man looks lost but tranquil. But then he tries to force his way past them and they struggle to hold him back.

Pinky is already on her BlackBerry screaming at the venue's management to get staff to clean up the mess while Bubbly and Pippi, looking tense and unsure, are moving guests away from the archway as it lets out another deep groan and shifts a few more degrees toward the floor.

Devinder sweeps glass with his shoe before he bends down to kneel beside Rupi. He can feel tiny remnants of glass cutting into his kneecap and is abruptly reminded of the throbbing in his left leg. He is reaching out to grab Iqbal's arm when he hears Karanpreet's voice in his ear.

"What is *he* doing here? Get him out, man!" Before Devinder can reply, Karanpreet steps away to assist his brothers who are leading Mr. Rai back to his table. As they leave, Amarpreet turns his head in Devinder's direction with a look of disbelief.

"It's a green Subaru station wagon," Rupi says as she presses a set of keys into his palm. "Take him to my place. Jeevan and I will be there as quickly as we can. Jeevan's brother will bring us home once I get Pappa calmed down."

Without hesitation Devinder takes Iqbal's arm and helps him stand. There is a surprising strength in Iqbal's muscles. As they stoop to pass through the leaning archway, Devinder takes note of the scrapes on Iqbal's hands. With every slow, careful step, jagged pieces of glass cut into the soles of their shoes.

Mr. Rai's shouting can still be heard as they descend the stairs toward the parking lot. Devinder frantically presses the car fob waiting to hear a beep. The Subaru located, he leans across Iqbal and fastens his seat belt before walking around to the driver's side. He adjusts the rear-view mirror and turns the key. It is only then that Iqbal speaks, mumbling through his tears.

"Please don't be mad at her, Dev."

SHE TAKES ONE last glance at her reflection in the window. Her eyes show a slight tinge of red, but she can blame that on the smoke machine. She is ready to greet Iqbal. She might even call him "Iqqi" for once.

As she turns and faces the entrance, Kuldip is horrified to see that Iqbal, who only a minute earlier walked with such purpose, is now cowering by the photo booth, hunched over at the shoulders. Mr. Rai, thin and angular, is confronting his son. The loud music drowns out what he is saying, but every few seconds he thrusts his index finger into Iqbal's chest. She is about to make her way toward them when Mr. Rai reaches his arms back and pushes Iqbal with both hands, with a fury and force that Kuldip has never witnessed before. Iqbal stumbles backward, his head hits the archway and in an instant mirror shards rain over him, splintering into smaller pieces as they hit the ground.

All around her, guests turn their heads in the direction of the crash, a sound like the roll of thunder. Mr. Rai, now bent at the waist, one arm held in the air, continues shouting obscenities at Iqbal who is kneeling on the ground, earlobes held between his fingers as if begging his father for forgiveness. The glass rains over them both.

Suddenly Rupi appears and kneels beside her brother. She tries to calm Mr. Rai but he ignores her.

The last thing Kuldip had wanted was for any harm to come to Iqbal. *I have made a terrible miscalculation*, she thinks, and the tears that had only subsided a few minutes earlier now well up again. She feels an urge to run to Iqbal but her shame holds her back. *I've done enough harm already.*

The music stops and Mr. Rai's dreadful and demeaning words echo through the ballroom.

With the lights turned brighter, Kuldip can see across the length of the hall. The party, which had been buzzing with dancing and chatter only moments earlier, has now come to a complete stop. The guests look shocked; this is not what they came for.

The scene shifts very quickly as Devinder and his brothers swoop in. Amarpreet and Navpreet hold Mr. Rai by his arms and try to lead him away. He resists fiercely and his shouting continues. His foul language and sheer rage have some parents leading their young children to the back corner, as far away from the disturbance as possible. Kuldip is grateful that Meena and Teena are outside with Alexis and have been spared witnessing Mr. Rai's violence.

Devinder lifts Iqbal off the floor, puts his arm around his waist, and holds one hand over his friend's head. They exit through the perilous-looking wooden structure, creaking and moaning, threatening to collapse. Through the window, she sees Devinder and Iqbal search the parking lot until eventually they drive away in an unfamiliar car. She should have guessed it would fall on Devinder's shoulders to look after his friend, but she never imagined anything like this would happen.

She wishes Devinder was not leaving; standing next to him would steady her. Without him, what role does she play in this family? Maybe a disruption is not what she wanted after all. She remains at the window for a few minutes after the car has pulled onto the street. The hall is filled with hushed conversations, but at least Mr. Rai is now quiet. Pinky and her team are busy on their BlackBerrys. Sonny Patel has his hand against the leaning wooden structure as if willing it to stay upright. A couple of facility staff are sweeping the shards of glass from the floor. At the photo booth the photographer is packing up his gear.

Auntie Deepa stands alone with her head bowed—a receiving line of one.

A handful of guests have put on their jackets while others are frozen in place.

Kuldip desperately wants to hold her daughters in her arms. She looks for them but they are nowhere to be seen. And there is a commotion by the row of cars at the street side of the playground.

"EMILY, I'M GLAD we've had this chance to talk. I feel that you will know what is best."

Emily is dazed. And the last thing she is certain of is what is best. Monty has asked her to keep their conversation private. "No one must know! I always meant to tell Deepa when the time was right but what good time is there to deliver such news? And now she is old and cannot take any more suffering."

But Deepa seems strong and healthy. Emily can still feel the force of her hand on her back as she and Sarah were led out of the prayer hall.

"And Devinder? I will leave it to you to decide what he needs to know and the best time to tell him. I never want him to feel that what we did for him was out of guilt or shame. He's been a blessing to this family. Such tragedy, to lose your mother and father so young. No one knows better than Devinder how a single day can alter the course of your entire life."

It occurs to Emily that guilt and shame are two sides of the same coin. She'd grown up with the Catholic concept of guilt, the awareness of having done wrong, and a commitment to contrition to overcome that sin. Confess, and forgiveness was yours. Shame was what being conscious of guilt led to. Guilt was personal but shame required others. Monty's shame was all-consuming—he worried about how he and his family would be perceived not only by God but by the community at large. His legacy must not be tarnished.

And the cause of Monty's shame and guilt? First there was the broken promise to Devinder's parents on the day of their accident. Monty had assured them that he would drive them to view a property in Pitt Meadows that had just gone on the market. Narinder had taken the afternoon off—they would leave right after lunch to return in time for Mira to pick up Devinder from the bus stop. They were excited about the acreage, a renovated farmhouse with a small barn and a spacious garden. The kitchen had been recently renovated. A tiny stream ran through the back. Monty thought it was underpriced. The ailing owners wished to move into the city to be closer to their children and grandchildren and were motivated to sell quickly. Deepa worried that Narinder and Mira were purposefully moving somewhere more remote, more detached from society, and how lonely it would be for Devinder. At least living in their basement, he might occasionally see their boys. But they had hardly seen Narinder and Mira in the previous months. Deepa complained that Mira no longer came upstairs to visit and scolded Monty for mentioning that they were thinking of selling the house they shared.

"Did you take a moment to think that it's their house, too?" Maybe that was the reason they seemed to be in such a hurry to move.

Narinder had recently received a promotion at work. They had saved up for a down payment. Narinder had a dream to buy a car. He'd need one if they chose to live in Pitt Meadows.

All this Monty recalled to Emily as though it had happened yesterday. He was no longer reciting from the memoir. These were the chapters he'd intentionally left out. It was obvious he thought of Narinder as a younger brother and had an admiration bordering on jealousy for his career, mentioning more than once that Narinder left the house each morning carrying a briefcase and wearing a suit.

And then there was the guilt over his priorities and its consequences. The snowstorm that day was more severe than forecasted, and the temperature dropped like a stone. A water pipe had burst in one of his laundromats. He received the news in the early morning. "I didn't even have time to tie a turban." He could have let his business partner look after it and kept his promise to Devinder's parents. Instead, he left the house in the dark, supervised his staff while they cleaned up the mess, and waited for the plumber to fix the leak.

In the midst of the chaos he lost track of time. When Deepa called the laundromat, she was standing beside Narinder and Mira, who were wearing their coats and waiting for Monty to drive them to the property. There was no way he could make it in time. Narinder suggested he could drive Monty's old station wagon, which had been parked behind their house since the previous summer. Monty didn't think it through. The engine on the old car had been acting up and the tires were worn thin. Narinder had never driven in snow. And yet Monty did not discourage them. "They were so eager to see the property and Narinder wasn't sure when he might get another afternoon off work!"

The RCMP called their home since the car was registered in Monty's name. The officer did not share the extent of Narinder and Mira's injuries, only that they were at Surrey Memorial Hospital. When Deepa called the laundromat she could barely get the words out. He had never heard her so upset. And it was only on the drive to the hospital that he realized how treacherous the roads had become. Blowing snow. Black ice. He couldn't see more than ten metres ahead and had to keep his hands firmly on the steering wheel to prevent the car from drifting.

The staff at the hospital would not let him see Mr. and Mrs. Gill. "For your own good," they said. An RCMP officer overheard his remonstrations and pulled him aside. He was writing a report on the accident and asked how well he knew Narinder and Samira. Did they have other family the police should reach out to? He marked down Devinder's school information for social services. But did Monty know where the boy was now and was he safe? The officer gave him a few minutes to call Deepa from the pay phone to make sure she would meet Devinder at his bus stop.

Then he wanted proof of car registration. Proof of insurance. But the papers were all in the car. The officer shook his head; the station wagon had caught fire after it veered off the road. The trauma surgeon interrupted them. He apologized that his team had done their best, but the internal injuries and third-degree burns were too much. There was nothing more to be done.

And the final strike that Monty had kept to himself all these years: "The trauma was too much for the baby, too, I'm afraid." Monty had never found a way to share that news with Deepa. Never had the courage to tell Dev. And now he wanted someone to know that had his parents lived, Dev would have had a younger sibling. It wasn't only Narinder and Mira that Dev lost that day.

Monty sighed deeply as though a weight had been lifted from his conscience. But he was on a roll and kept talking.

Monty was rattled by the surgeon's pronouncement and the officer's questions, which became more accusatory. "What was the condition of the car? Was it mechanically sound?" Monty wasn't clear on where the questions were leading and panicked in the moment. Narinder had taken the car without his permission, he'd said. He would never have allowed it if he'd been asked. Once the lie was out there, he couldn't find a way to take it back.

SUDDENLY THE BACK of the limousine feels small, stifling. Emily has sat patiently listening to every word, every painful detail. She loosens her scarf. Her fingers are knotted from gripping the stack of papers.

Monty does not pick up on her distress and says, as calm as a prayer, "I've kept you far longer than I intended, Emily. If Sarah is not around, I will have Pehalvan arrange a car for you." As though they'd just shared a casual conversation, a trivial chat about the weather. *After all he has burdened me with, this is his farewell? Job done.*

"I'm sure she's here somewhere," Emily says, barely able to get the words out.

Monty leans forward and whispers, "Please forgive me."

She sets the manuscript down, turns away, and opens the limousine door without another word. But then changes her mind. She must tell him what an impossible predicament he's put her in. His conscience may be unburdened but has he thought about the weight he's placed upon *her* shoulders? With one leg out the door she turns to face him and opens her mouth to speak, but he cuts her off. "Thank you, Emily. Devinder was much happier after he met you."

Speechless, she stumbles out of the limousine, the heat from the sun prickles her skin. Her legs feel weak as she walks around to the front of the building. There is a bitter taste in her mouth and her head is spinning. She leans against a wall to steady herself and closes her eyes to let it pass. But closing her eyes only gives her the sensation that she is adrift, floating in rough waters as they push her this way and that.

"Oh my. Are you okay?" Sarah is beside her, but Emily's vision is blurred and she cannot see her friend's face clearly.

"Just give me a moment," she says as she brusquely removes her scarf, unbuttons the top buttons on her kurta, and places her hand over her heart.

The moment of nausea passes and she leans her back farther into the coolness of the brick wall. She faces Sarah who is holding her by the arms, telling her to breathe.

"You are such a good friend," Emily mutters. "Were you here waiting for me this whole time?" She hears herself speaking but she's unsure where the words are coming from.

Over Sarah's shoulder, across the street, is a huge parking

lot leading to a shiny two-storey glass complex. Emily shields her eyes and squints as she reads the sign near the side of the road. THE ROYAL KING PALACE BANQUET HALL AND CONVENTION CENTRE. She'd thrown out the invitation card to the reception months ago knowing she wouldn't attend, but she can hazard a guess that this is the venue. Her mind clicks into the moment.

"Oh shit!" she says, panic growing in her belly. "We need to get out of here now!" She laughs at the absurdity of it. Of all places, Monty's driver has taken her to the one she had planned to stay far away from. Sarah leads her to the minivan.

"You can tell me what I've missed on the drive home," Sarah suggests.

"I'm not sure you want to know."

Sarah is opening the passenger-side door for her, still holding her by the arm, when a child's loud scream pierces the hot, still air. Instinctively, Emily looks to see where it came from. Across the street a small crowd is gathered beside a playground. She stands on her tiptoes to get a better look. And then another cry, a whimpering child.

"Did you hear that, Sarah?"

Before her friend can respond she is hurrying toward the distressed call, dodging in and out of traffic. A girl in a pink dress is weeping and clinging tightly to the skirt of a young woman dressed in black. Nearby is a yellow sports car, halfway out of its parking spot, its emergency flashers blinking. A young man stands by the open car door looking distraught, his hands over his head. A girl in a yellow dress lies on the ground behind the car. Beside her, a lone sneaker, turned on its side. Tiny bangles shattered and sprinkled across the pavement. The girl lies very still.

Before Emily has time to think she is kneeling by her side. She pulls Teena's hands away from her face and presses her scarf against the gash across her forehead.

"That's it. Keep the pressure on it." Sarah has arrived with her first-aid kit in hand.

Teena opens her eyes and tries to sit up.

"Stay there a minute, sweetie," says Sarah. "Can you see my finger?"

Teena gives the slightest of nods and Sarah moves her hand from side to side. Teena's eyes track her index finger perfectly. "That's good, sweetie. That's really good."

Sarah checks Teena's arms and legs for additional wounds. "Luckily it's only a couple of scrapes." She rechecks around the henna vines on Teena's arms, while Emily lifts the scarf to examine the cut on Teena's head once more. The blood has soaked into the material, but the flow has stopped. Sarah unpacks a piece of gauze and cleans around the wound with alcohol, gently squeezing a dab of antiseptic over the cut before ripping strips from a roll of surgical tape to secure a piece of gauze to Teena's forehead. Emily reaches out for Teena's hand and feels her squeeze back.

"What a brave girl you are."

Teena stretches out and throws her arms around Emily. Emily stands, Teena's head resting against her shoulder. She rocks her gently. Her legs are numb and weightless and move of their own accord toward the glass complex. She's halfway there when Kuldip is suddenly in front of them. Emily mouths the word *sorry* and lets Teena down just as the surprising force of Kuldip's hands set her off balance, tumbling backward, her head hitting the hard concrete.

By the time she opens her eyes, Kuldip is in the distance entering the building, Meena and the girl in black trying their hardest to keep up.

THEY ARE THE *centre. Nothing else matters.* The phrases repeat in her head but are never spoken out loud. Her head throbs from the rush of blood as she flies through the leaning mirrored gateway, oblivious to the shards of glass beneath her shoes. She strides down the stairs, pushes the exit doors open, and runs the length of the parking lot with her arms swinging by her side. Everything is a blur except for Teena in Emily's arms moving toward her.

They are the centre.

Kuldip sees Emily release Teena to the ground, but her arms are already in motion and do not slow their momentum. A strange power surges inside her, an accumulation of past silences and inaction.

Nothing else matters.

All those years of obediently playing her part, years of holding it all in, like everyone has expected her to. Her arms pull back, her hands open, and push hard against Emily's shoulders. A spring uncoiling. Her glass bangles jingle as they move swiftly through the air and then fracture.

They are the centre.

Tiny shards of bangle rain down onto the pavement.

Emily is falling backward, arms flailing wildly, but Kuldip does not wait to see her land. She grabs Teena and lifts her to rest her head against her shoulder. She looks sideways to make sure Meena and Alexis are still beside her.

It is only when she is inside and hears Teena mumble through her tears, "You're hurting me, Mom," that she relaxes her grip. She shifts Teena's body so she can see her face and notices the bandage on her head and the little red stain at its centre.

Nothing else matters.

ACT V

RAAT—NIGHT

DURING THE SLOW drive to Rupi's place, Iqbal confesses everything, beginning with the day Kuldip rescued him from his breakdown at the beach.

"I was frozen to the bone. Out of my mind. I really thought that day was my last. And then she appeared out of nowhere. I knew that day that something had to change."

He admits that he'd asked Kuldip to keep their meetings secret, that he feared his father would find out and be upset at her for helping him. "The last thing I want is for her to be blamed for any of this. Everything she did for me, she did out of kindness. She's an angel, Dev. She really is."

"You know I would have helped, too, Iqqi. Kuldip and I could have worked together. I could have met with your father. Prepared him. It didn't have to happen this way," Devinder replies.

Iqbal shakes his head. He is convinced that nothing would have prevented the events of the day. His father's reaction would have played out the same way no matter how much he'd been prepared or forewarned.

"His anger wasn't only about me showing up at the wedding today. It was about the past twenty years. For what

I've inflicted upon him. He was never going to take me back with open arms. His pride would never have allowed it. I'm just sorry that I ruined the reception. I should never have come. I'm not sure what I was thinking. I hope you and your family can forgive me."

IT WAS FOOLISH *to leave my BlackBerry at the reception.* Over an hour has passed since he and Iqbal arrived at Rupi's. His old friend snores quietly on the couch after having taken a shower and changed into a pair of Jeevan's workout clothes. Devinder had almost given up hope that he'd ever see Iqbal reconnect with his family, and despite what happened in the hall he feels a certain relief and optimism that this time his friend will stay off the streets. He's grateful that Kuldip found him and impressed by what she's accomplished.

He paces in front of the window, occasionally peeking out to check for Rupi and Jeevan. *What is taking them so long? What if I'm needed at the reception?*

Iqbal's clothes are piled on the coffee table and he bends down to take a closer look. Holding the trousers up, he thinks they look familiar. He checks the tag. FARAH. There was a time in his late teens when his brothers wore the brand to every special function or gathering. Was this the pair that had been gifted to him by Vaddé Maamaji when he first visited them? The shirt he doesn't recognize, but looking at the shoes it dawns on him that they are his, though he hasn't worn them in years.

He lifts the K-Way jacket and is surprised by its weight.

In the pocket he finds his missing Walkman with a mixtape Iqbal had made for him in their second year of university. OH WHAT A PERFECT DAY. *How did I not figure this out at the beach this morning? What other signals did I miss?*

As he piles the clothes together a folded photograph falls to the ground; Mrs. Rai with Rupi in her arms, Iqbal beside her. Once the post-wedding events are over he must smooth the waters between his family, Iqbal, and Mr. Rai; he's the only one capable of it.

Devinder has started to clean up the mess of Band-Aid wrappers and bloody gauze when he hears the sound of a car in the driveway. *At long last!* He opens the door and puts a finger to his lips to let them know Iqbal is sleeping. Rupi and Jeevan quietly remove their shoes. Their tired-looking boys follow their lead.

Finally Mr. Rai enters, with his head tucked into his chest. He struggles with the laces of his shoes and Rupi bends down to help him. Then he makes his way toward the couch. Devinder is about to step in front of him when Rupi signals for him to stay back. Mr. Rai sits on the armrest and stares at his son, gently touches his cheek and strokes his hair. He looks contrite. Chastened. Like a child exhausted after a tantrum. He does not utter a word. Seeing the bloody gauze on the table he puts his hands to his face and begins to weep.

He is still in tears as Rupi leads him upstairs. Jeevan hands Devinder his suit jacket and then also heads upstairs with the boys to get them ready for bed.

Devinder retrieves his BlackBerry from the inside pocket. One missed call and one voice message. He is surprised to see who they're from. He hits Play and hears Sarah's voice:

"Watch Teena for concussion. If there's a headache or vomiting, take her to emergency."

He hits Play again. And then again. No "hello" or "see you later." No explanation of why Teena might have a concussion, and more mysteriously no explanation of how Sarah would know about it.

He phones Sarah and leaves a terse message begging her to call him back.

When Rupi and Jeevan are back downstairs, he asks straightaway if they'd seen Teena before they left the hall. "Has something happened? Is she hurt?" They look at each other trying to decide who should speak.

Rupi says, "Dev, as far as we know Teena's okay, though there was an incident in the parking lot and Teena had some kind of fall."

Devinder's heart skips a beat. "What do you mean?" He is dialing Kuldip's number before they can respond. The phone rings as Rupi continues. "Teena looked a little scraped up but was walking beside Kuldip the last that we saw her. They were leaving the reception."

"Leaving?" He puts down his phone and waits for them to say more.

This time it's Jeevan. "Something else happened but we're not really sure what. Kuldip packed up her things and left in a hurry with Meena and Teena. Everything was happening so fast, Dev, it was hard to keep track. Your brothers were helping us with Pappa. But the whole room was on edge. I saw Kiran begging Kuldip to stay but she was determined to get out of there."

Devinder can feel his heart beating faster.

"There was also some kind of altercation with one of the guests. Alexis saw it but was too upset to talk. The poor girl looked shattered. Pete was taking her outside when we ran into them. When we told him that you'd brought Iqbal here, he ran back to grab your jacket, said he'd heard your phone ringing beneath the bar."

Devinder asks if he can borrow their car. Jeevan replies, "You won't find Kuldip at the reception hall. Probably best to try at home."

"I hope everything's okay, Dev," Rupi says as she hugs him at the door. "We're sorry that Pappa caused such a ruckus and that it took us so long to calm him down. Please forgive us. And thank you so much for taking care of Iqbal Bhaji. We owe you."

Once alone and sitting at the wheel he tries calling Kuldip again. Still no answer. He needs to see Teena for himself, to know that she is okay.

THE MOMENT HE opens the door he knows the house is not as they'd left it this morning—the quality of sound, a dull emptiness in the air. Even without turning on the lights, he can tell that the space between the two large windows in the main room is bare. The outline of the frame, the ocean painting that he had gifted Kuldip, a shade lighter than its surrounding. But the painting hasn't been taken away. Instead it rests facing backward on the floor, leaning up against the couch, the brown paper backing and the thin metal wire visible.

The toys and books that this morning lay on the floor have been picked over and rearranged. The drawers of the credenza are open wide. Moving to the stairs he listens for noises from above, hoping for the drip of a tap or the flush of a toilet. Anything to counter the desolation. Any sign of mundane routine. But there's nothing.

There are gaps in the row of family photographs that Kuldip carefully arranged along the stairwell. Pictures of Meena and Teena at various ages. Their recent portraits from picture day at school have been removed. In the girls' bedroom, still smelling of lavender, he finds clothes scattered across the beds. Dresser drawers have been left open. Breaks in the lines of dolls and book collections.

In the main bedroom the green-and-turquoise Punjabi suit that Kuldip had been wearing earlier lies jumbled on the floor. The kameez left inside out. Kuldip is never this casual. More half-empty dresser drawers left ajar. From the stack of suitcases on the top shelf of the walk-in closet, only his ragged backpack remains.

On the edge of their bed a single piece of paper, his name scrawled across the folded page.

He tries calling Kuldip's cellphone. Again, no answer.

He walks down the stairs and takes a seat on the lowest step. The streetlight illuminates the living room and hallway. The drawings of the Gurus hang at an angle.

He stares at the paper in his hand, runs his finger across the frayed edge, and slowly unfolds it. He sees Kuldip's tidy cursive.

Maninder and Tejinder are OK.

Don't call.

I'll be in touch when I'm ready to talk.

He feels a tremor in his feet, like the world is collapsing around him.

He decides he will confess to Amarpreet that he knew Iqbal would attend, that he meant to mention it but in the rush of the day it slipped his mind. A little lie but it will be better for everyone. He needs to give them time to cool down. Addressing Auntie Deepa and Uncle Monty will be trickier. He'll need to think it through.

From the stairwell he stares at the front door, willing it to open, willing Kuldip to walk in with Teena and Meena by her side.

His eye catches a golden glow from the hallway table and he walks over to pick up the kara from beneath his coiled headphones. He slides it onto his wrist. A reminder of the Gurus' words. *No beginning or end. A link in a long chain.*

Had it only been this morning that he'd seen Emily? Radiance on a pair of peonies. A plan to meet at Lighthouse Park.

The sight of Iqbal bathing at the shore could just as well have been days, weeks, months ago.

And then, driven by some unknown compulsion, he tightens the laces of his patent leather shoes and leaves the house, still wearing his suit trousers, his dress shirt and tie. He runs through the darkening summer evening; the cooling air feels crisp against his face. Through Hadden Park, past the Maritime Museum and the beach still packed with revellers. Silhouettes dance near the water, orange glow-sticks around their necks. A cacophony of laughter and song. The horizon of buildings across the inlet is illuminated, reflecting golden in the water. Where the seawall curves around, tall lampposts light up one by one as he runs beneath them.

To his left, the swimming pool is empty and a few seagulls have reclaimed their place for the night. Past the pool, between the brambles and the estates, the path is dark but he does not slow down. From above he hears more laughter and chatter. Jazz music. John Coltrane. A body splashes into a pool. On the sawn-off log by the water, the outline of two lovers, their bodies leaning into each other. He bounds two steps at a time up the concrete stairway toward Trafalgar Street. The click-clack of his leather soles and his breathing are the only sounds. He races up the wooden steps to Emily's apartment and picks up the aloe plant but finds nothing. He lifts the other planters in case he'd misplaced the key this morning. Still nothing. He knocks on the door. Two loud raps spaced apart, followed by three soft. No answer. No sound at all.

He tries the door, pushing with his hip. It does not budge. He leans over the side railing to peek into the kitchen. Only darkness.

He tries Emily's phone number. And then Sarah's.

A cold chill runs up his spine and he realizes his shirt is soaked through with sweat. His stomach rumbles and he remembers that he hasn't eaten since the two slices of toast at Amarpreet's.

Lost in his thoughts, it takes him a moment to react to the buzzing in his hand. He takes a breath before he looks at the screen. He clears his throat and then accepts the call.

"I'm sorry, Kuldip. I've been a fool. Please tell me Teena is okay!"

"Dev?" Kuldip seems thrown off by the immediacy of his declaration. "Slow down, Dev. Slow down. I'm not sure what you've heard but Teena's fine. She got spooked by the revving of a car engine, but the car never touched her. She tripped on her own laces and fell, hit her head. It's a small cut. She's going to be fine. She and Meena are at Kiran's place with Alexis. They're both okay. Where are you?"

Devinder lets out a sigh of relief and takes a moment before he responds. "I needed some air. Some space to think after I went to the house ..." He takes another moment to compose himself. "I saw you took ..." He chokes on his words.

"I asked you where you were, Dev, because I didn't want you to be driving when you hear this."

"Kuldip, we can sort this out. I'm not sure what's happened but ..."

"I need you to listen to me, Dev. Just please listen. I'm with Kiran and Karanpreet. We're on our way to Surrey Memorial."

Devinder's stomach drops.

"It's Uncleji. He had a seizure in the back of the limousine. Luckily Auntieji was with him at the time and had Pehalvan drive them to the hospital right away. Amarpreet and Navpreet are on their way, too. Deepa says Uncleji called your name just before he blacked out."

Devinder tries to respond but his throat is dry and he is having trouble breathing.

"Are you there, Dev? Say something."

"I'm here." And then very quietly, his voice cracking, "I'm on my way."

He runs down the wooden stairs, along the sidewalk to the end of the block, down the concrete steps to the pathway along the water. Brambles. Scratched skin and a ripped T-shirt. Past the pool and toward the beach. The half moon shines silver at the horizon. The North Shore Mountains have blended into a single dark shadow. The Twin Sisters keep watch. The tap of his leather soles echoes from the treetops. Still in his stride, he loosens his tie and in one smooth motion pulls it over his head. He undoes its knot, sticks an arm in the air, and lets the long ribbon of silk fall away behind him. He untucks his shirt and unbuttons it.

The lights from the new second-storey restaurant illuminate the path. He looks up at the cheerful families gathered at tables overlooking the ocean, couples wrapped in conversation.

By the willow trees, a neon-red kite appears in the sky ahead of him. The kite sways side to side, up and down. He remembers snowflakes on his mother's eyelashes, his father's business suit. He recalls his confusion and disbelief that terrible day, unsure of who would love him. His legs are moving at full tilt, his staccato footfalls still ricochet high above. And then suddenly a sound like the snap of an elastic band. He tumbles onto the grass and screams, holding his knee, which throbs and immediately starts to swell beneath his fingers. He tries to lift himself up, but the pain is too much, like a knife stabbing just below his kneecap.

He closes his eyes, takes several deep breaths, and senses his body meld into the ground. The grass grows over his torso and legs, tethers him to the earth. Another breath and his body sinks deeper. One more breath. Deeper still. Waves crash against the seawall. In the distance, a murder of crows caws loudly. A gentle guitar strum drifts up from the beach. The singer croons an old country song, a chorus of voices joins in. The melody is familiar. Yet just out of reach.

When he opens his eyes, the kite is floating directly above him, its diamond body static while the long luminous tail waves frantically in the high wind, red stars amongst the white. He imagines tracks between the stars, fashions celestial constellations. A hunted bear. Seven birds. And then a strong gust blows the kite downward, and it falls toward a clump of trees silhouetted against the charcoal sky. It crashes and hangs in the high branches of what he thinks is a silver maple, but he cannot be sure.

ACKNOWLEDGEMENTS

IT TAKES A pind, a village, to write a novel, or at least it did to write this one. The passage of time from concept to publication runs over nineteen years and there are many friends, teachers, and fellow authors deserving of gratitude for their contribution, advocacy, and encouragement. And I am sure I will forget to mention some names. To them I apologize.

Thanks are due for believing in this project and helping to bring it across the finish line: my agent, Carolyn Forde at Transatlantic Agency, and Doug Richmond and the entire team at House of Anansi Press; the Canada Council for the Arts, the Writers' Union of Canada, and the Ontario Arts Council.

Thank you for lessons in structure, specificity, style, and self-discipline: the University of Toronto School of Continuing Studies; instructors Kim Echlin, Barbara Radecki, Dennis Bock, and Ibi Kaslik.

ACKNOWLEDGEMENTS

Thank you for critical edits at critical junctures: Kim Echlin and Amrita Pal.

Thank you for fact-checks, clarity of language, and enriching the manuscript with detail and precision: Mohinderpal Pal, Sharanjit Padda, Sukhpal Pal, Pritpal Pal, Emily Cargan, Wendy Mendes, Mohan Gill, Par Sihota, Prof. Tess Maginess, Clare and Brendan McLaughlin, Michelle Patterson, Francis McKinley, Dr. Stephanie Fung, and Dr. Peter MacDougal.

For friendship, inspiration, and/or guidance over these many years: Anar Ali, Ann Shin, Richard Harrison, Aaron Tucker, Julia Polyck-O'Neill, Katrina Anderson, Ken Myhr, Robin Elliott, Julia Gaunce, Marcello Di Cintio, Nikki Sheppy, Ryan Falkenberg, Raj Parmar, Andrea Gust, Diana Blackmore, Caroline Cremer, Susanne Lyle, Nadia Shahbaz, Melany Franklin, Shawna Delgaty, Anthony Matthew, Paulo da Costa, Kevin Spenst, and Jacqueline Turner.

Thank you to Steven Gustafson of the 10,000 Maniacs for details of their 1986 Canadian tour and Tamara Lindeman, the Weather Station, for the kind use of her lyrics.

The poetry quoted on page 80 is from Rudyard Kipling's "If."

A *However Far Away* Playlist

1. Lovesong / The Cure
2. To Talk About / The Weather Station
3. Held / Smog
4. We Are Family / Sister Sledge
5. My Mother the War / 10,000 Maniacs
6. Grey Victory / 10,000 Maniacs
7. Into the Mystic / Van Morrison
8. Left Only With Love / Smog
9. Perfect / The The
10. A Case of You / Joni Mitchell
11. Out on the Weekend / Neil Young
12. The Morning Fog / Kate Bush
13. Well I Wonder / The Smiths
14. Didi Tera Devar Deewana / Lata Mangeshkar and S. P. Balasubrahmanyam
15. Yeh Dosti Hum Nahin – Happy Version / Kishore Kumar, Manna Dey, and R. D. Burman
16. Love Will Tear Us Apart / Joy Division
17. Desan Da Raja / Tarranum Naz
18. (I Can't Get No) Satisfaction / The Rolling Stones
19. Bhangra Fever / Midival Punditz
20. Black / Pearl Jam
21. A Love Supreme, Pt. 1 – Acknowledgement / John Coltrane
22. Untitled / The Cure

RAJINDERPAL S. PAL is a critically acclaimed writer and stage performer. He is the author of two collections of award-winning poetry, *pappaji wrote poetry in a language i cannot read* and *pulse*. Born in India and raised in Great Britain, Pal has lived in many cities across North America and now resides in Toronto. *However Far Away* is his first novel.